# LIE TO ME

# LIE TO ME

## KENDAL LOU DICKSON

Kendal Lou Dickson

# DEDICATION

This book is dedicated to my Mema, and in remembrance of my Pepa (March 10<sup>th</sup>, 1931 - July 26<sup>th</sup>, 2021).
If there are books in Heaven, I hope you choose to read mine.

# Contents

"All we have to decide is what to do with the time that is given us."
- J.R.R. Tolkien

# One

Celia sat in her agent's office, a small room covered in Pepto-Bismol pink colored paint. Even the candy dish, the same sickening shade of pink, only held pink Starburst candies. If a stranger walked in, they would assume this was an office belonging to a teenager, not a forty-five-year-old woman. In her pastel pink t-shirt dress, Celia almost looked like a decoration for the office.

She twirled her fingers in her bleach blonde hair, a nervous habit she's had since she was a child. Although she refused to admit it, her nerves were worse today than they had been in years. The role of the Witch Queen wouldn't be her first leading role, but it would be her first gig outside of her usual child dramas and family friendly films that she'd been acting in for almost eighteen years. She was chomping at the bit, worse than a nervous racehorse, to rebrand her career.

Amy, her agent, walked in attired in her usual pantsuit, a serious and stark contrast from her office and bubbly nature. Her brown hair was pulled into a ponytail. Black glasses, an accessory and not for enhancing her eyesight, sat on the bridge of her nose. She sat a caramel iced coffee down in front of Celia. Typically, Amy only brought gifts, like coffee, when she delivered bad news. Once when

Celia was a child, Amy gave her a stuffed bear before telling her she wasn't cast in a television series.

"So?" Celia asked before Amy could even take her seat.

"So, the director and producers decided they want to cast you as the Witch Queen."

Celia screamed, almost knocking the chair backwards as she jumped up. Happy tears fell down her cheeks as she clapped her hands together. She was tempted to pinch herself, but if it was a dream, she didn't want to wake up.

Amy set a thick stack of papers on the desk and pushed them towards her. "But..."

Of course, a 'but' was coming. Celia slowly sat down; afraid the happiest moment of her life was going to be torn away as quickly as it was given to her. She plunged a paper straw into the coffee and brought it to her lips. It was too sweet; the sugar and caramel syrup overtook any coffee flavor.

"One of the producers wants to amp up the public's connection to the two main characters, the Werewolf and Witch Queen. He thinks the best way to achieve this is a PR relationship between you and your co-star."

Celia nearly choked on her coffee.

"Wait! You're saying they want me to pretend to be in a relationship with someone to connect more with the audience?"

"Exactly!"

The color drained from Celia's face. She was in a relationship with her high school sweetheart, Brandon.

"For how long?" Celia asked.

"A few months before filming, during filming, and a few weeks past the release."

"But Amy, that could be two years or more."

"I know, I know. Listen this is a once in a lifetime role, something that could really set your career on the right path. I can tell them, but I can't guarantee you will get another opportunity like this. It could be career suicide. Face it, you're almost twenty-four, your days of playing the sweet young teen are coming to an end."

Celia knew Amy was right. She wasn't getting casting calls like she used to, and it was only a matter of time before she was another forgotten actress like Juliette Lewis.

"How much would I have to do in this relationship?"

Amy's smile widened. "You would never be asked to do anything past your comfort zone. It's all right here in the agreement. In public, you would need to portray a happy couple. This would include, but not be limited to, holding hands, being seen together in public at multiple locations, going on dates, and the occasional kiss."

"What about sex? That's not part of it, right?"

"Of course not! There is a specific line stating any and all sexual actions are forbidden."

Celia fiddled with her hair again, and her stomach muscles churned bile in her belly.

"Who is the actor?"

"That's the best part! It's Thomas Richardson."

Celia's eyes widened and her mouth dropped. *Why would a handsome and successful actor like Thomas need me as fake arm candy?* The almost forty-year-old actor with baby blue eyes and perfectly manicured hair, had been breaking hearts before she was even in high school. She wouldn't admit it to Amy, but she had always been a fan of his.

"Doesn't he have a wife or someone that wouldn't be okay with this?" Celia asked.

Amy shook her head. "As you may already know, he's very quiet about his personal life, but no, he's never been married and doesn't currently have a girlfriend."

Celia pulled a lock of her hair in between her fingers. She knew it was too good of a role to pass up, but still, she didn't know if she could break things off with Brandon. She wasn't happy, but she understood he was struggling. Brandon had become lazy and lost all his ambitions, spending most of his free time with a beer in his hand. His recent behaviors had severed multiple friendships, and she was one of the few people he had left.

"How long do I have to make a decision?"

"You only have—" Amy checked her watch— "fifty-eight minutes left. They want to know tonight in case they need to contact their second pick."


Celia sat on the tan couch in her apartment living room. She had changed into a tank top and shorts, removed her makeup, and her hair was in a messy bun. Her apartment was in the Southwestern part of Oxnard, California. It was in a lower-class neighborhood, the size and condition of the complex reflected that. Although the apartment was only a one bedroom, it was still expensive to rent. After all, it had come furnished and was walking distance to the beach. It's not where someone would expect to spot a famous person, but that's what drew Celia to living there. She was seldom recognized by her peers in the city, and it kept her humble. Honestly, it was a safe haven for her.

Celia scrolled through Thomas' *Instagram* on her phone. He didn't post much, but when he did, it was either a picture of him with his sister, his twin nieces, or of his adopted cat, Scooter. Someone knocked on the door and she sat her phone down on the couch next to her.

"Come in, it's open," she said.

Slowly the door creaked open, and Brandon walked in with a carton of assorted bottled beers. He was still in his work attire, slacks and a button up shirt. His blond hair was styled in its typical messy mop, and a grin sat on his round face. He closed the door with his foot and put the bottles onto a glass top table. As Celia didn't share the same taste in alcohol as him, he frequently brought beer over to stash in her fridge.

"Sorry, traffic was crazy," he said.

Celia smiled weakly. She had already made her decision but pulling the trigger wouldn't be easy. Brandon plopped down on the couch and fished a Miller Lite out of the carton. He said something about his job, he was a bank teller at a local bank, but Celia didn't hear him. Her mind was too preoccupied with the possible scenarios of how she could break-up him. Although she excelled at being an actress, she's never been much of a liar.

"Your lack of enthusiasm has me assuming you didn't get the role." He popped off the cap and took a sip. "Or is this an act?"

"No, I got the role."

"What? That's great. Why aren't you smiling? It's a good thing, right?"

"Yes and no."

Brandon sat his drink onto the table. The air in the room had shifted. It was tense and uncomfortable. *Lie, you have to.*

"Preparing for this role is going to keep me busy. I'm going to have to work with a personal trainer up to and during filming. I'm not sure where filming is yet, but I know that it's going to be in another country."

"Well, not seeing you every day would drive me crazy, but I'm sure we can fit in Facetime dates or something."

"Brandon, I'm sorry, but that's not going to work."

His smile disappeared. "Are you breaking up with me?"

She couldn't say anything, all she could do was feebly nod. Shock, sadness, and then anger flashed across his face. She reached out to touch his hand, but he yanked it away.

"Brandon please, don't be like this. If there was a way to have avoided this I would've, you know that."

"All I know is my girlfriend picked a movie over me."

Celia opened her mouth to speak, but he threw his hands up.

"Save it, I can't deal with this tonight. I need to go."

Brandon rose from the couch and knocked the bottles off the table and onto the floor, sending glass and beer everywhere. Celia followed him to the door, tears in her eyes.

"Please, just wait a second and let me explain. I didn't want to end things this way, but we've been struggling for months now," Celia said.

"No, *I've* been struggling." He held his finger in her face. "You have no idea what I've been going through these past months. I thought I could count on you to be here for me, God knows I've stuck around with you and all your family drama."

"Brandon, please don't be like this."

She reached out to touch his shoulder and he slapped her hand away.

"Save it. I hope this little movie of yours is worth it."

Brandon slammed the door roughly behind him, knocking a framed picture off the wall. Celia busted into tears; her entire body shook as she fell to the floor. As much as she hated to admit it, Brandon was partially right. She was given the choice of her boyfriend or a movie, and she chose the movie.

# Two

"Are you sure this isn't too much?" Celia asked.

She wore a black strapless gown with a side split that ran up to her thigh. Her hair was gently tousled, lips painted cherry red, and false eyelashes set atop her real ones. Strappy black heels sat on her feet, despite her reservations. Amy was next to her in the backseat of a silver limousine. Again, she was attired in a stiff pantsuit.

"No, you look great! You know how important first impressions are," Amy said.

"Even for a fake relationship?"

Amy rolled her eyes. "Seriously Celia don't act like this is a prison sentence. You're getting to date an A-list actor. This needs to appear *believable*, you don't want to be recast."

Celia sighed. "I know."

She checked her phone, it was a quarter until eight. No new text messages or missed calls. It had been almost five days and Brandon hadn't reached out to her. She had tried texting him to see how he was doing, but it appeared he hadn't even read the messages, so she stopped trying. He was probably hurting and needed space. Still, she worried about him and hoped he wasn't doing anything reckless, as alcohol was his favorite coping mechanism.

The limo screeched to a halt outside of The Glitz, an old opera house in downtown Los Angeles. It was built in the early 1900s and had recently been renovated to an upscale bar and lounge, only accessible to the rich and famous. No one could get past the bouncer without their name being on the list.

"Alright, I'm going to let his agent know you're here. He already has your number and is going to reach out to you. Now, go have fun," Amy said.

Celia's eyes widened. "You're going to leave me here by myself? Can't I at least stay in here and wait until he contacts me?"

"It's time to spread your wings, butterfly. Grab a drink, relax, and don't forget to have fun. If you need me you can always call but try to not need me."

Celia felt like a child being forced to go to daycare without their parents for the first time as she stepped outside of the limo. The warm, muggy air wrapped itself around her. A gentle breeze carried the scent of chicken from a nearby fast-food joint and the city was alive with chatter and the occasional sirens. It didn't sound or smell differently than the typical Los Angeles neighborhood, but it felt like she was about to cross into a different city, or world for that matter. The bottoms of her heels were slick as she walked to the unguarded entrance. The large double doors were a new addition, but modeled to look antique, as if they were a part of the original opera house. The pulse from the music vibrated the door handles. She took a deep breath and walked in. The air was bitter with stale cigarette smoke. A large man in a tuxedo stood behind the dark oak podium. Velvet ropes blocked the path to the lounge. The walls were a deep crimson and the lights tented blue, providing low visibility.

"Name?" the man asked.

"Celia Stuart."

He squinted as he turned the pages of a leather-bound binder. Celia twirled her hair in her fingers. She had eaten only an hour earlier, but her stomach already felt hollow. Her phone buzzed from inside her clutch. It was a text message from an unknown number that said, "Third floor". It sent a chill down her spine.

"Ms. Stuart?"

"Yes?" she turned her attention to the man she had momentarily forgot was there. The binder was opened on the last page. He unlatched the velvet rope and moved aside.

"You may enter."

Her eyes adjusted quickly under the lights. There was a large bar that stretched across the back wall. A handsome bartender was pouring drinks to the patrons at the counter. A red leather L-shaped couch was positioned in the far corner. In the opposite corner of the room were the stairs. She kept her head down as she crossed the room, not wanting to draw attention to herself. She couldn't help but notice Arnold Schwarzenegger sharing a cigar with his son. Everyone was dressed as extravagantly as she was, but she still felt out of place. Celia rarely went to bars, but when she did, they were casual college bars near Brandon's apartment. Frat boys were frequent, and no drink was priced more than five dollars.

Careful not to slip in her heels, she white knuckled the rail as she climbed narrow staircase. The lounge on the third floor was similar to the first, only the bar was smaller and there were small round tables with barstools and no couch. White curtain lights hung from the ceiling, illuminating the room better than downstairs.

Thomas, the only casually dressed person in the establishment in a t-shirt and jeans, sat at a table by himself. Even with a beard, he was easily recognizable. In one hand he held a dark drink and his phone in the other. He didn't appear to notice her walk in. There was a lump in her throat as she walked towards him. Too preoccupied with her own nerves, she took a misstep with her right foot and with as much grace as a drunk elephant, she fell to her knee. *Please please please say he didn't notice.* She looked up and met his gaze. *Shit.* Her face flushed cherry red and her ankle throbbed as she stood up.

"Hi, I'm Celia." She extended her hand to him. "Can we pretend like that didn't happen?"

His eyes traveled from her face to her waist and back. He didn't offer his hand in return.

"Should we also pretend you didn't rip your dress?"

"What?"

He gestured to her waist, where her dress's opening had split and rose, revealing the edge of her lacy black underwear.

Her face grew even redder. "You have got to be kidding me."

She quickly sat down and held her clutch over the opening. Thomas' attention returned to his phone. Awkward silence hung in the air, only partially masked by the jazz music emitting from the speakers. Thomas started coughing, and he brought his hand over his mouth. His eyes watered as he took a large sip of his drink. He cleared his throat and sat his phone down.

"Are you alright?" she asked.

"I'm fine. Would you like a drink or are you even old enough?"

Celia's mouth fell open.

"I beg your pardon, how young do you think I am?"

He shrugged his shoulders. "Eighteen, twenty tops."

"I'm twenty-three," she said.

"Could've fooled me. What's your poison?"

"Vodka soda is fine."

He walked over to the bar and spoke with the bartender, an older gentleman. A few inches taller than six feet, Thomas looked even taller in person than he did in his movies. Celia considered texting Amy, telling her she needed a ride home. A ripped dress *had* to be a good enough reason to leave early. She didn't even have to mention how aloof Thomas was acting.

"Here." Thomas sat the drink in front of her on the table.

Celia took a generous sip, hoping it would help calm her nerves. Thomas fiddled with the glass in his hand. There was a noticeable look of sadness in his eyes.

"Why'd you agree to do this?" Celia asked finally.

"I could ask you the same thing. You're not even twenty-five and you want to be bogged down in a fake relationship? My twenties were wild, I don't think any agent or producer could've talked me into something like this."

Thomas had been known to the public eye, courtesy of *TMZ* and other trashy media outlets, as a party boy. Almost every other day he was highlighted in photos by various paparazzi. Most pictures were of him shirtless, revealing his washboard abs, often drunk, and always with some young pretty model by his side. It wasn't until he turned thirty that his name stopped appearing in tabloids. The only news that ever came out about him was about his film roles and professional appearances. His personal life was left a mystery. The only glimmers into it were from his and his sister's *Instagram* accounts, and even those were few and far between.

"Regardless, I was thinking a few nights a week we should go out to public places to be seen and photographed. I don't need you blowing up my phone, but you can call or text if something comes up. I don't know how good of an actress you are, but you need to *play* the part. Understood?"

Celia nodded. All hopes that this was going to be an enjoyable experience had evaporated. It seemed that he didn't want to be part of this even more than she did. Thomas stood up and walked around to her. He draped his arm over her shoulder. His cologne, earthy and strong, was a welcome surprise.

"Can you take a picture of us?" he asked the bartender.

The man nodded and took Thomas' phone.

"Now make sure you smile pretty," Thomas said.

Celia relaxed into his touch, his warmth inviting her in. She smiled and the man snapped two photographs. Thomas took his phone and retreated to his seat. His cologne still lingered in the air.

"Alright, now to add this to *Instagram*. What's your handle? We need to follow each other," he said.

"It's my first and last name— Celia Stuart."

She didn't want to admit that she was already following him on social media, or that she had been for years.

"And so it begins." Thomas sighed.


Celia's phone hadn't stopped buzzing since Thomas posted the picture. Friends all the way back from middle school were messaging her. Even her mother, who was on the other side of the country for a luxury cruise, had called three times, and left a voicemail with each call. She hadn't responded to any of the messages or calls, but she was aware of the attention the photograph was getting. Most of the comments were positive, even from Thomas' stalker fans, but the comment that mattered most was Brandon's. Somehow in the sea of, "So cute," and "Congrats," his comment was the one that caught her eye. One sentence, "You have got to be kidding me".

Celia rolled over in her bed. It didn't matter how many times she tossed and turned, she wasn't able to fall asleep. The analog clock on her nightstand glowed. It was only four o'clock in the morning. Suddenly her phone buzzed, a text message from Thomas.

"Want to go to the beach?" it read.

She rubbed her eyes and reread the message. Still, curiosity intrigued her.

"When?" she asked.

. . .

"I will pick you up in twenty."

*Seriously?* She peeked again at the clock. It wasn't like she was able to sleep anyway, but still part of her wanted to say no.

Especially after how *well* their first meeting had gone. Some part of her, perhaps the small glimmer of hope that this could end up being a positive working relationship, persuaded her.

"I'll be ready."

She threw off her covers and went to the bathroom. The walls were covered in eggshell white paint, and the tile was as equally bland. The only color came from her Pusheen shower curtain and green rugs. She brushed her tangled hair, threw on some waterproof mascara, and brushed her teeth. She wasn't sure what to wear. It was four in the morning, after all, but still they were going to a beach. She went with her black bikini, cut off shorts, and a white crop top. Staring at her reflection, she was suddenly self-conscious. She was thin and petite, lacking any curves, and didn't feel like someone Thomas would be seen with. *Are people actually going to believe this?* Her phone buzzed, signaling his arrival. She took a deep breath, grabbed her bag, and headed downstairs.

Thomas was sitting in the driver's seat of a red Mustang. Its windows were tinted so darkly that she couldn't actually see him, but it was the only vehicle with its lights on, so she knew it had to be him.

"Good morning," he said as she climbed into the passenger seat.

He was wearing a Los Angeles Dodgers ball cap, solid black t-shirt, and pineapple print swimming trunks. A cartoon Edgar Allen Poe air freshener hung from the rearview mirror, filling the vehicle with an airy forest aroma. He changed the radio station, stopping on an oldies rock group Celia didn't recognize.

"How'd you know I was awake?" Celia asked.

He turned out onto the desolate service road. "*Instagram.*"

"Oh."

A man walked his Great Dane on the empty sidewalk as they drove by. The only light was provided by the streetlights overhead and the thin crescent moon.

"How'd you know where I live?"

"Your agent, Annie, told me."

"Amy," Celia corrected.

*Of course, she did.* The car turned on a side road towards the pier.

"It must be nice living this close to the beach," Thomas said.

"It is, but I don't go as often as I used to."

"Why not? Afraid someone will recognize you?"

She shook her head. "People around here don't usually recognize me. I'm not anywhere near as famous as you are though."

Thomas parked the car in the empty beach lot and got out. Celia followed him to the edge of the shore. The air was humid, but the water was icy cool. The beach was as vacant as the parking lot, save for a few seagulls. The gulls' chirps and the sound of the crashing waves echoed through the morning.

"My sister called me the day after I posted that picture." Thomas started walking. "Apparently my two nieces are fans of yours."

"Really?" Celia kept pace beside him.

"Yeah, saw some movie with you and a horse and were fans ever since. They've seen all your movies apparently."

"That's sweet." She stopped. "Do they know?"

"Know what?"

"This is fake."

He sighed and shook his head.

"The contract," she said.

"Besides." He kept walking. "If they knew, it would break their little hearts. They're more excited that I'm dating you than when I took them to the premiere of *Kungfu Panda 3*."

She laughed and a genuine smile spread across his face.

"Sounds like you're really close to them?"

He nodded. "I love them like they're my own."

"Can I ask you something?"

"Sure."

"Why did you never settle down and have kids? I'm not saying you're too old or it's too late, I just figured someone like you would have a family by now."

His smile faded and the sadness she saw before reemerged in his eyes. Celia's chest tightened, and she immediately regretted asking.

"I'm sorry, it's none of my business. I shouldn't have asked," she said.

He didn't say anything. His gaze was far off, as if he wasn't there. She didn't know what was wrong, if anything, but she wanted to bring him back out of his head. She reached for his hand. It was rough and warm to the touch. He returned his focus to her as she pulled him deeper into the sea. She stopped when it was a little over waist deep for him and the water came up right under her chest.

"What makes you confident that I know how to swim?" he asked.

"*IMBD* said you did all the under-water stunts in *Shark City*."

"You read my profile? I thought only crazy stalker fans did that."

Celia took a step back and splashed water onto his face. His lips curved into a mischievous smile.

"Oh, so that's how it's going to be?"

Again, she splashed water towards him. He returned fire, utilizing a wave to amplify his attack. Her hair was soaked flat against her head, and her shirt clung to her.

"You're taller than me, this isn't fair!"

"Tough shit." He sent more water her way.

Both of their faces were red from laughing. Celia lurched forward and into his arms as something brushed against her leg. Maybe it was the side-comment about his role in a movie with sharks, but her smile faded as her mind filled with endless possibilities of what had touched her.

"What's wrong?" he asked.

"Something touched my leg."

"Do you want to go back to the shore?"

She nodded. Silently they walked back to the water's edge. Thomas pulled a small piece of seaweed from her hair. His hand lingered on her shoulder.

"Careful, there's no one around. I could start thinking you actually care about my feelings."

"What is that supposed to mean?" he asked.

"You were so cold when we met. It was like I was literally the last person you wanted to be around."

"I wouldn't say last, maybe second or third to last."

"Can you be serious for one second?"

"Look, there's a lot going on in my life right now. There's more to me than what you read online."

"You know, that's fine, I'm not asking you to be a perfectly open book. I just want you to be civil. It's not like I'm not going through my own stuff. I chose you over my boyfriend."

"Celia, let's get one thing straight. You chose a *movie* over your boyfriend, not me."

She pictured Brandon's face when he saw the picture of her and Thomas. It was probably a mixture of disbelief and sadness, or perhaps he was angry.

"You know what, you're right, and that's a decision I will live with."

Celia walked up the beach and sat down. She combed her fingers through her wet, tangled hair. After a moment, Thomas followed and sat down next to her.

"I love acting, I always have, but sometimes it forces you to choose between your personal life and your career. One thing I've learned over the years is how valuable forgiveness is and how infrequently we forgive ourselves. This won't be the last time you're forced to make a tough decision. My advice to you would be to start learning to forgive yourself," he said.

Tears slid down Celia's cheeks. The guilt for abandoning Brandon was overwhelming. Thomas placed his arm tightly around her and pulled her head into his chest. His heartbeat echoed in her ear.

"Can we stay like this for a little bit, please?" she asked.

"We can stay here as long as you'd like."

# Three

Celia sat in the backseat of the limousine next to Thomas. She wore a silver gown covered in delicate crystals, and her hair was pulled into a fishtail braid. Thomas, for once, was dressed up as well, sporting a blue velvet suit.

"Are you nervous?" he asked.

"No, why do you ask?"

He sighed. "I hope you're a better actress than you are a liar. You have a tell. Whenever you're nervous you play with your hair, and you haven't stopped touching your braid."

Celia immediately brought her hand down to her side. No one had noticed, or at least admitted they had noticed, her nervous habit in years.

"Okay, I'm a *little* nervous. This is our first public outing as a couple and it's not like we're going to a restaurant or bar."

"It's just an awards show."

"Do you really consider the *Academy Awards* just some awards show?"

He shrugged his shoulders nonchalantly.

"You do realize the biggest awards show I've ever attended was the *Teen Choice Awards*, right?"

"Listen, I'm going to be by your side the entire time. If someone, press or otherwise, throws an uncomfortable question at us, I'll handle it. All you need to do is smile and look pretty, like you always do."

The heat rushed to Celia's cheeks, as the limo slowed down and pulled off next to the curb. It was like her heart was literally going to burst out of her chest.

"You ready?" he asked.

She nodded. He opened the door and the crowd of bystanders roared. Photography flashes were intense like strobe lights.

"Thomas! Mr. Richardson! Over here," they all shouted.

Thomas held his hand out to Celia and helped her out of the vehicle. Suddenly the crowd was shouting *her* name too. Hand in hand they walked down the red carpet and lined up behind the crowd of stars. Richard Madden, Chris Evans, and Octavia Spencer were standing close by, cracking inaudible jokes between themselves. Although Celia had been around high-profile stars before, she never ceased to be in awe around them. They were regular people, like her and fans, but seeing Captain America standing merely a few feet away still was strange.

"What happens next?" Celia asked.

"Well, we're going to shuffle through this line to get photographed. We can mingle with people, and then eventually we will be ushered inside and can find our seats," he said.

A model carrying a tray of Fiji Water walked over to them, her eyes locked on Thomas. Her long gown was a bright blue, and her heels were silver. She pushed a lock of her brown hair behind her ear, and her thin lips curved into a smile.

"Would you like a water?" she asked in a thick British accent.

"No thank you," Thomas said.

"Are you sure?" she asked again, taking a step closer to him. She lightly placed her hand on Thomas' shoulder. Her long fingers stroked the velvet fabric. Thomas took a step back, and the model took a step forward. He cast a nervous glance at Celia.

"He said he was good," Celia said.

The model turned to Celia, and her smile was gone. Her glare made Celia uncomfortable, but she refused to break eye-contact and crossed her arms. After what felt like an eternity, the model winked at Thomas before walking off. He straightened his tie and sighed.

"Thank you," Thomas said.

"Anytime." Celia smiled. "She acted like I wasn't even here. I think she was the *thirsty* one."

Thomas chuckled. "I didn't realize you could be so tough. No wonder they cast you as the rebellious rancher's daughter."

"Were you reading my *IMBD* profile now?"

"No, I watched your movie. You look really good in a cowboy hat."

He winked and a weird warm feeling enveloped her stomach. *Don't even think about it Celia. This is for PR and he's being a good actor... a really good actor.*

Thomas led her in front of the white wall and the cameras and crowd intensified. Thomas was a natural and the cameras loved him. It was impossible to photograph him at a bad angle. Celia's confidence blossomed being next to him. She was glowing and Thomas must've noticed as he couldn't stop staring at her.

"Can we get a kissing shot of the new couple?" one of the photographers asked.

Celia looked to Thomas, this *had* to fall under the category of uncomfortable questions. Without appearing to give it a second thought, he pulled Celia into his arms and kissed her. It was electric, shooting warmth throughout her entire body. She wasn't sure how long they had been kissing, but when he started to pull away, she pulled him back in. There was an eruption of clapping and whistles from the photographers, but she was only concerned about him.

Thomas took a step back and he was smiling, but his eyes looked pained. A knot formed in her stomach and an overwhelming wave of self-consciousness washed over her. As if he saw the light drain from her eyes, he gave a quick wave and pulled her away from the cameras.

"I'm sorry, I shouldn't have done that," she said. She was on the verge of tears.

"Don't be ridiculous, it's fine." Thomas pulled her into a tight embrace. "I promise—it's fine."

Before either of them could say anything else, Robin Roberts walked up with a small camera crew. She was dressed in a suave leather pantsuit, toting a microphone.

"Hey Thomas, I was wondering if I could get a quick interview with you and your new beau?" Robin asked.

"Uh, sure, if it's alright with you, Celia?"

Celia nodded and forced a smile. She still didn't feel right. No matter what he said, her gut was telling her something was wrong. Thomas shifted to Celia's left side, so he was between her and Robin. His hand rested on the small of her back. One of the camera crew members counted down from five and sent a thumbs up.

"Good evening everyone, I'm Robin Roberts and I'm coming to you live from the *Academy Awards*. Currently with me is one of my favorite action movie stars, Thomas Richardson, and his girlfriend, actress Celia Stuart. So, tell me, how are you both doing tonight? I understand that this is Celia's first time here at the *Academy Awards*. Can you tell me what it's like?"

"Good evening Robin, we're doing great, thanks for asking. It's an honor to be here," he said.

They both turned their attention to Celia.

"Honestly, Robin, I was a little nervous on the way over here, but Thomas has really kept me at ease. I couldn't have asked for a better date. Like he said, it's an honor to be here."

"Good, I'm glad to hear it. Now a little birdy told me you two will be staring in the new romantic thriller, *The Werewolf and The Witch Queen*. Is there anything that you can tell us about that?" Robin asked.

"I can't say too much other than I'm excited to be working with director Vincent Monticello again and I think you guys are going to love it," Thomas said.

"Awesome, I know I for one am looking forward to it. Thank you both for your time tonight and it was a pleasure meeting you, Celia. Alright, back to you Bob," Robin said.

"And scene," one of the crewmen said.

Robin shook both their hands and disappeared into the crowd with the crew.

"They already put out the casting information? Doesn't that make *this* obvious?" Celia asked.

"Not at all, you're a *very* convincing actress."

Celia smiled half-heartedly. "Fake it until you make it, right?"

Celia was on her couch, deep into reading *Outlander* when someone knocked on the door. It was a little after one o'clock in the afternoon and she wasn't expecting anyone. Curious, she sat down her book and went to the door. It was Brandon.

"Hey, Celia. Can I come in?" he asked.

Celia hesitated for a moment. It wasn't pretty the last time she saw him, and part of her feared him acting out and doing something worse.

"Please?" he asked.

"As long as you promise to be civil, yes, you can come in."

He followed her to the couch and sat down. He had bags underneath his eyes and his hair was messier than usual, evident that he probably hadn't been sleeping well. He was wearing cargo shorts and a t-shirt, his typical wardrobe choice when he wasn't working.

"You look good," he said.

"Brandon, I don't mean to be rude but, why are you here? I won't lie and say it isn't nice to see you, but you never responded to any of my messages. It's weird for you to show up out of the blue after ghosting me for over a month. I was under the impression that you didn't even want to be friends anymore."

"Celia, I don't think you realize how much I care about you. I know this has been a hard few months for me and things haven't been ideal, but I've been trying, really. I was hoping by the end of this year I could get back into school and we could've moved in together."

"Oh."

Celia looked down at her hands. She couldn't deny how much she once cared or how much she *still* cared about Brandon. If he had asked her to move in before all of this, she might've said yes.

"Why are you telling me all this now?" she asked.

"I was talking to my cousin, telling her how you broke up with me and then started dating some actor. She told me that guy is thirty-seven-years-old, and it was weird, unbelievable actually, that he would date someone extraordinarily younger than him. I shrugged it off until I heard about the speech at the *Academy Awards* and looked up the casting call for myself. That's when it *hit* me. You didn't breakup with me because the film prep or the schedule, you were *forced* to so you could take part in some fake relationship."

"That's not true."

"Don't bullshit me Celia, you and I both know you can't lie to save your life."

A lump sat in her throat. Her hands shook, fighting the overwhelming urge to fiddle with her hair. She knew it would give him all the proof he needed. She had to think quickly.

"Brandon, I'm sorry, but that's not the case. Thomas and I met at my final audition. We exchanged numbers and things progressed from there."

Brandon slammed his fists onto the couch. "Why are you lying to me?"

"I'm not lying."

Brandon lunged forward, grabbed Celia by the shoulders and pulled her into a kiss. It wasn't the way she remembered. It was rough and his lips tasted like stale whiskey. He released her and sat back. Her face was expressionless.

"Tell me you didn't feel something now, anything. Tell me you don't still have feelings for me, and I'll go."

Celia was torn. She didn't feel anything when they kissed, but she did still have feelings for him. They had been entwined in each other's lives for so long that she would probably always care for him to some extent.

"I'm sorry Brandon, but I've moved on. I will always care for you, but as a friend and nothing more," she said.

He blinked slowly, as if he was processing her words. He stood up and went to the door. This time she didn't try to stop him, and he left quickly and silently. Celia sighed and pulled a pillow over her face. Breaking up with him the first time was hard enough, but this was the final nail in the coffin, and she knew there was no coming back from this. Even after all this, if he somehow managed to forgive her for lying, there would always be a lack of trust.

Celia's phone buzzed. Reluctantly, she dropped the pillow and picked it up. She had expected it to be Amy or Thomas texting to remind her of the dinner date, but it was from Brandon. She held her phone up to unlock it, and her stomach dropped.

"I know you're lying and I'm going to prove it," it read.

# Four

Celia sat across the table from Thomas at Osteria Mozza, an Italian restaurant. She was wearing a solid red dress with wedge sandals. Her hair was gently curled. Thomas wore jeans and a black button up shirt. The lighting in the restaurant was dim, the staff were mainly relying on candles and wall sconces as they tended to the patrons.

"Are you okay?" Thomas asked.

"I'm fine." Celia took a sip of wine. "Why do you ask?"

"You haven't said much all night. And just so you know, I've been around women long enough to know when a lady says she's fine, she's not. I have a sister, remember?"

Celia sighed. It was no use keeping it a secret from him. She pulled out her phone and handed it to him. His eyebrow raised as he read the message.

"Who's Brandon?" he asked.

"My ex. He showed up earlier today and called me out. I don't think he's doing well. It's been a really rough year for him, and I know me breaking up with him didn't help. He reeked of whiskey when he kissed me, and he never drinks whiskey."

"He kissed you?"

"It's not a big deal. We were in my apartment, no one saw."

"So, you were alone with a guy in your apartment?"

The waiter approached in an attempt to take their order, but Thomas held his hand up and the waiter quickly retreated to a different table. The restaurant wasn't busy, only about half of the tables were full, so the waiters and waitresses were more attendant than needed.

"Why do you care?" she asked.

"Hey, keep your voice down. I care because if we're dating how is it supposed to look if another guy, an ex-boyfriend at that, is alone at your apartment with you."

"I didn't even think about it. This relationship is one of the last things on my mind."

Thomas appeared slightly offended.

"You know what I mean. It doesn't take the time or energy that a real relationship does. We don't talk unless there's something on the schedule," she said.

"You know you *can* always contact me," he said.

"I'm not supposed to blow up your phone, remember?"

"Come on Celia, don't be childish. That's what I said before."

"Before what?"

"Before I got to know you. You're not what I expected, and I mean that as a compliment. I prematurely judged you and I'm sorry I did."

"It's okay, I'm sure this wasn't your ideal situation in the first place."

"How about we start over and wipe the slate clean? You can contact me as much as you'd like." He reached his hand across the table and placed it over hers. "And don't worry about this punk Brandon. Let him try."

Celia smiled. "I would like that."

"Do you want to get out of here?" he asked

"Where would we go? I thought the purpose of tonight was to be seen on a date together."

"We will be seen, but it'll be somewhere else. I saw a carnival set up on the way over here. I think it would be more fun. Besides, a greasy corndog sounds way better than overpriced spaghetti."

"Okay, let's go."

Thomas set fifty dollars underneath the menu and stood up. He offered his hand to Celia and she took it. They didn't wait for the waiter to return, and Celia didn't bother to notify Amy of the change of plans. The spontaneity was intoxicating. Although the sun had set a few hours earlier, the outside air was still warm. Arms locked with one another, they walked on the sidewalk amongst the crowd. A few people took their picture from afar, but no one approached them.

"Do you ever get approached?" she asked.

"Sometimes, but it depends on the location. Honestly, I'd rather them come up instead of slinking in the distance and stealing pictures. It feels like an invasion of privacy, and it reminds me that I'm not considered a regular person. I like to think I'm like everyone else, but some fans put me on this pedestal that I can't live up to."

"The price of fame, I guess."

The carnival was only a few blocks away from Osteria Mozza. The gentle breeze carried the scents of fried dough, and sweaty animals throughout the streets. A Ferris wheel, decorated with flashing chaser lights, peaked over the neighboring buildings. A tent housed a petting zoo with exotic animals as well as a horse-walker with miniature horses wearing tiny saddles for kids to ride on. There were at least a hundred booths, housing a variety of games and serving greasy foods and alcoholic beverages. There was a small rollercoaster, a swing carousel, bumper cars, haunted house, tunnel of love, house of mirrors, and a space themed orbiter. Music of all different genres and time periods shuffled through the speaker system, dulling the roar of conversations between the patrons.

"Can we ride the Ferris wheel?" Celia asked.

"Only if we don't eat first... I'm slightly afraid of heights."

Celia couldn't help but laugh and Thomas frowned.

"Hey, it's a common phobia."

"I didn't imagine you being afraid of heights of all things."

They walked over to the Ferris wheel and got in the short line. It creaked as it slowly brought its riders down. Reluctantly, Thomas relinquished two tickets to the pimpled teenager and took a seat. Celia sat next to him, and the teenager checked the bar before turning his attention back to the line. Thomas' eyes were wide, and he was slightly trembling. Celia grabbed his hand.

"It'll be alright, I promise," she said.

He nodded but didn't look convinced. He closed his eyes as they ascended from the ground. The higher they rose, the cooler the air was around them. Celia's arms were covered in chill bumps. The wheel stopped, swinging their seat as it did, and Thomas squeezed her hand tightly. Slowly he opened his eyes. The entire carnival as well as the nearby park were visible from their seat. The stars glittered above them. The music and crowd's chatter below were inaudible. It was calming.

"If you weren't an actor, what would you be?" Celia asked.

"Growing up I wanted to be an artist. It's hard to find a picture of me as a child without a sketchpad or some drawing paper in my hand. Unfortunately, those dreams went out the window when I realized I couldn't draw worth a damn. No one had the heart to tell me though, and my mother *still* has some of my 'masterpieces' hanging in her house. What about you?"

"A counselor or some sort of mental health professional." She looked away from him. "My dad committed suicide when I was ten-years-old. My parents were going through a nasty divorce, but he seemed fine. I had spent time at his house two days before, and I had no idea what he was planning. I used to think about our last day together, trying to piece together any signs I might've missed... I used to blame myself. Surely, there had to have been something he said or did that should've let me know what was going on."

"Celia, you were a kid, there's no way you could've known."

She nodded and a tear slipped down her cheek.

"When you lose someone close to you unexpectedly, it's hard to comprehend. Your mind looks for answers, sometimes a person to blame, and it happened that I was the last person to see him, so I blamed myself. I know now, there wasn't anything I could've done differently. He had demons he was battling on his own, and he didn't see a way out."

"I understand that completely. Sometimes it's easier to keep things to yourself than to burden others with your problems."

"If someone cares about you, they won't see it as a burden. They'll try and help you, but you have to be willing to help yourself first. I think that's where things went sour with Brandon. He was struggling but didn't want to help himself and things got progressively worse. I'm not going to sit back and watch someone drown if they're not willing to take the lifeboat that's given to them."

Thomas looked away, towards the road and passing cars. The Ferris wheel resumed its rotation briefly, bringing them to its peak.

"What if it's too late?" he asked, still staring at the road.

"What?"

"What if someone changes their mind, decides they want the lifeboat, but it's too late so they end up drowning?"

Celia knew they weren't talking about Brandon or her father anymore. *Have you lost someone too?* She interlaced her fingers with his and scooted closer to him. His heart was beating slowly.

"I don't think it's ever too late," she said.

"I hope you're right."

The Ferris wheel brought them back down and Thomas was visibly relieved. They walked towards a concession stand whose sign said, "The best fried food in ALL of America". Pretzels rotated in a glass display and the grease cried as various food items were dipped into it.

"What can I get you two?" the stocky man at the register asked.

"Corndog and lemonade sound good?" Thomas asked.

Celia nodded.

"Alright, we'll take two corndogs and two lemonades."

"That'll be twelve-fifty."

Thomas handed the man a twenty. Someone lightly tapped Celia on her shoulder. She turned and saw a woman in her early forties with a young daughter.

"Ma'am are you Celia Stuart?"

Celia nodded and the young girl's face lit up.

"My daughter is a huge fan, would you mind if she took a picture with you?" the woman asked.

"Of course not, I'd love to."

Celia walked over to the girl who was shyly toying with the hem of her polka dot dress.

"What's your name?"

"Lily."

"Nice to meet you Lily," Celia said.

The little girl smiled wildly. Celia kneeled and put her arm around her waist. They smiled as the mother snapped several photographs. The mother thanked Celia and the pair disappeared into the crowd. Thomas handed Celia her corndog and lemonade.

"That was sweet," he said.

"Most of my fans are really kind and I'm fortunate."

"I wish I could say the same. I've had a few stalking instances and when I've dated before, I've had some stalker fans harass my girlfriends. Shoot, I was a groomsman in my friend's wedding once and some girls started harassing the bridesmaid I walked down the aisle with on social media. It was ridiculous."

"Maybe someone should've warned me about your crazy fans before I agreed to this," Celia joked.

Thomas shrugged his shoulders and they both laughed. Celia took a bite of her mustard drizzled corndog.

"Is this the best corndog you've ever had in America?" Thomas asked.

"Definitely top five, can't say it's the best though."

"It was, as predicted, better than the spaghetti would've been."

"True, but it's not very romantic."

"Oh don't underestimate me, I can make it romantic."

He grabbed her hand and pulled her through the crowd of carnival goers. Hastily they weaved in and out of clusters of people. He stopped in front of a game booth. For five tickets, a person could attempt to throw rings onto different colored bottles. Red bottles were worth five points, black were ten, and white were one point each. After throwing all ten plastic rings, points were added up and could be exchanged for a prize. The prizes ranged from bouncy balls, various stuffed animals, and live goldfish. The most coveted prize was a large unicorn plush, similar to the one in *Despicable Me*.

"Are you ready to be romanced?" he asked.

"How?"

"Watch and learn."

Thomas handed the booth attendee, an overly enthusiastic elderly male, five tickets. He chewed the end of a cigarette while Thomas held the cup of rings. He leaned over, turned his head, and squinted his eye as if he was calculating the perfect strategy to ensure the most points. Celia stood beside him, her hand covering her face in a poor attempt to conceal her laughter.

"Laugh all you want, but I'm winning you that unicorn," he said.

He stood back up straight and threw his first ring. It bounced off of a black bottle and landed on the ground. Zero points. His next three tosses were slightly better, successfully landing on one red bottle and two white bottles, but then his luck ran out. All the remaining throws ended up on the ground.

"Seven points will get you a goldfish or one of these little stuffed animals. What will it be sir?"

Thomas looked to Celia, but she simply shrugged her shoulders. This was his idea after all.

"How about the smaller unicorn? Let's do... the pink one," Thomas said.

The attendee handed him the unicorn plush, it was at least five times smaller than the grand prize, but it was equally as cute. It had a fuzzy rainbow-colored mane and tail and a sparkly silver horn. Thomas got down on one knee and extended the unicorn to her. The people around them had stopped and were staring. A few started taking pictures with their cellphones. Her face flushed and heat rushed to the back of her head.

"Celia, will you do me the honor of accepting this lovely unicorn?" he asked.

"Yes, now *please* get up," she said.

He grinned madly and stood up. The bystanders cheered as she took the unicorn from him.

"I'm going to kill you," she whispered.

"What? So soon? We haven't even done part two."

"What's part two?"

He didn't answer, instead he grabbed her hand and started walking again. They passed the tent with animals, where a small child was crying for their father, scared to be alone on the miniature horse. The smell of sawdust shavings and sweaty animals overtook the aroma of fried foods. He stopped at the end of the path, in front of the tunnel of love, haunted house, and house of mirrors.

"You're kidding... right?" Celia asked.

Thomas shook his head. "You asked for a romantic date, so you're getting a romantic date. Now, do me a favor and close your eyes."

Celia sighed but did as she was told. Thomas put one arm around her waist and kept her hand in his other. He guided her forward slowly and carefully. She felt safe, like he wasn't going to accidentally walk her into a wall.

"Alright, there's a step here and then we're going through a door," he said.

Celia stepped up onto the wood and it creaked. Thomas opened the door and the air inside was warm. Eerily sounding classical music spewed from the speakers.

"Open your eyes."

He hadn't taken her to the tunnel of love. He had chosen the haunted house instead. Faux cobwebs hung from the wooden ceilings. White strobe lights flashed on and off. A middle-aged woman stood behind a wooden counter to take tickets. She wore a witch's hat, and there was something lumpy under her shirt, giving her a humped back. A large mole was on the side of her nose, and it wasn't evident if it was real or part of the costume.

"Ten tickets... if you dare," she said.

Thomas pulled out the ticket reel, giving her the remainder they had. She forced a cackle and pointed towards a small door. The anxiety of going inside overwhelmed Celia.

"Are you ready for this?" he asked.

Celia shook her head. "How is this romantic exactly?"

"Because I presume you're going to be scared so you'll for one hold my hand, and two cling to me. I figured we would get 'closer' here rather than in some cheesy tunnel. Now come on."

Begrudgingly she followed him through the door. It was pitch black, absent of the strobe lights. Thomas took a step in, and a small red light lit up on the floor. He took another step and a scream shot out of a speaker as the image of a clown lit up the side wall. Celia practically climbed in his arms, and he started laughing.

"It's not funny Thomas, I hate jump scares!"

"Like how I hate heights?" he asked, smirking.

She gently punched his arm. *Now I see what this is. Payback.*

"No need to worry, I'll protect you."

Celia rolled her eyes. "My hero."

Thomas led her into the next section. It was a small tunnel like area where there was a bridge. The walls and floor were lit up in brilliant red and orange hues that moved in a circular motion.

"Well, this doesn't look scary," Celia said.

"Walk on it."

Celia took the lead. Her legs wobbled as if the bridge was moving. She white knuckled the railing. Dizziness consumed her. Her stomach became queasy, and the corndog was in danger of resurfacing. Thomas came up behind her, and put his hands on her waist.

"The bridge isn't really moving. Concentrate on the ground, not the walls," he said.

Celia stared at the bridge below her and took another step, it was still wobbly but manageable. As quickly as she could, she crossed the remainder of the bridge. Thomas was close behind. The door opened to a brighter room. It was staged like a bedroom with a small bed, dresser, television, and a collection of mutilated dolls. The walls and floor were splattered in fake blood. The television was set on static, and it echoed throughout the room. One of the dolls was placed directly in front of the television and its head cranked around as they stepped forward. Its wooden mouth opened and giggled.

"I'm getting *Poltergeist* vibes in here," Thomas said.

"I didn't realize you were a horror connoisseur," Celia said, stepping over a doll.

Thomas smiled. "You never asked."

The final room was a mock graveyard, fitted with turf grass, foam tombstones and rubbery zombies clawing out of graves. An actor dressed as an undead grave keeper stood in the corner of the room. His face was caked with white and grey paint. He wore a black trench coat riddled with holes and covered in fake blood. He wore white contacts that hid his pupils and carried a severed arm prop. He groaned at Celia and Thomas.

"He seems lovely, maybe we should invite him to spend the rest of the night with us," Thomas said.

"I guess you can let me drive your Mustang home and I can leave you here to get acquainted with him."

Thomas laughed. "In your dreams. My sister doesn't even get to drive my car."

"I bet I'll be driving your car before the movie is finished filming."

"I wouldn't hold your breath."

Thomas held the exit door open for her and they walked outside. The night air was cooler and most of the carnival's crowd had diminished. The majority of the booths had shut down, while others were in the process of closing.

"What time is it?" Celia asked.

"Eleven fifteen. I should probably be getting you back home," he said.

Celia reluctantly nodded. Truthfully, she wasn't ready for the night to be over. Thomas took her hand and they started walking back towards the restaurant. The sidewalks were mostly abandoned now, save for a few night owls and homeless people. Thomas' car was the only one in the restaurant's parking lot. He held the door open for her and she got inside. He stood there, staring at her, a smile across his face.

"For the record, I'm not ready to go home either. If I didn't have a doctor's appointment tomorrow morning, we would've done something else. This has been the best night I've had in a long time. Thank you," he said.

# Five

When Thomas asked Celia to tag along while he took his nieces trick-or-treating, she couldn't say yes quick enough. Halloween had always been a big deal for Celia, even when she was a child. From the art of dressing up to the act of handing out candy to trick-or-treaters, Celia never failed to participate. As her fame grew, Halloween became more important as she could freely walk among her peers without any recognition or attention.

Thomas picked Celia up a little before six o'clock in the evening. He was attired as a pirate, complete with an eyepatch and rubber hook to hide his left hand. Eyeliner heavily lined his visible eye. Celia was dressed up as a cat. Large homemade ears were fastened to the top of her head. She also wore matching gloves and a tail. Her face was painted with whiskers and a heart-shaped nose.

"Is it a good idea to be driving with that thing on?" Celia asked.

"Don't worry, cats have nine lives."

Celia rolled her eyes and buckled the seatbelt. Thomas was noticeably staring at her. The heat rushed to her cheeks, and she was suddenly self-conscious. *I knew I should've gone the sexy route, he probably thinks I look ridiculous.*

"You look cute."

"You do too."

Thomas chuckled wildly.

"Sorry that was... weird," she said.

"No, it wasn't. I haven't been called cute in a long time, that's all."

The roads were busier than the morning of their beach visit. People of various sizes, shapes, and ages flocked on the sidewalks. Almost everyone out and about wore a costume, save a few reluctant parents of trick-or-treaters.

It was a forty-five-minute drive to Thomas' sister's house, and the quiet neighborhood was as busy as the city. Costumed children weaved in and out of the street as Thomas put the vehicle in park. He shut off the ignition, but didn't move. Celia studied his nervous expression.

"Listen, I haven't brought anyone over in quite some time. It's been more than a few years. My sister is... protective. I told her to be on her best behavior, but there's no guarantee. Shoot me a look or something if it gets to be too much, okay?" Thomas said.

"How about we have a safe word instead?"

"Like what?"

"Pineapples."

He laughed. "Pineapples?"

She nodded and returned his smile.

"Alright, pineapples it is."

Celia and Thomas waited for the crowd of kids to take their candy before approaching the doorstep. A plastic pumpkin dish filled with various candy sat on a stool outside. A handwritten sign that said, "Take one," was taped to the dish. A smiling skeleton was pressed against the glass door. Thomas rang the doorbell twice, his anxious expression unwavering. Celia grabbed his hand and his face immediately softened. The door opened to two six-year-old twin girls, one dressed as a butterfly and the other as a bee.

"Uncle Tom is here," they shouted in unison.

Their eyes fell on Celia and they started jumping up and down.

"Celia is here too!"

"Alright, stop shouting," Thomas' sister said as she appeared in the doorway.

She was tall like Thomas and shared his blue eyes. Her dark brown hair was styled in a bob. She wore a black t-shirt that read, "This is my sexy witch costume," and jeans. She scooted the children aside and opened the door. Immediately she pulled Thomas into a hug.

"Gwen, this is Celia. Celia this is Gwen. The bee is Delilah and the butterfly is Danielle," Thomas said.

Celia extended her hand to Gwen, but Gwen pulled her into a tight hug instead. A group of giggling children slipped past them and took their share of candy. The twins resumed their bouncing, their hands grabbing at Gwen's shirt.

"Can we go trick-or-treating now?" Delilah asked.

"Yeah Mommy, can we?" Danielle echoed.

Before she could answer, Thomas broke off into a coughing fit. His face reddened and he doubled over as he coughed. He put his hand on the brick exterior of the home and took a few breaths as he regained his composure.

"Are you okay?" Gwen appeared concerned.

"I'm fine," he said.

"Are you taking your medicine?" she asked.

Thomas shot her a stern look. "Yes. Can we please talk about this later?"

Gwen nodded and took a deep breath. Her expression slightly relaxed.

"Come on girls, get your pails so we can go," Thomas said.

They scrambled into the house and returned with two pumpkin-shaped plastic bins. Thomas started towards the sidewalk and the girls followed quickly behind. Gwen grabbed Celia's arm before she could join them.

"Is he doing okay, like really? Will you please be honest with me?" she asked.

"As far as I know, yes," Celia said.

"Thank you, Celia. I know I'm the little sister and sometimes he sees me as nagging, but I can't help my worrying." She forced a smile. "Please make sure he has the girls back by eleven."

Celia slowly caught up with them. She kept a smile on her face, but something about Gwen's concern for Thomas' cough had made her stomach queasy. *What medicine? Is he sick? Why would he hide it?*

"Everything okay?" Thomas asked.

"Yeah, she simply asked that we bring the girls back by eleven."

"We better hurry then," he joked.

Celia forced a smile and Thomas took her hand. Together they walked in silence behind the twins, who marveled at each piece of candy they received. With every house they visited, their pails got fuller and heavier, slowing their pace. The later it got, the colder the air grew. Porch lights started turning off and the children trick-or-treating were slowly outnumbered by mischievous teenagers. Thomas carried a sleeping Danielle in his arms while Celia held hands with Delilah as they walked back to the house. Gwen opened the door before they even had the chance to knock.

"Right on time," she said.

"Could've scored a few more houses if this one hadn't conked out," Thomas said.

"I'm not conked out, I can do it," Delilah said.

"Nice try kiddo, but it's already past your bedtime." She took the pumpkin pails. "I bet if you ask nicely, Uncle Tom will tuck you in."

Her little eyes widened. "Really?"

"Sure," Thomas said.

He offered his freehand to Delilah and together they went into the house. Gwen went inside and Celia followed her down a narrow hallway into a spacious living room. Pictures of the twins, Thomas,

Gwen and her husband, were hung on the walls. Toys littered the hardwood floors. An L-shaped pleather couch and matching recliner were pressed against the pale-yellow walls. The television was paused on a black-and-white movie. A half-glass of red wine was sitting on the end table.

"Please excuse the mess, my husband is out of town, so I've had my hands a little full. Would you like a coffee or anything?"

"No thank you, I'm good."

Gwen sat down on the couch and Celia sat down next to her. She turned off the TV and set the remote next to her wine glass.

"It's been a really long time since Thomas has had a girlfriend."

"I didn't know," Celia said truthfully.

"After he was diagnosed, he said he would never date again. You must really be special to have changed his mind."

"I promise, I'm not."

Celia nervously touched her hair. She felt guilty lying to his sister. It was one thing to trick the public, lying to family was a different matter. It made her stomach queasy.

"Have you guys been... you know, intimate?" Gwen asked.

Celia almost tore a piece of her hair out. Red-faced, she quickly shook her head. *Fucking pineapples. Where's Thomas when I need him?* Gwen put her hand over Celia's.

"Please know that it is an option as long as he keeps up with his medication and uses protection."

Celia's mouth fell open. This was not the direction she expected the conversation to go. Before she could respond, Thomas walked in.

"Kids are in bed and on their way to snooze town." He looked from Celia to Gwen. "Is everything okay in here?"

"Yes, like... pineapples," Celia said.

Thomas' eyes widened and Celia hoped he saw the please-get-me-out-of-here expression on her face.

"Why don't you sit down for a bit and we can all have a

conversation? I know you have a bit of a drive back, let me fix you some coffee or something," Gwen said.

"Actually, it's getting late. I think it would be best if we went ahead and got back on the road. You know how people can get on Halloween," he said.

Celia sighed, relief washing over her. She mouthed, "Thank you," as she stood up. Gwen stood up as well, visibly disappointed.

"But—before we go, can you grab a picture of us?" Thomas asked.

Gwen nodded and took his phone. Thomas put his arms around Celia's waist and pulled her into him. Celia forced a smile. His touch was comforting, but it wasn't enough to shake her queasiness.

"Please make sure you come back soon," Gwen hugged them both. "And Celia, please know that you're always welcome here."

Thomas took off his eyepatch and removed his pirate cap as soon as they got back in his Mustang. Celia removed her gloves and took a deep breath. She stared out the window, unable to meet his gaze. She was afraid to look at him. Afraid he would know something was wrong. Afraid he was going to tell her he was sick, sick enough to be concerned about.

"That wasn't too bad, right?" he asked.

"No, I really enjoyed it. Thank you for inviting me," Celia didn't look at him when she spoke.

The roads and sidewalks were eerily empty. Michael Jackson's *Thriller* played softly on the radio. They hadn't been driving for more than a few minutes when Thomas pulled off onto the shoulder of a random street. Her heartrate increased, but she refused to show any expression.

"Alright, what's going on?" he asked.

"What do you mean?"

"For starters, you haven't said much since we left, and normally, I can't get you to stop talking. Not to mention, you won't even look at me."

Celia looked at him. "Better?"

Seemingly unamused, he shook his head. Celia shrugged her shoulders nonchalantly.

"I swear to God, you're going to make me crazy. One minute I think I'm—" his voice trailed off.

"What?"

"Nothing."

Celia reached over and grabbed his hand. It was quivering and tears were in his eyes.

"What is it Thomas? You can be honest with me."

"I think I'm falling for you," he whispered.

He unbuckled his seatbelt and turned towards her. Her heart was beating so loud, she thought her eardrums would burst. Slowly he leaned in, touching his forehead to hers briefly before kissing her.

# Six

Celia stood on the balcony of her apartment with Meghan, one of the few friends Celia trusted. Meghan was a Broadway performer, and her fiery red hair matched her fierce personality. She held her phone in her hand, mindlessly scrolling *Twitter*. Celia leaned over on the railing, watching the traffic beneath them. Both girls were casually dressed in shorts and t-shirts.

"So you think he's sick?" Meghan asked.

Celia nodded. Thomas' surprise confession and kiss had left her feeling high, but it hadn't been enough to curb her concern—or curiosity. There's no way Gwen would've reacted the way she did if he was suffering from a common cold. Plus, the intimacy question brought up red flags.

"Have you thought about flat out asking him?"

"Yes and no. I don't know if we're at that point in our relationship. Sometimes he seems genuine and caring, but other times he'd aloof and distant."

"I looked at some of those stalker sites like you asked, but there isn't much to go on. There were some 'concern articles' where he had been documented having a few of those coughing fits, and he's cancelled two appearances for 'undisclosed health reasons', but that's about it."

Celia sighed and Meghan put her arm around her.

"I'm sure he's fine. His sis mentioned medication, right? I'm sure if he's on medicine, whatever it is, is manageable."

"I know, I'm probably being paranoid."

"Has Brandon still been bothering you? I've seen him commenting on all the pictures of you and Thomas, it's pretty creepy."

Celia shook her head. "I don't think he's finished though. You know how stubborn he is."

"You mean *manipulative*. I swear he's always been like this, you're just now seeing it."

"Maybe... I'm trying not to worry about it because I've got so many other things going on. Thomas is going to be a guest on *Jimmy Kimmel Live*, and he's asked me to tag along. I don't know if it's going to be as smooth sailing as our first interview was."

"Sounds like you have a lot to look forward to, not stress about. Enjoy your time with Thomas, embrace the limelight a little, I'm sure Brandon will find some other girl's life to ruin."

Celia hoped she was right, but with the way Brandon had changed, there was no way to know for certain. She went inside her apartment and Meghan followed close behind. The air conditioning coolly embraced them.

"Are you going to invite Thomas to my wedding?" Meghan asked.

"I'm not sure... I don't want his presence to bring any unwanted attention to your big day. I could always go stag."

"I don't think there's a way he could bring any unwanted attention. Besides, I don't want one of my closest friends sitting alone at a table while everyone is dancing. Promise me you'll at least ask him to come?"

Celia nodded. She knew Meghan was already planning on her bringing a date, since she was dating Brandon whenever she asked her to be a bridesmaid; however, she truthfully had been so busy, Meghan's wedding had been one of the last things on her mind, let alone replacing her date. It would only make sense for her to bring Thomas.

"Now are we going to go eat? I'm starving," Meghan said.

"Yeah, let's go."

As soon as Celia and Meghan stepped outside of the complex, they were ambushed by a swarm of paparazzi. Men and women, all with cameras and recording devices, huddled around the front steps. Like moths under a porch light, they came alive as soon as they realized it was Celia.

"Celia! Celia, over here," they shouted.

The flashes and shutter sounds were more intense than at the *Academy Awards*.

"Celia, what's it like dating one of Hollywood's most eligible bachelors?"

"Are you really involved with Thomas or is this a PR stunt?"

"Is it safe to say the age gap affects the relationship?"

"Who is Brandon and what's his involvement here?"

"Care to comment?"

"Celia?"

She suddenly was wobbly as the heat rushed to her head. Her vision blurred and she fell to the ground, unconscious.

Celia woke up in her bed covered in a cold sweat and with a throbbing headache. She was stripped down to her bra and panties, her clothes folded neatly on the fabric bench at the end of her bed. A damp rag was laying across her forehead. The sun was peeking in from the blinds, and the clock read four o'clock in the afternoon. Celia pushed the rag off and slowly sat up.

"Meghan?" she called out.

"Actually, it's Thomas."

Thomas walked in and Celia blushed. She scrambled to pull the covers up. He wore his Los Angeles Dodgers ball cap, a navy-blue t-shirt, jeans, and cowboy boots.

"Where's Meghan? What happened?"

"She went home after I got here." He sat on the edge of the bed. "You fainted. You've been out for several hours, I was worried."

"Oh my gosh... wait, what about the paparazzi?"

"The cops came, and they cleared out, but they did get some pictures. My phone wouldn't stop buzzing with notifications, I had to turn it off."

"Is it bad?"

Thomas casually shrugged his shoulders. He wasn't convincing.

"I need to see this."

Without thinking, she got up to retrieve her phone. Her face reddened as she realized she wasn't dressed and dove back under the covers. Thomas didn't bother hiding his amusement and doubled over in laughter.

"Do you mind?" she asked.

"Not at all."

He winked at her before leaving the room. She waited a few seconds before getting up and closing the door. Her head still throbbed and standing made her dizzy. Slowly she pulled on her shirt and shorts before joining him in the living area. He was sitting on her couch, still wearing a smirk. She grabbed her phone off the glass top table. Three missed calls from Amy, over thirty text messages, and hundreds of social media notifications.

"Was it really that bad?"

"Well, your ex-boyfriend sent an anonymous tip about us being in a fake relationship and he was kind enough to include your address."

Celia's stomach fell to the floor. Brandon knew how important it was for her to remain out of the public's eye. Perhaps if she wasn't involved with such a high-profile actor, no one would care, but now she had to worry about the paparazzi, and maybe even visits from Thomas' stalker fans.

"What should I do?" she asked.

"First and foremost, I think you need to look for new living arrangements. The apartment complex's security can only do so much, and eventually they're going to get tired of playing police."

"I still have almost two months left on my lease... I guess I could find another place but paying for two different apartments at once will murder my savings. I guess I could stay with Meghan for a few days, I know she wouldn't mind letting me crash on her couch, until I can come up with a game plan."

"Why don't you move in with me until your lease is up?"

Celia's mouth dropped. "What? No, I couldn't possibly do that!"

"Why not? What better way to steamroll his accusations than for us to move in together? Plus, once filming starts we won't even be in the country. It's not like we would be sharing a bed, I have a guest room and plenty of space."

"You're serious, aren't you?"

Thomas nodded. Celia set her phone down and walked over to the balcony window. As much as she didn't want to admit it, he had a good point. But this went far beyond the agreement. The closer they became the worse this could end up after the film was done. She looked over at Thomas expectantly waiting for her answer. *There is no possible way that this could end well.* Celia didn't want to admit it, but she was starting to have feelings for him, and she was scared to even entertain the idea. Sure, he seemed to genuinely care, but this all stemmed from an agreement. It wasn't real.

"I may come to my senses and change my mind but give me a few minutes so I can pack my bags," she said.

A grin spread across his face. "Take all the time you need."

Located in a gated community in Los Angeles was Thomas'

house. The large houses, although cookie cutter, were built with different brick and stone variations. No two combinations were the same. All the yards were well manicured, no blade of grass out of place. Thomas' house was fashioned with grey and white stone. Large oak trees shaded the yard and square shaped shrubs inhabited the flowerbeds. His house was one on the smaller end for the neighborhood, but equally as nice as the others.

Thomas pulled his Mustang into the garage while Celia parked her Volkswagen VW Beetle against the curb. Thomas retrieved her two bags from the trunk and she followed him to the front door. Her nerves intensified as he unlocked the door. They had been alone together before, but never like *this*. Brandon was her first and only boyfriend, so she had never gotten the chance to live with a man before. Immediately upon entering the house, the smell of lavender surrounded them. Thomas' cat Scooter, a three-legged fluffy Siamese mix, came up meowing. Curiously, he sniffed Celia's leg before rubbing against her. Celia bent down and scratched the cat's head. His eyes were even bluer than Thomas'.

"I know I said there's enough space for both of us, but know that Scooter thinks he owns all the space," Thomas said.

"I don't think I'll mind." She stood up, taking the purring cat in her arms.

"Let me give you a quick tour," Thomas said.

The entrance led into a short hallway that branched off into the living room and kitchen. Past the kitchen was another hallway that led to the guest bedroom and a bathroom. On the other side of the living room was the master bedroom and bath. There was an office, which Thomas admitted he rarely used, next to his bedroom. All the walls were painted a soft beige and the floor was lightly stained hardwood. Both bathrooms had tan tile in place of the wood, and the two bedrooms had carpet. The walls were scarcely decorated, save for a few cat shelves and pictures of his family. The living room was furnished with two white couches, a television, a recliner, end table, and a cat tree. In the backyard was a small pool and gazebo.

The guest room was large and if she hadn't known better, would've assumed it was the master bedroom. It had a queen-sized bed, two nightstands, an armoire, and a television stand that doubled as a bookshelf. The comforter was a deep tree green and the curtains were a dark brown. There was a painting of a white horse above the bed and a fan-drawn picture of Scooter was on the wall in between the two windows. Next to the television were two framed pictures, one of Delilah and one of Danielle but it wasn't obvious which was which. Thomas sat her bags down in the corner of the room.

"Alright, I'll leave you so you can get settled." He lingered in the doorway. "Everything is going to be alright, I promise."

*I wish I could believe that.* She sat Scooter down and he ran after Thomas down the hallway. She laid back on the bed and stared at the popcorn ceiling. Although she had been out for a few hours and it was only half past seven, she already wanted to go to bed. She was mentally and physically drained. Her phone buzzed from inside her purse and she groaned. *What now?* Lazily she dug it out. At the top of the sea of notifications was a text message from Brandon. Seeing his name sent an uncomfortable shiver down her spine. Wearily, she opened it and almost dropped her phone. It was a picture of her right before she fainted. It wasn't one taken by the paparazzi, no, this one was snapped by a cell-phone in the crowd. Brandon had been there.

# Seven

Celia walked into Thomas' living room, half asleep. It was a little past nine o'clock in the morning and the sunlight harshly refracted through the windows. Unsure of how casually she should dress in his house, she wore a black t-shirt and cut-off shorts. Thomas was lying on the couch, a bag of frozen peas lying across his forehead. He was shirtless, only in sweatpants, and Celia couldn't help but stare. He had a phoenix tattoo on the right side of his ribs, a paw print on his right shoulder, and a Roman numeral sequence above his left peck. She knew the numbers stood for the twin's birthday as he had spoken about his tattoos previously in interviews, but she hadn't known about the phoenix tattoo. It was breathtaking, outlined in black and filled with brilliant shades of orange and red like a watercolor painting.

"Thomas?"

He slowly sat up and the peas fell onto the ground. Scooter jumped off his cat tree and ran over to investigate, the bell on his collar jingled with each step he took.

"Hey good morning," Thomas said.

"Are you alright?"

He nodded. "Woke up with another headache, nothing out of the ordinary. Did you sleep okay?"

"Yes, thank you. Scooter kept me company most of the night and that was nice. I didn't realize cats were so affectionate."

"He's definitely a special one."

Celia walked over and sat on the other end of the couch. She stared at Scooter, afraid if she looked at Thomas her eyes would be drawn to his chest and she'd start staring again. Thomas picked up the peas and held them to the side of his head. There were bags under his eyes and he looked exhausted.

"How long have you been up?" she asked.

"Since about seven, I think. Normally I jog in the mornings, but today I didn't feel like it so I've been in here trying to rid myself of this headache."

"Do you need some Tylenol or anything?" she asked.

"No, I took something earlier, it hasn't started working yet unfortunately."

Something was different about him today. Maybe it was the headache, but he didn't seem like *himself*. He was similar to an empty shell, his smile lacking its usual luster. He looked... sick. Celia repressed the urge to toy with her hair.

"Did you take the medicine your sister had mentioned?"

Thomas sat the peas down. "What?"

"On Halloween, your sister mentioned medication. I was wondering if that's what you took."

"Christ, what all did she say?"

The atmosphere in the room changed. It became overwhelmingly awkward and tense. Celia didn't know what to say, her chest was heavy. It was like the night at the beach all over again.

"Celia, what did she tell you?"

"Nothing really... she asked how you were and then if we had been, um, intimate."

"She asked WHAT now?"

Celia threw her hands up defensively. "Listen I didn't say

anything, but that's when she said it would be okay, so long as you were on medication and we used protection…"

"I'm going to kill her, I'm literally going to kill her."

Thomas stood up ran his fingers through his hair. His face was red. Aside from his performances in movie roles, Celia had never seen him angry before.

"What else? What else did she say?" he asked.

"Nothing, you walked back in before she had the chance… should I be worried about you?"

Thomas turned and looked at her. The anger that was in his eyes evaporated and his expression softened. He sat down next to her and took her hands into his.

"I appreciate your concern, but you don't need to worry about me. My sister likes to make a big deal out of things she shouldn't. This whole thing was blown out of proportion," he said.

Celia nodded, but she didn't feel reassured. There was more to this than he was letting on, even if Gwen had been overreacting. Maybe it wasn't her place to worry in the first place, but she couldn't help it. The more time she spent with him, the more she cared about him. As much as she didn't want to admit it, she was falling for him too.

"Would you like some breakfast?" he asked.

"Sure."

Thomas kissed her forehead before retreating to the kitchen. Celia picked up Scooter off the floor and sat him next to her. He purred loudly.

"Eggs and bacon sound okay?" Thomas asked.

"Sure, I'm not picky," she said.

Thomas retrieved two frying pans from the cabinet and started heating up the stove top. The kitchen was small but had a large island and plenty of counter space for cooking. The countertops were a light grey marble, meshing with the slate tile backsplash on the kitchen walls. All the utensils and appliances were black. It was, arguably, the only room with a dark color scheme as if it had been a part of a completely different home.

"How do you feel about weddings?" Celia asked.

Thomas shrugged his shoulders. "They're alright, I guess. Why?"

"Meghan is getting married in a little over two weeks and I'm one of her bridesmaids. She kindly reminded me yesterday that I no longer have a date. She suggested that I should ask you since we're together and all."

Thomas slapped bacon onto a sizzling pan and turned around.

"Is this your way of asking me?" he asked.

"Well yes, but it's in Chicago, so we'd have to fly... and then there's the matter of us having to share a hotel room."

"That's fine with me. If you want me to go, I'll go." He turned around to tend to the eggs. "But I'm going to be honest with you, I'm not much of a dancer."

Celia smiled. "Well we have a little bit of time to practice. I'll let Meghan know."

Scooter kneaded his paws on her lap, demanding attention, but Celia was more focused on Thomas' muscular back. How could someone who was *that* fit possibly be sick?

"If you want to grab something to drink and some silverware, it shouldn't be much longer till this is done. There's orange juice and milk in the fridge, but I have a Keurig if you'd rather have coffee."

Celia sat Scooter down and went into the kitchen and retrieved two sets of plates and silverware. She filled a glass with orange juice and took it to the dining room nook. It was a small area with a white square table. The long wall was consisted of three large windows, giving a generous view of the backyard. A navy blue China cabinet sat in the corner. Inside were various aged bottles of liquor, wine, and whiskey. It also housed various glassware, probably to keep Scooter from breaking anything.

Thomas brought over the plates with generous helpings of eggs and bacon and sat them on the table. He brewed a pod of blonde coffee into a mug that said, "I'm not single, I have a cat". He didn't add any sugar or creamer before placing it on the table.

"I'm going to go put on a shirt real quick, I'll be right back. I'm sorry, I didn't realize I was half-dressed," Thomas said.

Celia didn't say anything, refusing to admit that she didn't mind him being shirtless. She took a bite of her eggs. It was nice to actually have a cooked meal for breakfast. Celia didn't know how to cook anything that didn't involve being tossed into a crockpot, and even those options were limited. She didn't eat breakfast often but when she did her choices were limited to whatever could be popped into a toaster oven or eaten cold. Thomas returned wearing a solid grey t-shirt. As soon as he sat down he broke into a coughing fit that brought tears to his eyes.

"Sorry." He took a drink of coffee. "As hard as I try, I can't control those."

"You don't have to apologize. Have you always had coughing issues?"

He shook his head. "I've only been dealing with this for a few years, but it seems like it has gotten worse recently."

*Maybe this is what he takes medicine for? Or could the coughing be a symptom of something else?* Curiosity haunted her, but she didn't want to press him again about his health, at least not yet anyway. It would probably come up again eventually, especially if she saw Gwen.

"How long have you had your tattoos?" Celia asked.

"I've had the twin's birthdate for about three years, Scooter's paw print for two, and I actually got the phoenix done a few months ago. I feel like every time I get a tattoo I immediately want another one, but I have so many ideas running through my head it's hard to make a decision. My go-to artist, Mason Brown, works at a shop called Pins and Needles in downtown Los Angeles. Do you have any?"

Celia shook her head. "I would like to get one, something small on my wrist that would be easy to cover up if need be; however, I don't know what I would get. I think if I ever got one, it would have to have some serious meaning behind it."

"Would you ever get a tattoo with a co-star? Like how all the original *Avengers* actors got one together?"

"To be fair, Mark Ruffalo sat that one out. I don't know if I would though. I guess it would depend on a lot of factors."

"So I shouldn't count on us getting matching tattoos?"

She laughed. "Definitely not."


Saturday brought rain and humidity. The skies were shrouded in dreary shades of grey, keeping the sun at bay. Thomas had been quiet for most of the day. Celia had assumed he was thinking about his upcoming interview, but part of her feared something else was going on too. Still, she didn't want to pry, so even on the way to the studio Celia kept quiet. She had concerns of her own to deal with anyway. Amy had lectured her about the "fainting incident", even accusing her of breaking the contract and telling Brandon the truth. Celia had spent the better part of an hour convincing her it was a lucky guess, showing her the text messages he had previously sent. Regardless, Amy had stressed how it brought negative attention and suspicions they didn't need, and that damage control needed to be done ASAP. Their picture from Halloween was posted on every social media outlet with the same blurb describing how "happy" the couple is and that the claims were the words of a bitter ex. Most fans seemed to comment in support, but there were a few who were doubtful.

Immediately upon arriving at the studio, Celia and Thomas were separated and sent to their own dressing rooms. Both marked with a whiteboard and their names written on it. The room was small with a large mirror lined in bright LED lights. The carpet was beige and the walls were a crimson red, making the room appear even smaller. A rolling coat rack sat against the corner with three sealed garment bags. Celia took a seat in the director chair and pulled out her phone. Thomas had texted her, "Time to get pretty".

She smiled but before she had the chance to reply, there was a quick knock on the door.

"Can I come in?" a voice asked.

"Yes," Celia said.

A woman in her mid-thirties walked in toting a large black make-up bag. She was wearing tight black pleather pants, heels, and a solid red crop top. Her platinum blonde hair was pulled into a high ponytail and square-shaped glasses sat on her thin nose. She heaved the makeup bag onto the counter and extended her hand to Celia.

"Hi, I'm Elena and I'll be doing your makeup and hair today."

"Celia." She took her hand and shook it. "Is this all necessary? I was under the impression I was going to be in the audience."

"I was told to get you camera ready. I wouldn't assume you're sitting this one out sweetie."

Celia's stomach dropped. She had been optimistic that this was going to be all about Thomas, but of course that would've been too easy. Elena unzipped the bag and pulled out a twirling wand, straightener, and smaller makeup bags. It was a lot of different products, but the harsh lighting in the room made Celia feel ugly and like she was going to need a bit of all of it. It was like every imperfection on her face was magnified.

"Do you have any skin sensitivities I need to be aware of before we begin?"

"Not that I know of."

"Good."

Celia sat quietly while Elena worked. First she did her hair, a half up-do with gentle curls, and then she did her makeup. From primer to foundation and fake lashes to blush, she was made-over. She wasn't contoured to look different, Elena had merely accentuated her features. The final touch was a colorless gloss that made her lips shine.

"Your bone structure is to die for," Elena said.

Celia blushed. "Thank you."

"Now, your agent coordinated with us to have some dresses sent over. You can wear whichever one you would prefer, but I think the yellow one would suit you best."

Elena unveiled the yellow gown and Celia's mouth fell open. It was floor length and had a plunging neck line that was held together with lace. There was a thin band of lace that went around the waist as well as two high slits. It was the most beautiful dress that Celia had ever seen.

"That is stunning, are you sure I should wear something like that? It seems like a bit much for a talk show interview..."

"I won't lie to you sweetie, I saw the video of you fainting and I've read the articles buzzing around the internet. I know that's going to be brought up tonight, regardless of if Thomas is asked about it or you are, there's no way it won't be. You want to make a hell-of-an impression, something that shows you're not concerned with the accusations or embarrassed by the photographs. This is the dress to make that impression."

"Okay, I'll wear it."

Celia stripped out of her casual t-shirt and jeans, and Elena helped her into the dress. After she zipped it up, she took a step back and turned Celia towards the mirror. Celia's eyes widened.

"You look amazing sweetie."

There was another knock on the door. Elena opened it and a man walked in. He was wearing a white collared shirt and black slacks. He held a clipboard in his hand and he had an earpiece with a walkie.

"Is she ready?" he asked.

"What do you think?"

The man shrugged his shoulders. "I'm just a producer."

Elena rolled her eyes.

"Men don't know anything. Go on, and dazzle them," she said.

Celia followed the man out into the hallway. The white walls featured pictures of Jimmy and Guillermo with past guests. In between the pictures with Scarlett Johannsson and Robert Pattinson was one with Thomas. He was at least ten years younger in the photograph, his hair was a little past his ears and he had a mischievous smile. He looked happy, genuinely happy, something Celia rarely saw in person.

"We're about twenty minutes from starting. You and Thomas are going to be the first guests tonight. You can wait in this room and we will come get you when it's time," the man said.

He let her into a room with two fabric couches, a table with magazines and a television on the wall. The television was set to show the stage. Celia sat down on the couch and took a deep breath. She wished she had brought her phone so she could've kept herself distracted. Waiting was one of the hardest things for Celia. It never mattered what she was waiting for, it always made her anxious.

The television was muted, only the air conditioning's hum played in the background. Celia hadn't even realized the show had started until she saw Thomas sitting on a couch. Jimmy was at his desk. Thomas was wearing a maroon suit, and his hair was spiked up. Jimmy was in his typical attire, a black suit. She stood up and walked to the television, fiddling with the small buttons until she heard his voice.

"Thank you so much for having me," Thomas said.

"No, thank you for being here. It's great to see you again, it's been a while! I feel like a lot has changed in your life with *The Spy* franchise ending, getting cast as the lead in *The Werewolf and The*

*Witch Queen*," he leaned forward and lowered his voice, "and having a girlfriend."

Thomas laughed. "Yes, a lot has changed."

Jimmy leaned back in his chair. "Three movies over the course of twelve years, some might say that *The Spy* was a defining role of your career. How does it feel now that it has come to an end?"

"It was bittersweet, but I think I was ready. It was my first big role and I can honestly say it taught me a lot, but I've been ready to move on for a few years now. I wanted something different, a challenge. I will say I have grown incredibly close to the cast and crew these past years and I will miss working with them."

"That's understandable, and you will be missed as John Malcom. I think it's safe to say you gave Agent 007 a run for his money. Now, speaking of something different, why don't you tell me about your upcoming role in *The Werewolf and The Witch Queen*? I understand that filming is set to begin in a couple of months."

"I am extremely excited to be a part of such a unique film and getting to work with Vincent Monticello again. This film combines my favorite genres, horror, and romance. I think it's comparable, but more daring, than the *Underworld* series. I am going to be playing the role of The Werewolf and Celia Stuart will be The Witch Queen. It so happens that Celia is also my girlfriend, so I think filming is going to be fun."

"I'm not sure if fun would be the appropriate adjective in this situation."

The audience and Thomas laughed.

"Now, I know we don't normally talk about your personal life, so this is new territory."

The door opened and the producer walked in. Celia didn't even notice him, her eyes still glued to the television.

"Ms. Stuart it's time." She jumped at the sound of his voice.

"Right, sorry," she said.

Celia followed him down the hall. They weaved in and out through the production crew and filming equipment. Celia's heart beat faster with each step she took. *It's just an interview. It's just an interview.* She stood behind the door to enter the stage. She could hear the audience's muffled applause. The door opened, but her feet were frozen to the ground. There was silence, and she was afraid the whole audience could hear her heartbeat. Guillermo approached her and offered his arm, she took it hastily and he escorted her out.

"Celia Stuart, ladies and gentlemen," Jimmy said.

The audience resumed their applause. Thomas' mouth fell open, his eyes locked on her. She mouthed, "Thank you," to Guillermo and shook Jimmy's hand before taking a seat next to Thomas.

"You look... amazing," he whispered.

Celia's face flushed. She took his hand into hers and gently squeezed it. The audience settled and Jimmy sat forward.

"Thank you for coming today Celia, it's very nice to meet you," Jimmy said.

"Thank you for having me," she said.

"So, let's dive straight into this. I'm sure you're aware how private Thomas has been about his personal life in the past, so this is my first time interviewing one of his girlfriends. For all his female fans out there, what's it like dating him?" Jimmy asked.

"I've never met someone so compassionate. As you know, I've had some personal issues come up recently, and he has really taken care of me. I don't know where I'd be living right now if it weren't for him," Celia said.

"Wait wait wait, are you saying that the two of you are living together?"

Thomas and Celia both nodded.

"Wow, this *is* serious. So, since you mentioned your issues, I have to ask, what was that all about?"

"Honestly Jimmy, I'd rather not go into details. My address was leaked to the press by a disgruntled ex-boyfriend."

"Not only that, but he also claimed that your entire relationship was a PR stunt. What do you have to say about that?"

Thomas turned and kissed Celia. Her stomach filled with butterflies and her face reddened again. The audience clapped and cheered. Thomas pulled away slowly and winked at her.

"Well that answered that." Jimmy laughed. "Alright so enough with the serious stuff. We're going to play a game to see how well you two know each other. I'm going to ask each of you a series of questions about the other and you will both write your answers on a whiteboard. If your answer matches, you will get a point. The person with the most points win bragging rights *and* the honor of delivering a pie to the face of the loser. Sounds fun right?"

Guillermo brought each of them a small whiteboard and marker while a man from the production crew rolled out a larger whiteboard and set a large pie onto Jimmy's desk. The pie was actually a thin pie crust topped with a thick four-inch layer of whipped cream. Celia looked over nervously at Thomas and mouthed, "Pineapples". While it was described as a game, she was afraid it was more of a test.  Seemingly unfazed, Thomas laughed and blew her a kiss.

"Alright first question is for Celia. What is Thomas' favorite color?" Jimmy asked.

Celia pursed her lips. It was a simple question, sure, but it wasn't something they had ever discussed. She was going to have to guess. Thomas watched her sheepishly from behind his board.

"Alright, Celia please reveal your answer," Jimmy said.

Celia turned her board. In big, boxy letters she had written, "Red".

"Okay, Thomas, now it's your turn."

Thomas flipped his board around. It said, "Red", and a wave of relief wash over her. The audience applauded enthusiastically.

"Okay that's one point for Celia." Jimmy paused while Guillermo scribbled a point under Celia's name on the large board. "Okay, so Thomas the next question is for you. What is Celia's favorite kind of dessert?"

Again, something they had never talked about. Thomas looked cool and collected, if he was nervous, he didn't show it. Maybe he thought of it more as the game it was intended to be. He winked at her, and her posture relaxed. Test or game, she wouldn't want to be doing it with anyone else. After a moment, both Celia and Thomas wrote on their boards.

"Please reveal your boards."

Thomas went first. He had written, "Hot fudge sundae". Celia's said, "Banana ice cream". Thomas playfully grimaced, hiding behind his whiteboard and Celia pretended to wipe sweat off her brow.

"It's a good thing *your* favorite is pie," Celia teased.

The audience laughed.

"Alright no points this round. My final question for Celia, what is Thomas' favorite animal?"

Celia smiled. *Too easy.* She had known it long before she had met him, when she was just a fan. Before he had adopted Scooter, Thomas had been active in promoting the Trap, Neuter, and Return program for feral cats in California. He had even appeared alongside Jackson Galaxy on an episode of *My Cat from Hell.*

"Reveal your boards."

Both of their boards said, "Cat". The audience applauded and Guillermo added a point to Celia's score.

"Thomas this is your final question. What is Celia's favorite type of flower?"

Thomas looked confident, as if he knew the answer, but Celia knew he didn't. If he was right it would have to be some sort of lucky guess. Either way, she was relieved she wasn't going to have to be picking whipped cream out of her hair.

"Time for the final reveal."

Thomas had written, "Roses," a safe guess, but Celia's answer was, "Sunflowers".

"This explains why she threw away the bouquet of roses I gave her last week. I assumed it was because they were the wrong color," Thomas said.

Celia simply shook her head and the audience laughed.

"It looks like our winner is Celia, congratulations," Jimmy said.

Guillermo brought over a plastic medal and placed it around her neck. The audience cheered and clapped.

"Are you ready to do the honors?" Jimmy asked.

Celia grinned. "You have no idea."

Thomas covered his face and sunk into the couch as far as he could as Guillermo handed her the pie. The audience laughed as he peaked from behind his fingers. Celia pressed her knee into the couch and leaned towards him. He reluctantly withdrew his hands, and she smashed the pie into his face. Everyone, including the audience, broke into maniacal laughter as the foil tin fell onto his lap and revealed the damage. Whip cream was everywhere from his hairline down to his chin. He wiped it off his eyelids and put a dot onto Celia's nose. Celia grabbed his face and kissed him, transferring a chunk of the whipped cream from him onto her. They both laughed as she pulled away.

"And to think, I was trying to save you from a date with pie," Thomas joked.

"If that isn't cute, I don't know what is. Thank you both for coming out today. It was nice meeting you Celia and it's always a pleasure seeing you Thomas." Jimmy stood up. "Ladies and gentlemen, Celia Stuart and Thomas Richardson!"

The audience stood and clapped. Thomas took Celia's hand into his and they waved as the filming cut for a commercial. One of the production team members brought out a towel for each of them to clean their faces. Jimmy wiped away the sweat on his forehead with a handkerchief.

"Seriously guys, thanks for coming. I know it was spurred on you last minute Celia," he said.

"Anytime, it was fun," Celia said.

Thomas nodded. They both shook his hand, were captured in a quick photograph by one of the crew members and left the stage. Thomas was quiet as they walked down the hallway. He went into the waiting room and sat down on the couch. Celia lingered in the doorway, studying him.

"Are you alright? You've been... quiet today," Celia said.

Thomas nodded. "Sorry, I've had a lot on my mind."

He patted the cushion next to him and Celia came and sat down beside him. He wiped off a dab of whipped cream she has missed above her eyebrow. She leaned in and pressed her forehead to his.

"You know, you can always talk to me," she said.

"I know." He kissed her softly. "Being around you helps."

Celia caressed his cheek.

"Are you ready to go home?" he asked.

"Yes, as long as we stop for food on the way, I'm starving."

Thomas stood up and held his hand out to her. She took it and he pulled her to her feet. Together they walked back towards their dressing rooms.

"Sunflowers, huh?"

"Did you really think I would be basic enough to prefer roses?"

He playfully pushed her. "I guess it's safe to say I don't know you very well."

"It hasn't even been two months, I can't say I expected you to. Besides, you have plenty of time to get to know me."

"I hope so."

# Eight

A few days after their appearance on *Jimmy Kimmel Live*, Thomas and Celia boarded a plane and flew to Chicago for Meghan's wedding. It was late in the afternoon by the time they were checked into their hotel. It was an older hotel in the process of being remodeled. There was only one elevator in the entire building, and it moved slowly, as if it would break if it went any faster.

"I'm *so* glad we're on the third floor," Thomas said.

"I know, this is going to be pain if we're ever in a hurry," Celia said.

She was wearing jeans, a hoodie and red sneakers. He was in his usual casual attire of jeans, boots, and a t-shirt. His familiar Los Angeles Dodgers ball cap was on his head. The elevator stopped abruptly, shaking as it reached the third floor. Their room was directly across from the elevator. It was large in size but was only one room. There was a kitchen area, a small space for the couch, and then a queen-sized bed was pushed against the wall. Mirrored sliding doors hid a makeshift closet, and a small bathroom was in the corner. An old heater hummed in the background, trying to keep up with the cold Chicago air.

Celia sat her bags down and walked over to the bed. Its mattress was firm and springy. The couch was worse, as if they had covered rocks underneath the fabric instead of cushions. It wasn't quite the luxury hotel that was promised on the booking website.

"I can sleep on the couch, if you'd be more comfortable," Thomas said.

"I don't mind sharing a bed with you. Besides something tells me it gets cold at night and I'm going to need all the warmth I can get."

Celia hung up her clothes in the closet while Thomas rested on the bed. She had brought a black dress for the rehearsal dinner and her peach flowy bridesmaid dress along with some other casual clothes. They were only supposed to be gone for two and a half days, but she had over packed just to be safe.

"Are you going to unload your suitcase?" Celia asked.

"Eventually." He opened his eyes. "Probably while you're getting ready."

Celia sat down on the edge of the bed. It was strange being alone with Thomas in a hotel room, like she shouldn't be there. Her stomach was twisted in knots. She pulled out *Outlander*, unfolding the page where she had left off, and started reading. Diana Gabaldon was supposed to distract her, but all she could think about was Thomas.

"How many times have you read that?" Thomas asked.

Celia dog-eared the page and closed it. Thomas scooted forward on the bed, moving close to her.

"The entire series maybe three times... this book, I can't tell you how many times. Why?"

"You've about worn the cover off."

"It's my favorite book. Usually, I bring it with me on set so I have something to entertain myself in between filming. Have you read it before?"

"No, but I watched the first season of the show, if that counts."

"I think the book is better."

"Not a Sam Heughan fan?"

She laughed. "I *never* said I wasn't. I just prefer the book, that's all. I'm going to get ready so we can go to the rehearsal dinner. It's about a ten-minute walk from here."

"Alright. I'll get changed in a minute."

He took the book and started reading it while Celia was in the bathroom. It had only a small shower, toilet, and single sink. There was barely enough room for her to even change and little counter space for her things. She curled her hair, put on some mascara, and reapplied her lip gloss. Her dress was short, the hemline falling several inches above her knees. It was a halter style top that tied at the back. The flared skirt was adorned with lace. Not wanting to embarrass herself or Meghan by falling at the dinner or wedding, she played it safe by bringing only flat shoes. She walked out of the bathroom and found Thomas still reading, but he had changed into black slacks, a grey button up shirt, and a black leather jacket.

"Ready?" she asked.

His eyes lit up when he saw her. "Yes, you look beautiful."

Her cheeks reddened. She tried to hide her face from him, hoping he wouldn't notice her blushing, as she pulled her black faux-fur coat from the closet. She had forgotten its mirrored doors.

"You're being awfully shy, are you alright?" he asked.

"Yes, I'm fine—alright, I'm alright."

"If you say so."

The outside air was merciless. The temperature was in the low fifties and a heavy wind swept throughout the entire city. Chill bumps covered Celia's arms and legs. She huddled close to Thomas as they walked. Meghan and her soon-to-be husband Eric were standing outside of Giordano's away from a crowd of tourists. She wore a long ivory dress and faux-fur shawl. Eric was wearing a suit. His curly blond hair was partially hidden by a black knitted cap. Meghan started waiving frantically when she saw Celia. Her face was beaming, as was Eric's.

"I'm so happy you guys are here," Meghan said.

She pulled Celia into a tight embrace. Thomas shook hands with Eric.

"We have a corner section by the window seats, it's the four tables pushed together. We're still waiting on a few more guests, but you're more than welcome to go on in and grab a seat. We already ordered some pitchers and several pizzas," Eric said.

"Alright see you in a bit," Celia said.

The interior of Giordano's was even more packed than the exterior. All the tables were full and the waiting area was cramped with people as well. Waiters and waitresses weaved in and out of patrons, maneuvering trays heavy with beverages and pizzas. Meghan's maid of honor, Sarah, and her two other bridesmaids were at the table speaking with Meghan's mother, while Eric's parents sat quietly to themselves. Celia didn't have to introduce Thomas, they already knew who he was. Sarah was wearing a daringly low-cut blouse and tight pleather pants. Her chocolate brown hair was straightened and fell past her hips. Her eyes were fixated on Thomas.

"It's so nice to meet you in person. I'm a huge fan. Would you mind if we got a picture together?" Sarah said.

Thomas shrugged his shoulders, and she handed her phone to Celia. Thomas put his arm lightly over her shoulder, while she rested one hand on his lower back and the other on his stomach. Celia took two pictures and handed the phone back, but Sarah didn't remove her hand from his back. Something about the way she was looking at him made Celia uncomfortable. Celia had only been around Sarah a handful of times, and she hadn't really spoken to her except at the bachelorette party and dress fittings. She was closer to Thomas' age and was undeniably beautiful.

"You're going to have to tell me all about filming *The Spy*, I heard you did your own stunts," Sarah said.

"I did a few, but I can assure you that the John Malcom you saw jumping through glass was my stunt double," he said.

Sarah pulled out one of the chairs and sat down, gesturing him to join her. He looked over at Celia, but she was preoccupied with helping Eric's mother clean up spilled beer. He sat down and Sarah poured him a glass of beer. She leaned in close to him as if she didn't want to miss out on a single word he said. Meghan and Eric walked in with his best man, his brother Eli, and his three groomsmen. They sat down, pushing Celia to take a seat on the opposite side of the table where she couldn't hear what Thomas and Sarah were talking about. She poured herself a glass of beer and toasted with Meghan, but her smile was forced. Insecurity plagued her and her stomach was queasy.

Sarah reached over and placed her hand on Thomas' forearm. Celia suddenly was frail, like the wind had been knocked out of her. She stood up and headed towards the bathroom at the back of the restaurant. Unlike the dining area, the bathroom was completely empty. Her eyes watered as she gripped both sides of the sink. She stared at her reflection, a lone tear slipped down her cheek. *Why are you acting like this? It's not like you're really dating Thomas.*

Celia quickly wiped away the stray tear as the door opened. Sarah walked in with a smirk on her face. Quickly, Celia cranked the faucet, burning her hands with hot water. Sarah stood in front of the mirror. She uncapped a tube of red lipstick and brought it to her lips.

"It's pathetic you know," Sarah said.

"I beg your pardon?"

"Oh please Celia, it's written all over your face. You can't stand the fact that Thomas is more interested in me than you." She rubbed her lips together. "I don't get why you're so bent out of shape, I know this whole relationship is a publicity stunt. Hell, I knew it all along. Brandon didn't want to believe me at first, but he came to his senses."

"How do you know Brandon?"

"I'm his cousin."

Celia's mouth fell open.

"I figured you didn't remember me after you didn't say anything when we were at the bridal boutique. You and I, we've met before. I was at his graduation party."

Celia looked at her, dumbfounded. She remembered that day too well, she had been upset, as her own mother had forgone her graduation ceremony to take a spur of the moment trip to Mexico. She had given her five hundred dollars, a graduation present, but no words of praise or apologies for being absent. Brandon had done his best to make her feel welcome at his own party, but it was in vain. She was isolated, surrounded by his family members, all strangers save for his mother and father. There were more than one-hundred people there, all their faces blurred together. Except one. Sarah had been there. Only, she was practically unrecognizable. She was heavier set, her hair was streaked blonde, and she wore glasses. A far cry from the woman that stood before her.

"I'd say it's nice to see you again, only it isn't. You broke Brandon's heart. He has been struggling for months now, he didn't need anything extra added to his plate," Sarah said.

"I didn't intend to hurt him, but I'm not sorry for breaking up with him. It had been coming for a long time. I tried helping him, but he didn't want to help himself. As for my relationship with Thomas, you shouldn't speak about matters you know nothing about. Don't assume because you look plastic, you know what's fake and what's real. Now if you'll excuse me."

Celia went for the door, but Sarah grabbed her arm, holding her in her place. Her nails dug into her skin.

"We're not finished."

Celia yanked her arm free. "Yes, we are. This weekend is about Meghan and Eric, not me nor you. Stop acting like a bitch and let them have their moment."

Celia rubbed her arm as she walked back to the table, Sarah's indentions were still visible. Thomas stood up, his face was concerned.

"Are you alright?" he asked.

"No." She turned to Meghan. "Actually, I'm not feeling well. I think the flight tired me out. Would you mind if I went back to the hotel? I don't want to be tired tomorrow."

Meghan frowned. "I'd rather you stay, but I understand. Get some sleep and I'll see you at nine o'clock sharp."

Celia hugged her and retrieved her coat. Thomas followed her out. The temperature had dropped by more than ten degrees and the wind was unforgiving. Celia walked quickly, not waiting for Thomas to catch up.

"Celia slow down," he said.

She kept her pace. She couldn't hear him, the passing cars, or even the chatter of the people on the sidewalk. She was too engulfed in her own thoughts. *How did I not recognize her? Has she been spying on me for Brandon? What is she going to tell him?*

Thomas grabbed her arm in front of the hotel, pulling her to a stop. Concern reflected across his face.

"What are you doing?" he asked.

"What am I doing? What about what *you're* doing?"

He blinked slowly. "I don't understand."

"You can't tell me you didn't notice how Sarah was treating you. She was all touchy-feely. Not to mention she was fucking you with her eyes from the moment you walked in." She hooked her arms behind her head. "I have never felt so insecure... so jealous, in my entire life."

"Do you really think I was paying attention to her?"

"It doesn't matter, Thomas. I don't think I can do this anymore."

"Do what?"

"*This*." She gestured towards him. "This was supposed to be easy, play the part of the girlfriend, get the role I wanted and move on with my life. It's all in the contract, black and white."

"You can't tell me you're acting like this because of that stupid document we both signed. You know this goes beyond that."

"That's the *problem*! I'm over here letting myself be vulnerable and getting attached to you when this isn't real. None of it is real. It feels real, sure, but you're an actor, a damn good one at that."

Celia turned to the hotel's doors, but Thomas grabbed her hand. Tears were streaming down her cheeks.

"Look me in the eyes and tell me you think this is all an act," Thomas said.

She turned to him. The familiar pain haunted his eyes. His brow was furrowed and his cheeks reddened. Celia didn't say anything, she only stared. A homeless man tugging on the leash of an old dog walked past them.

"Do you really think this is an act?" he asked.

"I... don't know."

"You're the first thing I think about when I wake up in the morning, and the last thing before I fall asleep. My heart beats faster every time you look at me, sometimes I swear it's going to beat right out of my chest. And when you kiss me my entire body goes weak. I'm hopelessly wrapped around your finger and you don't even realize it."

"Your words are beautiful fiction, Thomas. Maybe you should pursue a career in writing instead."

"It's not fiction, I'm telling you how I feel."

"Then prove it."

"How?"

Celia shrugged. "I don't know and quite frankly, I don't care. I'm tired of playing games."

Thomas grabbed her shoulders and pulled her into him, pressing his lips roughly against hers. It sent a warm feeling throughout her entire body. It was like the kiss they shared at the *Academy Awards*. He pulled away, but this time, there was light in his eyes. He scooped her up into his arms and carried her through the hotel lobby. They squeezed into the elevator with an older gentlemen. He stood in the corner, looking down at the ground while Celia, still in Thomas' arms, kissed him.

He carried her into their room and gently set her on the bed. She grabbed his jacket collar and pulled him down on top of her. He pulled off his jacket and slid out of his shirt. She hastily pulled off her jacket and tossed it aside. She brought his hand to the zipper at the back of her dress.

"Are you sure you want to do this?" he asked.

She nodded. Slowly he unzipped her dress, stripping her down to her red lace underwear. His hand caressed her cheek and moved down her side, stopping at the hemline of her panties. His fingers hesitated, tracing the delicate lace pattern. He took a deep breath.

"I have to be honest with you... I haven't done this in years, so I may be a little rusty," he said.

"Don't worry about it." Celia sat up and gently kissed him. "It's been some time for me too, so we're even."

He pressed his forehead lightly against hers. She fumbled with his belt buckle until it was undone. He pulled down his pants, leaving only his black boxers. Celia scooted back on the bed and he climbed on top of her. Her fingers brushed down his spine as they kissed. Heat radiated off his skin and onto hers. The smell of his earthy cologne wrapped around her like a blanket.

Celia woke up to her alarm going off. Seemingly undisturbed by the rhythmic beeping, Thomas was asleep next to her. She went to hit snooze, but the time rattled her awake. It was nine forty-five in the morning. She was supposed to be at Meghan's hotel at nine. There were three missed phone calls and several text messages. *Shit!* She threw off the covers and ran into the bathroom. Her hair was a tangled mess and the makeup from the previous night still sat on her face. She sat her phone on the bathroom counter, dialing Meghan's number while she hastily dumped toothpaste on her toothbrush.

"Where are you?" Meghan answered.

"Meghan I am *so* sorry, I'm leaving right now. I have to brush my teeth and throw on some clothes," she said.

There was a pause followed by an audible sigh. "You're lucky I love you."

"I know." she spoke between mouthfuls of toothpaste, "I promise, I'll be there soon."

"You better."

Celia reached to hang-up the phone, but accidentally knocked it into the bathroom trashcan. *Seriously?* She rinsed out her mouth and set her toothbrush down. The trashcan was disgustingly full with tissues and other trash. Thomas' used condom sat at the top. Of course her phone had ended up in the bottom of it all, it was her luck. She took a deep breath, as if she could suppress her gag reflexes, and reached into the trash. Her fingers touched a hard object wrapped in tissue that was next to her phone. Slightly curious, she pulled it out. Her stomach fell to the floor and a wave of nausea washed over her. It was a syringe. The syringe's needle was slightly bent as if it had been used and discarded. There had only been two people in that hotel room since they checked in, she and Thomas, and it wasn't hers.

Thomas' phone started ringing from the other room. She panicked, rewrapping the syringe and plunging it to the bottom of the trash can as hard as she could. She washed her hands, the water was steaming hot, but she didn't feel it. Too many thoughts were swirling around in her mind, she didn't have room for the pain. She threw on a hoodie and jeans before slipping out the door. Her bridesmaid's gown fluttered behind her as she ran down the hall. She had not bothered to say anything to Thomas. It's not like she even knew what to say to him anyway.

By the time Celia arrived at the hotel, the makeup artist was finishing with Sarah. Everyone else had already had theirs done and were in the process of changing into their bridal dresses. Meghan sat in a velvet armchair, her hair pulled tightly into rollers. She didn't smile when she saw Celia, her expression was a mixture of anger and anxiety.

"Where have you been? You know you were supposed to be here at nine," Meghan said.

"I'm so sorry. I had a long night, and I must've hit snooze in my sleep," Celia said.

"You left *early*. How did you have a long... oh." She looked Celia up and down. "Did you and Thomas have sex?"

Sarah stiffened in the chair, causing the artist to smudge her lipstick above her lip. Celia grabbed Meghan and pulled her aside.

"Yes, we did."

"If I wasn't so mad right now, I'd be happy for you. Okay, I'm happy for you, but I'm still mad. You're going to have to tell me about it after you're ready."

She pointed to the empty chair where the makeup artist was waiting. Sarah had moved to the corner, pretending to be on her phone while she attempted to eavesdrop.

"Okay that's fine, but not today and not in front of Sarah," Celia said.

"Why?"

"It's a long story, but today is about you and Eric, so don't worry about it. Okay?"

"Okay."

The wedding ceremony was quick, or at least it was to Celia. She had spent the entire time thinking about Thomas and not paying attention to the ceremony itself. She had caught him staring at her a few times, offering a few winks, but she had been unresponsive to his gestures. Her mind was running a million miles a minute, trying to figure out why there was a syringe in the trashcan. Sure she knew he was taking medication for something, but she didn't know how that went together. *Diabetes? Or could it be something more serious? What if he has a drug problem?* All the scandalous paparazzi headlines flashed in her mind. He had been a partier throughout his twenties, maybe some of his old habits still shadowed him.

The wedding reception was held in a large banquet hall only a few blocks away from the church where the ceremony was held. Guests had walked to the venue, while the bridal party had hung around for pictures with the bride and groom. Celia had arrived to the hall almost an hour after Thomas. By this time most guests were already at their tables sampling the caterer's menu. A few brave souls had even ventured onto the dance floor with the encouragement of the DJ. The lights were dim and gave off a blueish tint. White curtain lights lit up the walls. Each table had a small vase filled with peach-tinted carnations. Celia had barely walked in the door when Thomas approached her.

"Hey," he said.

"Hey."

He pulled her into a hug. The awkward tension in the air was suffocating. He looked nervous, sweat rested on his brow. Celia smiled as a waiter approached them with glasses of pink champagne. She downed hers like a shot, grabbing another glass before he went to other guests. Thomas put his arm around her shoulder and guided her to a secluded corner.

"What's going on?" Thomas asked.

"Nothing."

"Is this about last night? I warned you it had been a long time beforehand…"

Celia shook her head. "Last night was great, I promise."

"Then what is it? You snuck out this morning without saying anything, refused to make eye-contact pretty much the entire ceremony, and now you're not acting like yourself."

"I don't think this is the place."

"The place for what?"

Celia looked around. Everyone was preoccupied with Meghan and Eric as they made their entrance as husband and wife. Conversations were loud, and the music was even louder. This wasn't the most opportune time to ask, but it was the best chance she was going to get.

"Are you on drugs?" Celia asked.

Thomas nearly dropped his champagne glass. "What?"

"Are you on drugs?" she asked again.

"Please, keep your voice down." He grabbed her hand and led her out into the hall. "I heard you the first time."

Thomas went over to the faux-leather white couch and sat down. Celia followed him. Footsteps echoed off the tiled floors. The midday sun shone through the ceiling's windows. A few waiters and guests passed by them, but they were pretty much alone. Celia twisted a loose piece of hair between her fingertips.

"I'm not on drugs Celia, why on earth would you even think that?" Thomas asked.

"Please be honest with me."

"I am being honest with you."

"What about the syringe then?"

Thomas looked at her. His eyes held a look she had never seen before. A combination of disbelief and anger. Her chest tightened.

"Did you go through my things?" he asked.

Celia shook her head.

"Don't sit there and lie to me." He stood up. "Why did you go through my things?"

"I didn't—I found a syringe in the trash."

"You went digging through the trash? What were you trying to find?"

"You're not letting me explain. I wasn't trying to find anything, I didn't even know there was something to find. I was rushing around this morning and accidently dropped my phone into the trash. When I went to grab my phone I found it. I don't understand why you're upset, when I'm the one who's been lied to."

Thomas sat back down without a word. He stared at the white wall in front of them. Celia fought the urge to cry. It was like her entire relationship with Thomas had peaked and then came crashing back down all within the span of a few hours. She hadn't even had time to wrap her head around the night before. Everything had gone downhill too quickly.

"I'm not on drugs," Thomas said quietly.

Celia didn't respond. His words didn't bring her the comfort she had hoped for. Thomas turned to her and placed his hand on her cheek, wiping away a lone tear.

"Then what are you hiding?" she asked.

"I'm not hiding anything from you. There's some stuff you don't know about. I promise, I will tell you someday. I'm just not ready... it's complicated. Do you trust me?"

"Of course... where do we go from here?"

"I think we should pick up where we left off last night. I meant everything I said, and if you're open to it, I want to explore the idea of a real relationship. Would that be okay with you?"

Celia nodded and a smile spread across Thomas' face. He stood up and pulled her up into a tight embrace. She rested her head against his chest. His heart raced in her ear.

# Nine

Celia sat on the couch in Thomas' living room, reading *The Werewolf and The Witch Queen* script. She was casually dressed in a faded t-shirt and distressed jeans. Scooter was curled up beside her, occasionally kicking her with his back leg as he dreamt. The afternoon sun beamed in through the blinds. It was quiet save for the lawn company outside working on neighbors' yards. Thomas had left several hours earlier to go run some errands, leaving Celia to entertain herself. She had started reading the script, as filming was starting in only a few weeks she needed to immerse herself in the storyline. A doorknob rattled, pulling her from a steamy scene between her character and Thomas'. Scooter hopped off the couch and ran towards the back door.

"Thomas did you forget your key?" Celia called out.

No answer. There was a brief pause and the door rattled again. She sat the script down and stood up. When Thomas left that morning, he had gone out through the garage, his usual habit. *Why would he be trying to get in through the back?* She covered her hand over her mouth, as the realization suddenly dawned on her—it wasn't Thomas.

She grabbed her phone and texted Thomas, "Please hurry back, I think someone is trying to get inside."

As soon as she hit send, the sound of glass shattering echoed throughout the hall. Scooter ran past Celia into Thomas' bedroom. The backdoor clicked as it opened. Celia followed after the cat as quietly and as quickly as she could, shutting and locking the door behind her.

Thomas' bedroom was large. A king-sized bed sat in the middle of the room, light stained oak nightstands stood on either side of it. The comforter was a chocolate in color and absent of design other than Scooter's loose hairs in random places. On the opposite side of the room was a large dresser that matched the nightstands, and a television set. The double doors leading to the bathroom were open, as usual, for Scooter to access his litterbox that was hidden in the closet. Celia pried Scooter out from underneath the bed and went into the closet with him, quietly closing the door. It was eerily quiet, only her heart's rapid beating was audible. She jumped as her phone buzzed from inside her jean pocket.

Thomas had texted her, "Security guard is on the way. I'll be there in fifteen."

Celia slipped her phone back into her pocket and sat down on the carpeted floor. Fifteen minutes was an eternity to be alone with a stranger in the house. *Why would someone want to break in?* She pulled her knees to her chest. Thomas didn't keep anything of value that Celia knew of. His house was in an expensive neighborhood, and the house itself was nice, but the inside was furnished as if belonged to an average working-class citizen. There was nothing special that stood out about it, other than it belonged to an actor. Perhaps it was chosen at random, there were no visible signs of anyone being home except her car out front, but other houses had cars sitting on the street as well. Either they were smart for timing their break-in with the lawn service, or stupid for not considering the extra witnesses.

The silence was severed as a large crash echoed throughout the house. There was a short pause followed by another crash and the ripple of glass shattering. The next sound was unrecognizable, rattling followed by what sounded like condensed air being released. Celia was sick to her stomach. *What if I don't have fifteen minutes?* She turned on her phone's flashlight and started looking through Thomas' large closet. Scooter's eyes glowed from a shelf, his body hidden behind shirts. There were shoes, shoe boxes, various clothing articles, and some cat supplies but nothing appeared feasible to be a makeshift weapon. Her mind flashed to the syringe at the hotel. It wouldn't be an ideal weapon, but it had to be better than nothing.

She took a deep breath and opened the closet door as quietly as she could. It was hauntingly quiet outside, not a trace sound of the intruder whatsoever. Using her phone as a light, she started digging through his bathroom drawers. There was a shaving razor, but no syringes or needles in either drawer. She opened the cabinet above the sink and her eyes widened. It was full to the top with different types of medications. A pile of disposable syringes sat next to several small vials. She carefully picked up a vial. The prescription name was Fuzeon, something she had never heard of before.

Someone knocked outside the room. Startled, Celia dropped her phone but narrowly managed to save the vial from slipping.

"Celia? Are you in there?" Thomas' voice was a welcome comfort.

She hastily put the vial back in the cabinet, careful to turn it the way she found it. She picked up her phone, and the glass screen was shattered. *Dammit.* She rushed to the door and unlocked it. Thomas pulled her into a tight embrace. She wrapped her arms around him, her head tightly pressed against his chest. His heart was racing almost as quickly as hers.

"Are you alright?" he asked.

"Yes. I grabbed Scooter and we hid in your closet."

Thomas sighed. "Well I'm glad you two are okay. I can't say the same for the house."

Celia stepped out into the hallway and shut the door behind her. There were glass shards all across the floor leading towards the living room area. Red spray paint marked the beige walls in unrelated circular patterns. The living room television was smashed to pieces, as if a baseball bat was taken to it. Celia's script had been torn into fine pieces and thrown about as if it were confetti. The blue display case was overturned, its bottles broken with their contents mixing together as they pooled on the floor.

The neighborhood security guard, Officer Sam, was standing by the back door. He was young, not much older than Celia, and green on the job. He rubbed his thick fingers across his forehead.

"I'm going to have to talk to the neighbors and lawn service employees and see if they saw anyone suspicious coming or leaving the area. It appears that he climbed your fence to gain entry into the backyard." He looked at Celia. "I'm going to need a statement from you. Thomas suggested this was possibly done by an ex-boyfriend of yours. Are you able to give me a description of the perpetrator?"

Celia shook her head. "I have no idea who did it. I heard someone trying to get in and as soon as he broke through the glass I went and hid. I was reading and hadn't heard anything beforehand."

"Alright. I'm going to call some of my buddies down at the station so we can make a report. We'll need to get some pictures as evidence, so it might be best if you guys stay somewhere for the night at least and you can clean up tomorrow. I'll try and make sure the vehicle is taken care of first," he said.

"Vehicle? Did something happened to my car?" Celia asked.

Sam and Thomas exchanged nervous glances. Celia walked to the front and opened the door. "Whore," was painted in big, bulky letters across the side of her vehicle. All four tires were flat, and the mirrors were broken. Celia stumbled back, shock and anger boiled inside of her.

"Brandon Loften is the name of my ex-boyfriend." She approached

Sam. "He's been sending me threatening text messages and he leaked my address to the press."

"Do you have these messages still on your phone?"

Celia nodded. She pulled out her phone and handed it to Sam. He slowly scrolled through the messages. He jotted down Brandon's number and handed her phone back to her.

"I can assure you we will talk with him, but I can't make any guarantees that he will be charged or arrested for the crimes that happened today. After all, he may not have been the perpetrator. It may be in your best interest to file a restraining order," Sam said.

"I will think about it," she said.

Sam pulled out his phone to call the station. Glass cracked under his boots as he walked to the kitchen. Thomas pulled Celia aside.

"Would you be more comfortable in a hotel or would you rather stay at Gwen's house? I'm pretty sure the twins went out of town to stay with Brett's parents. I know she made you uncomfortable last time, so I am okay with us staying in a hotel," Thomas said.

Celia shook her head. "I wouldn't mind staying with Gwen."

"Are you sure?"

"Positive, I promise."

Celia was quiet during the drive to Gwen's. She spent most of the time looking out the window, watching the different people and cars they passed. Thomas was quiet too. His eyes were on the road but his attention appeared to be elsewhere. Scooter was howling unhappily from his carrier in the backseat. His distaste for car rides was blatant. Thomas parked his Mustang in front of Gwen's house and turned off the ignition. Celia unbuckled her seatbelt, but Thomas didn't move. His fingers were still around the steering wheel.

"Are you okay?" Celia asked.

"Right now or in general?" he asked.

Celia bit her lip. He turned towards her, his eyes were bloodshot.

She had been so distraught earlier, she couldn't recall if they had been like that.

"I'm sorry—" He unbuckled his seatbelt— "It's been a rough day all around."

"I know... do you want to talk about it?"

He shook his head. "Maybe later."

Celia didn't push. She opened her door and got out. She had packed a bag for two days, just in case they needed to be away longer than Sam anticipated. Gwen met them at the door. She was casually dressed in a solid black t-shirt and jeans. She hugged Celia first and then Thomas.

"Are you guys okay?" Gwen asked.

"Yeah, we're fine. Can't say the same for the house. Not looking forward to cleaning that up," Thomas said.

Celia's face flushed. *Does he blame me for what happened?* She knew he had every right to, after all she was the one responsible for bringing Brandon into his life, but part of her hoped he didn't. They walked into the living room. Gwen's husband, Brett, was sitting on the couch watching a football game. He appeared at least fifteen years older than Gwen. His black hair was thinning and peppered with grey hairs. He wore athletic shorts, and a red t-shirt that said, "This is my drinking shirt". He was shorter than Thomas, but was almost as muscular. Two empty beer bottles sat on the end table beside him.

"Celia this is my husband Brett. Brett this is Celia," Gwen said.

Brett didn't get up from the couch, but extended his hand to her. He smiled as they shook hands.

"Nice to meet you. I've heard good things about you," he said.

"Thank you, it's nice to meet you as well."

Brett turned his attention back to the game, not even acknowledging Thomas. Thomas sat down Scooter's crate and released him. The cat immediately ran to Gwen and rubbed against her legs.

"Who's playing?" Thomas asked.

"San Francisco 49ers and Los Angeles Rams. The 49ers were in the lead for the first quarter, but they've slowly gone downhill. It's been almost an hour since either team has secured a touchdown," Brett's attention stayed on the television as he spoke. "Can't say it's been the best game."

There was a long pause, and Celia felt the tension in the air. It was suffocating.

"Would you like me to show you to the guest room?" Gwen asked.

"Yes," Celia said almost too eagerly.

Gwen led them down a back hall to a large bedroom. It had a full-sized bed, a nightstand, and an armoire that served as a television stand. The room's walls were painted a soft yellow, and the carpet was beige. Pictures of the twins were hung on the wall like a disorganized collage. A clear tub filled with cat litter sat in a corner of the room next to two stainless steel mixing bowls to serve as makeshift bowls for Scooter. A rocking chair with a purple afghan blanket sat in the opposite corner. Both of the windows had the curtains drawn and blinds closed. Thomas sat his bag down on the bed.

"Thank you for letting us stay, I'm sure there was some arm twisting involved," Thomas said.

Gwen shook her head. "Please don't worry about it. I'm glad to have you both here. I am going to finish cooking dinner, you two get settled and I'll let you know once it's ready."

Thomas pulled his clothes out of his bag and moved them to one of the vacant drawers in the armoire. Celia sat her bags down by the rocking chair and peered out the closed blinds. The sidewalk was vacant, no neighbors in sight, the complete opposite of Halloween. She turned around and started unpacking.

"What's the deal with you and Brett?" Celia asked.

Thomas sat down on the bed. "It's a long story."

"We have time."

Celia walked over to the bed and sat down next to him. He closed his eyes and laid back on the purple comforter.

"How much did you know about me before we met?" he asked.

"If I'm being honest, I was a fan of yours for a long time. I already followed you on all on all the social media sites."

His lips curved into a smile. "That's cute. I'm assuming you know a little about my twenties?"

"Yes."

"When I was cast as the lead in *The Spy*, it gave me quite an ego boost, especially after it became a hit at the box office. I had strangers approaching me left and right for autographs, beautiful women throwing their numbers at me, stores giving me free shit if I'd get photographed with it. It was something I'd never experienced and I was enamored with all the attention. Honestly, I did some things I shouldn't have. I drank too much, partied too hard, and got myself in stupid situations. I felt invincible and I got careless."

"How were you careless?"

"Had a few pregnancy scares and one too many car accidents."

"Oh... I didn't know."

"Yeah, Gwen helped me keep it out of the press's hands. She acted more like the older sibling, always there to clean up her irresponsible brother's messes. It took a toll on her." Thomas opened his eyes. "If Brett hadn't been there for her, I don't know how things would've turned out. After she got pregnant, Brett gave me an ultimatum. I had to choose between my poor lifestyle choices or my sister and nieces. I chose them, but it was too late. The damage was already done."

"You were the one who was drowning—"

"What?"

"The night at the carnival, you asked me what if someone was drowning and it was too late to take the lifeboat. I thought maybe you had lost someone too, but you were really talking about yourself."

"You're right, and I'm still drowning."

Before she could respond, Gwen appeared in the doorway. "Dinner is ready."

Gwen had cooked spaghetti, cheese-covered garlic bread, and made a salad. The large rectangular table in the dining room was set for four with plates, bowls, silverware, and glasses already filled with red wine. Gwen brought the basket of bread and salad to the table, while the noodles and sauce sat on the granite kitchen counter. As the football game had ended, the television was set on a local news channel. The weatherman didn't say anything they didn't already know, it was going to be another hot and humid week. After getting a portion of spaghetti, Celia joined them at the table, taking a seat next to Thomas.

"Aside from today's scare, how has everything been with you guys?" Gwen asked.

"Good. We flew down to Chicago last week for my friend's wedding and that was nice. Although I can't say Thomas is much of a dancer," Celia said.

They all laughed and Thomas' face turned red.

"I warned you what you were getting into before we went. Besides, I only stepped on your foot twice," Thomas said.

"You would think a grown man would realize he did something wrong the first time and know better than to do it again," Brett said.

The smile disappeared from Thomas' face.

"Brett, stop it. This isn't the time," Gwen said.

"For Christ's sake Gwen, it's never the time. I hate how every time he comes over we have to play the part of a happy family. I know he's been better, but that doesn't make up for all these things he's done over the years."

"He's suffered enough, let him be," she said.

"No, this isn't suffering, this is karma." Brett dropped his fork. "I'm going to go stay at my brother's tonight, I can't deal with this right now."

Brett left the kitchen and went to the master bedroom. Gwen gave an apologetic look to Celia and Thomas before following after him. The door slammed behind them and they were inaudibly arguing. Thomas didn't say anything, His gaze was focused on the untouched breadbasket, but it was obvious his mind was somewhere far away. Celia gently placed her hand over his. He looked at her briefly, and stood up. Without a word, he walked back towards the bedroom. Brett appeared with a backpack slung over his shoulder. He went out the front door, slamming it so hard behind him that the pictures on the wall shook. Shortly after, Gwen came back into the dining room and sat down. Her eyes were puffy and red as if she'd been crying.

"Where's Thomas?" Gwen asked.

"I think he went back to the guest room."

Gwen nodded slowly. She took a bite out of a piece of garlic bread. Celia just stared at her plate. She was hungry, but her appetite was gone.

"Please eat." Gwen wiped a tear from her cheek. "I don't want the food to go to waste."

Celia forced herself to take a bite of the spaghetti. The noodles had gotten thick and heavy from soaking in the sauce, but it was still good. After they finished eating, Celia helped Gwen clean. Gwen didn't say anything, but Celia didn't mind. She wouldn't have known what to say. The television in the background was the only noise. Celia went into the guest bedroom and found it empty. Thomas was in the small bathroom, and had left the door cracked. Celia wanted to talk to him, comfort him somehow, but she also didn't want to intrude on his space. She lingered in the bedroom doorway. Thomas had a syringe in his hand and was draining the contents from one of the small vials. She closed her eyes as he plunged the needle in his left upper arm.

"Are you okay?" Gwen asked.

Celia hadn't heard her walk up. Thomas opened the door wider, looking from Gwen to Celia. His expression was suspicious. Celia quickly nodded.

"I just was trying to remember where I left a book. I thought I had brought it, but couldn't find it in my bag," Celia said.

"Alright, well if you need anything, please let me know." Gwen looked to Thomas. "Can I borrow you for a moment? We need to talk."

Thomas followed her down the hall towards the living room. Celia waited about twenty seconds before following them. They were sitting at the dining room table. Thomas' fingers traced the swirled pattern of the red table cloth.

"How did the appointment go today?" Gwen asked.

Thomas shrugged. "Same as usual."

"I see."

"I'm sorry, I know you're hoping that one of these days I'll be better all of the sudden, but that's not going to happen. This will be the death of me someday, and all we can do is hope it's not anytime soon." Thomas sighed. "Brett's an ass, but he has a point. I'm only living with consequences from my own actions."

"That's not true. You weren't doing anything different than most young men at that age, and it's not fair that you have to live an abnormal life. I don't understand why Brett has to be like this— he has to see how much you've struggled," Gwen started crying.

Thomas scooted his chair closer to her and put his arm around her shoulder. Celia's stomach fell to the floor. She turned to go back into the bedroom, but accidentally stepped on Scooter. He yowled and ran down the hall. *Dammit.* The chair screeched against the tile floor as Thomas stood up.

"Celia?" Thomas said.

She turned around. Both Thomas and Gwen were staring at her. Gwen was trying to regain her composure to no avail—she was inconsolable. Celia was nauseous not only for what she heard, but for intruding on their conversation in the first place.

"I was just grabbing my phone," Celia said.

It was only a partial lie. Her phone was sitting on the kitchen counter, next to the dish drying rack. She went to the kitchen and grabbed it as quickly as she could without appearing suspicious. Thomas touched her shoulder. She couldn't force herself to make eye contact with him.

"What all did you hear?" he asked.

"Enough," she said.

Thomas bit his lip. Celia briskly walked past him and retreated to the bedroom. She shut the door and locked it. Back against the wall, she slid down to the floor. Her hands were shaking to the point that she barely unlocked her phone. She pulled up *Safari* and went to *Google*, typing in Fuzeon. The words, "HIV antiviral," hit her like a ton of bricks. Everything suddenly made sense.

# Ten

Celia stood at the end of the pier, the wind blew her hair wildly about. The waves crashed against its wooden beams, guided by the full moon. Thomas stood beside her, his attention focused on her instead of the water. It was a little after midnight, and the air was cool but humid. Seagulls cautiously gathered behind them. Celia hadn't said a word during the drive from Gwen's house. Thomas had attempted small talk, but had given up after each attempt was met with silence.  He had never been one for small talk anyway.

"Were you going to tell me?" Celia asked.

"Yes."

"When?"

Thomas sighed. "I don't know. I was waiting for the right moment to bring it up."

"When would that have been? After you were too sick to hide it anymore?"

He didn't say anything.

"Do you think maybe it would have been wise to mention it before we had sex?" she asked.

"I'm not ignorant about my own disease, Celia. I sure as hell wouldn't intentionally give this to someone else." He lowered his voice. "I knew it would be okay as long as I was careful and used protection."

*It was like what Gwen said on Halloween. How could I not have known what she meant?* Celia shook her head.

"How long have you been dealing with this?"

"I can't say for certain. It progressed to AIDS before I even realized I was sick. I didn't have any symptoms at first. All of the sudden I started getting headaches, fevers, and I would end up in these horrible coughing fits. I was tired all the time, and it made filming, let alone just doing my normal day to day routine, difficult. Doctors didn't know what was going on, so we tried a bunch of different medications, but nothing helped. They didn't even fathom that someone like me would have a STD. I was tested as a last resort, and low and behold, my results came back as positive for AIDS."

Celia felt like she was going to throw up. She shut her eyes, hoping the melody of crashing waves would settle her stomach. Thomas looked up at the glittering stars. Their presence still powerful, despite the moon's brightness.

"Does anyone else know besides Gwen?"

"My agent knows, a few close friends, and of course Brett. If you ask Brett, I got what I deserved. He can't forgive me for putting my sister through hell. I can't fathom how many sleepless nights she had worrying about her stupid brother. Who knows, maybe he's right."

Celia opened her eyes. "Don't say things like that."

"Why not? Celia, you have no idea what I was like when I was younger. If I stood here and told you I wasn't a terrible person, I'd be lying. I was selfish and reckless. I don't even know if I infected anyone else, and I haven't bothered to even try and find out." He looked out at the ocean. "Before you say 'it's not too late', let me clarify. I was so fucked up, I don't remember who all I slept with. I don't know if they were they fans, actresses, or models."

"Why are you telling me all of this?" she asked.

"I figured if you were interested in knowing the truth, you'd want to know everything, not bits and pieces. Even if it changes how you see me, you deserve that much."

"Were you afraid it would change things between us?"

"Hasn't it already?"

Celia looked at him. Tears glistened in his eyes. The recognizable sadness she had seen so many times, finally had a reason. Thomas was mistakenly viewed as a man who had everything, when in reality he carried a heavy burden. He wasn't just an actor on screen, he had a character he had to portray all the time. He wore a mask that never came off. Celia walked over to him and wiped a tear off his cheek.

"Nothing has changed. I still care about you as I did before. Honestly, it's *scary* how much I care about you. I've never felt like this about anyone in my entire life, not even Brandon. I don't know what's going to happen in the future, with filming, our relationship, or anything really, but losing my Dad made me aware of how precious time is. Life is too short to worry about what's going to happen or dwell on what has happened," Celia said.

"You need to know that I'm fighting a losing battle. I'm on medication, but it's not meant to cure my disease. If you want out of this at any time, I understand, I won't hold it against you. I refuse to be selfish, even if it means losing you."

Celia wrapped her arms around him, resting her head against his chest. His heart beat slowly in her ear, its rhythmic pounds overshadowed the crashing waves. *You won't lose me. I promise.*

Thomas moved the shattered remains of what used to be the television into a large trash bin while Celia swept glass pieces into a dustpan. Celia was in jeans and t-shirt that said, "La vie est belle". Thomas wore athletic shorts and a solid-white t-shirt. The cool

December air seeped in from the raised windows. Coldplay hummed softly on the radio.

"I'm glad I have homeowner's insurance," Thomas said as he wiped sweat off his forehead.

"I'm sorry this happened," Celia said.

"You don't need to be, it wasn't your fault."

Celia shrugged. "I'm the reason Brandon did this, although after speaking with some of the witnesses, the police don't think he acted alone."

"Brandon did this because he's a punk that can't get over the fact he was dumped. Eventually he's going to have to face reality and act like an actual adult. I just hope that's sooner rather than later. Who do you think would've helped him?"

"Sarah, maybe? She was pretty nasty at the rehearsal dinner."

"I can't wrap my mind around the fact she's Brandon's cousin. I don't know if I should be baffled by how small the world is or sickened by the irony."

"The world is a strange and unusual place. I will say, I haven't gotten any more threatening messages since filing the restraining order."

"I hope it lasts."

"Me too."

Thomas leaned over the bin and stared intently at Celia. He didn't say anything, as if he was waiting for her to notice. Her cheeks flushed when she realized.

"What are you doing? Do I have something on my face?" she asked.

"Have you ever been to Scotland?"

She shook her head. "Why?"

"Well, I suppose I shouldn't spoil the surprise, but I got a call from my agent today. They've finalized the filming locations and lodging. We're filming in Scotland."

Celia's mouth fell open. "Are you serious?"

"As a heart attack."

Celia set the broom against the wall and walked over to Thomas. A wild grin sat upon his face as he took her shaky hands into his. A mixture of nervousness and excitement danced underneath her skin. She had never filmed out of the country prior to this, her passport had just been collecting dust in a desk drawer. It was more of a trinket, something she had acquired in case she needed it. Quite frankly, she had worried it was a waste of money and time, that she was never going to get the chance to use it.

"We're going to start filming on January third. The plan was for us to fly down on January second, but I have an idea—it might sound crazy but hear me out. It's going to be a mess around here for a few weeks, I'm going to have to have some repairs done and furniture replaced." He gestured to the paint stained couch. "So I thought maybe we could fly to Scotland two weeks early and spend the holidays there. We could visit some touristy stuff and see Scotland's beautiful countryside. I went ahead and asked production if we could fly out earlier, and they didn't seem to mind. They're not covering our accommodations until filming, but that's not a big deal—I can cover it. I've thought this through, honestly, it kept me up thinking about it. Gwen already agreed to keep Scooter for the duration of filming, the girls love him, I mean—what's two weeks longer?"

"Correct me if I'm wrong, but you're saying you want to spend Christmas and New Years in Scotland, with *me*?" her voice was barely above a whisper.

He nodded. "What do you think?"

"I think you're crazy." A smile spread across her face. "But I can't imagine a better way to spend the rest of 2016—let's do it."

Thomas' eyes lit up, his grin matched hers. He took her into his arms and spun her around. Joyous laughter escaped both their lips.

This was undeniably crazy, but what about their relationship had been normal in the first place? Celia's phone buzzed from inside her back pocket. Her smile faded as she saw the caller ID. It was her mother, Beth. Her mother had called three times over the past hour and had sent several text messages. Celia had elected to not answer the previous calls. She knew it would be some long-drawn-out phone call talking about her latest adventure, ending with the "why don't you call me more often," question as it always did. Reluctantly, she put the phone to her ear.

"Why haven't you been answering your phone?" Beth asked.

"I've been busy," Celia said.

It was true. She and Thomas had spent the better part of the day cleaning the mess left behind by the intruder as well as the officers.

"Will you let me in so we can at least speak face to face?" Beth asked.

Celia's stomach churned. "What do you mean?"

"I've been standing outside your apartment complex for half an hour. Security won't let me in because you aren't answering the buzzer."

"I'm not there..."

"Then where are you?"

Celia hesitated. Thomas was staring at her, the stress in her tone was obvious. She didn't want her mother around Thomas, at least not anytime soon. Celia knew how she would be, how she *always* is.

"Can you meet me at Carole's Coffee Shop in about thirty minutes?" Celia asked.

Beth sighed. "Yes."

She slid the phone back into her pocket.

"Everything okay?" Thomas asked.

"I don't know. My mother is in town, which is strange. She never shows up, not even when she's actually invited. She went to my apartment, but they wouldn't let her in so I'm going to have to go meet up with her... shit, I forgot about my car."

"I could drive you," Thomas offered.

"There's still so much to do here though. I don't mind calling an Uber."

He shook his head. "I have a few things I need to pick up, I could drop you off on my way to the store, and then swing by and grab you on the way home."

"Are you sure you don't mind?" she asked, somewhat hoping he would change his mind.

"Positive."

Carole's Coffee Shop was only a twenty-five-minute drive from Thomas' house. Traffic was light, despite it being a Sunday afternoon. The sun was harsh against the cloudless sky. Celia hadn't said much during the drive, only offering an occasional one-word response whenever Thomas asked a question. The shop's parking lot was full, and people clustered around outside on the sidewalk. Beth stood by herself at the corner. She was in her mid-fifties, but her wrinkled face was smooth thanks to her skin care rituals and a highly recommended plastic surgeon, making her appear almost ten years younger. Her short hair was unnaturally as light as Celia's and her skin was a fake orange tone. She wore a hot pink blouse, white capris, and rhinestone covered sandals.

Celia twirled her finger in her hair. The sandwich and chips she had for lunch tried to claw their way up. Thomas grabbed her hand and squeezed it.

"I'm sure you'll be fine, but if you need me you know the safe word," he said.

She smiled. "Pineapples."

Beth didn't appear to notice her get out of the car, her focus drawn to her cellphone. Celia took a deep breath and walked towards her. She contemplated jumping back into the car and leaving with Thomas, but Beth looked up and it was too late.

"Celia," she said.

"Hi Beth," Celia said.

Beth came over and threw her arms around Celia, pulling her into an uncomfortable hug. Celia stiffened under her touch. Beth never was one for affection, unless it was with one of the many male counterparts in her life. Whenever she acted warm towards anyone else, Celia knew it was for show. Beth took a step back and pursed her lips.

"I've been so worried about you," she said.

"Why?"

"You haven't been answering my calls or texts. I didn't even get as little as a turkey gif on Thanksgiving. I have to find out about my own daughter from watching *E! News*. Do you know what that feels like?"

Celia shrugged. "I've been busy."

"*Clearly.*"

"What's that supposed to mean?"

"We have a lot to catch up on."

The coffee shop was as busy on the inside as it was outside. Groups of various sizes lounged on the brown pleather couches and arm chairs. Almost every circular table was occupied, with empty stools being stolen for additional seats as soon as their occupier got up, even if it was just for a quick bathroom break. Celia managed to snag two seats at the long counter that stretched across the north wall. The wall was almost solid windows, allowing the harsh sunlight inside. Its reflection on the silver counter was almost blinding. Celia wished she had agreed to meet Beth at a bar. At least then she could have drank to dull her senses. Caffeine would only amplify her anxiety.

Beth sat a vanilla latte down in front of Celia. "Extra sugar."

"Thanks," Celia said. *At least she remembers how I like my coffee.*

Beth took her seat. She placed her large leather tote bag on the counter next to her, as if it would be a barrier between her and the stranger next to her.

"So is it true." She took a long sip of her peppermint flavored coffee. "That you're living with that thirty-seven-year-old man?"

"His name is Thomas."

"Do you realize how bad that looks? You're not even thirty and you're shacking up with some older man you don't even know."

Heat rushed to the back of Celia's head. "Appearances were the last thing on my mind when strangers suddenly had my personal address. You should be more concerned with my *safety*. I had to take out a restraining order against Brandon after he broke into Thomas' place when I was there alone. He trashed the place as well as my car."

"That doesn't seem like something he would do. He was always a nice kid. I don't understand why you broke up with him in the first place."

"How would you even know? You were barely around him because you were never home."

"Keep your voice down, people are staring," Beth said.

She was right. Several people had stopped talking altogether, their gazes fixed on Celia and Beth. Celia shook her head. Anger was boiling beneath her skin. She knew it was a waste of breath to even attempt to argue with her mother. Beth had selective memory, and for some reason seemed to believe she was some PTA mother that was actively involved in her daughter's life all the way through grade school.

"Why are you even here?" Celia asked.

"To figure out what is going on with you. You haven't been responding and I've been worried, especially with your recent behavior. I know you've been distant in the past, but I figured you'd at least let me know when you make life changes that could affect your career."

"So you're worried about my career?"

"Yes and you should be too."

Celia sighed and rubbed her temples. It didn't matter how much time had passed, her mother was the same person she'd always been. Beth was the reason Celia was an actress. When Celia was barely old enough to walk, she started sending headshots of her to various castings calls and agents. When Celia booked her first commercial, she was elated. She bought her various gifts ranging from stuffed animals to candy bars. Whatever she wanted, it was hers. On the other hand, when Celia was recast as a child actress on a day time soap opera, Beth was a nightmare. She yelled, took things away, and made Celia feel worthless. Beth developed a toxic routine. When Celia's career was thriving, she was her biggest supporter; however, when it struggled, she was her worst critic.

"You know I have your best interest at heart."

"I don't think you do. Thomas coming into my life has been the best thing that's happened to me in a long time."

"What about the movie deal?"

Celia shrugged. "I'm happy about that too."

"Listen, this isn't my first rodeo. I know what PR relationships are, what they look like, and the incentives. I can see what you're getting out of this, but I don't understand what a man like Thomas Richardson gets out of this. What's his payoff?"

"It's not a PR relationship and there's no payoffs for anyone. Can you please just drop this already?"

Beth shook her head disapprovingly. "I don't believe you."

"I don't need you to. I know what it is and so does Thomas, that's all that matters. I think this concludes you're figuring out what's wrong with me." Celia pulled out her phone. "When is your flight out? I can get you a ride to the airport."

"I haven't booked one."

"What do you mean?"

"There's more than one reason I'm here."

Celia sat her phone down. Her attention focused on Beth. While plastic surgery had done wonders, it hadn't been able to erase everything. The expression that plagued Beth's face since the separation from Celia's father, a mixture of sadness and anger, was still there. Beth didn't have to say anything, Celia knew there was some part of her that would always love him.

"Jeff and I have decided to take some time apart," Beth said.

Jeff was Beth's soon-to-be sixth husband. It seemed like every relationship she had moved too quickly and then fell apart even quicker. Celia's father was her longest relationship, spanning nearly twelve years. Jeff had made it to almost six months, which in itself was no easy feat.

"I'm planning on moving back to California full time while Jeff and I sort things out. I thought maybe I could stay with you until I found a place on my own."

Celia's mouth fell open. If she had been drinking her coffee she would've spit it out. *She can't be serious!* Beth looked at her expectantly.

"I'm not asking Thomas if you can move into his house."

Beth shook her head. "I'm not asking for that. I was thinking about your apartment. I mean, you're not living there right now anyway. I could take over the rent until the lease is up. Surely, that would give me enough time to find a place of my own."

"Oh... What's the catch?"

"There isn't one Celia. I'm just trying to find somewhere to live. This is a difficult time for me and I could use some support. I figured you'd think it was a great idea..."

Celia couldn't argue that it was a bad idea—in all honesty, it wasn't. It would help her out. She could use her money to rent a different apartment and get out of Thomas' house. Regardless of how much she liked staying with him, she knew that was never meant to be a permanent living solution. Once they returned from Scotland, she could find a place of her own.

"Okay."

"Okay...?"

"Okay as in you can take over my lease, but we're going to do this the right way." Beth's face lit up but Celia ignored her. "I don't want it to be a secret from the apartment managers in case something happens. I don't know what the process will be, but know there will be documents to fill out."

"We can do whatever you want. Thank you, you have no idea how much this means to me."

"Do you at least have somewhere to stay tonight?"

Beth shook her head. "I was assuming you were still at your apartment when I came down and that I could just stay with you."

Celia sighed. *How typical.* She checked her phone. It was only three-fifteen, and the leasing office didn't close until five.

"If we hurry, we can get this all sorted out today and you can just stay at my apartment."

"I'm ready to go now, if you'd like. Although I'm hoping you'll stay and help me get settled after the paperwork is finalized. I don't want to rush, it's been such a long time since we've seen each other."

"So long as you promise not to say anything more about my relationship with Thomas, and as long as it's not too late, I will stay for a bit."

"I promise," Beth said.

# Eleven

The Los Angeles International Airport was busy, as usual, despite the late hour. The lines to check-in spilled out into the walkways. The deafening hum of excited conversations echoed throughout the entire facility. Celia sat on a bench in terminal four, her foot nervously tapped the floor. She wore jeans, riding boots, a sweater, and a puffy brown jacket—a stark contrast to her normal attire. After a handful of *Google* searches and visits to tourist websites, she had realized how cold it would be in Scotland, and that a new wardrobe was essential. While she was normally hot-natured and rarely cold, she wasn't sure how she would fare with the average temperatures being around forty degrees Fahrenheit.

"I thought I was the only one afraid of heights," Thomas said.

He handed her a hot latte, courtesy of Dunkin' Donuts, and sat down. He was dressed equally warm in a white cable knit sweater, jeans, boots, and a wool trench coat. He took a sip of his black coffee.

"That's not it." She twisted the latte cup in her hand. "I'm anxious, yes, but in a good way. It's not just that I'm going to a foreign country for the first time, I'm going with you. That makes it special."

Thomas smiled and placed his hand over hers.

"If someone had told me last year, heck even a few months ago, this is where I would be today, I would've laughed and told them they were crazy. I never thought I'd get the chance to work with someone like you, let alone date you."

"Stranger things have happened, right?"

Celia laughed. "Yes, yes they have."

"In all seriousness, I'm really happy things have turned out the way they have. When I was first diagnosed, I swore I'd never date again. I didn't want to risk infecting anyone else. I channeled all my energy into my career. What free time I had was devoted to working with feral cats, and spending time with my family. Staying busy was a nice distraction, but I was still depressed. This is the happiest I've been in... I honestly can't tell you when—it's been *that* long."

Tears glittered in his eyes, but he was smiling. It was at that exact moment Celia knew what that strange feeling that had been festering inside her mind and spreading throughout her entire body was. She knew one hundred percent, without a single doubt, she loved him. She had fallen slowly like descending into the deep waters, but as soon as she fell, she was engulfed. There was no turning back now. She was at his mercy.

"Group A, it's time to line up. Please have your boarding passes ready," a flight attendant called over the intercom.

Thomas wiped a stray tear from his cheek and helped Celia stand. Together they walked to the boarding area. It was the loudest area of the airport, as if the excitement to travel reached its peak for the travelers. Thomas' hand shook nervously in Celia's as they waited to board.

"I don't know if this coffee was such a good idea," he admitted.

"Don't worry, we can watch a movie until your nerves wear off."

"I don't know if there is a movie that lasts over fifteen hours."

"I'm sure we can figure something out, we always do."

He smiled. "You're right, we do."

The flight attendant, a blonde woman in her late fifties, scanned their boarding passes. An overly enthusiastic smile sat upon her powdered face.

"Enjoy your flight," she said.

Thomas forced a smile and Celia nodded before following strangers into the air bridge. The echoes of conversations faded to a loud whisper as they got closer to the plane. The interior of the plane was spacious. The seats were a dark grey, almost black, in color and lined the aisle in pairs. Wide screens were positioned behind each seat at the top. An array of buttons sat on the left side of the armrest, most for reclining and adjusting the seat's position.

Celia took the seat closest to the window. The window itself was foggy and covered with raindrops. Thomas sighed heavily as he sat down. His hands were trembling worse, the metal on the seatbelt clanked loudly as he attempted to buckle it.

"Here, let me." Celia leaned over and fastened the buckle. "I know the worst part is the taking off and landing. You can squeeze my hand as hard as you need to. I don't mind."

"I'm going to take you up on that. I'm sorry I'm so jittery. I don't know what's the matter with me."

"I understand now why you insisted on those shots before our flight to Chicago."

"It was only one shot... and a beer."

Celia playfully rolled her eyes. "Sure."


It was a little after seven o'clock in the evening when their plane landed in Edinburgh. A cab driver had picked Celia and Thomas up from the airport. He was an older gentleman, probably in his mid to late fifties, with a thick Scottish accent. The interior of his car smelled like lavender and Christmas music emitted softly from the speakers.

"Where would you like to go?" the man asked.

Thomas turned to Celia. "What do you think?"

Her stomach gurgled, overshadowing Gene Autry's *Jingle Bells*.

"Are you hungry?" he asked.

She nodded, her face a deep red. Besides the latte at the airport and a small package of sweetened peanuts, she hadn't eaten.

"Since our bags are already headed to the hotel, we have two options. We could go to the hotel and order something in and rest or we could grab something around here and maybe explore for a couple of hours. First time international traveler's choice, what do you say?"

"I say the latter. We can always sleep in tomorrow."

"Good choice." Thomas turned to the driver. "Do you have any dining recommendations for two tourists?"

He stroked his chin thoughtfully. "Aye. I know a really good pub downtown. With Christmas coming up, it's right in the heart of the festivities. Plus they have the best Scotch pies. The recipe made it to the finals for World Scotch Pie Championship a few years ago."

"Works for me. Celia?"

"Let's go," Celia said.

"Alright, buckle up then. We should be there in ten minutes or so, depending on traffic," the driver said.

Celia took Thomas' hand into hers as the car merged into the airport traffic. She was exhausted from the flight, but arguably more excited. Goosebumps covered her flesh. The sky was dark, enveloping the countryside. Stars were masked by a thin layer of clouds. Thomas and the driver chatted softly. He said he had lived in Edinburgh all his life, and had been a cab driver for almost four years now. He kept mentioning how *familiar* Thomas looked. Thomas said he must have one of those faces and Celia stifled a giggle. If Thomas wasn't going to reveal his identity, neither was she.

The closer they got to the pub, the more festive the city became, as if it was alive with Christmas spirit. Christmas lights glittered on every building and light post. Small markets selling everything from holiday crafts to different foods lined the streets. Snow rested upon the ground, treetops, and rooflines. The sidewalks and paths were crowded with people of all ages, tourist easily blending in with the locals. It didn't feel like they were in another country, it felt more like another world.

"I've never seen something so amazing." Celia's hands were pressed against the foggy window.

"Come on now, you've seen me naked."

Celia playfully shoved him and they both laughed.

"We're here," the driver said.

He parked against the curb outside Highlander's, a small pub nestled in between a bakery and clothing store. Thomas fished out his wallet and paid the man, tipping him generously. The cool air engulfed Celia as soon as she exited the vehicle, sending a shiver down her spine.

"I hope you both enjoy your time in Scotland," he said.

"Thank you, we will," Celia said.

Thomas wrapped his arm around Celia, and they walked into the pub. It was larger than it had initially appeared to be. A rectangular wooden counter fenced in the bartender at the right corner. There was a small wooden stage in the opposite corner, where a woman stood drunkenly singing along to some unfamiliar Christmas song. Her friends, who appeared equally drunk, were filming her from their smart phones. Round tables were scattered across the floor. Some larger square tables sat near the bar. Paper snowflakes and sparkling silver tinsel were fastened on the brick wall.

A fir tree sat next to the entrance. It was decorated with handmade ornaments, popcorn garland, and blinking chaser lights. Stockings, presumably with the names of the employees, hung on the mantle of a gas fireplace near the restrooms. The servers and bartender were dressed casually in different t-shirts and jeans. Their only contrast to the patrons were their matching blue Santa hats and the black aprons tied around their waists. A chalkboard sign, lined in tinsel, said, "Please seat yourself."

Thomas and Celia chose a round table catty corner to the stage, giving them a first row seat to the karaoke participants. With menus in hand, one of the servers, a petite woman with dark brown hair, approached their table.

"Good evening! My name is Monica and I'll be taking care of you guys tonight," she said. Unlike the cab driver, she had a heavy English accent.

She handed both Thomas and Celia a menu. "Would you guys like to start off with something to drink? Or perhaps some chips?"

"What would you recommend for two tourist who've never been to Scotland?" Thomas asked.

"We have quite a few different Scottish beers, ciders, whiskey, and gin. I would definitely recommend the chips, and of course our minced mutton Scotch pie."

"How about two Scotch pies, an order of chips, and a beer for me. Any brand works, I'll leave it to your choice," Thomas said.

Monica nodded and turned to Celia. Celia didn't bother to look at the drink menu. If Thomas was going to be spontaneous, so was she.

"I'll take a Scottish cider. I'll leave the choice to you as well."

"Alright, I'll get started on those drinks and get your order to the kitchen."

As Monica walked off, a young Scottish guy stepped onto the stage. He couldn't have been older than twenty, an impish grin sat on his face as he began to sing along to Elvis Presley's version of *Blue Christmas*. He was terribly out of tune, but his bar mates cheered him on nonetheless.

"Would you do that?" Celia asked.

"Karaoke?"

She nodded.

"Can't guarantee I'd sound any better than him, but yeah I'd be down. You?"

"No, I'm terribly self-conscious about my voice. I'm pretty sure the only person who's ever heard me sing was Meghan, and that was after one too many shots of tequila."

Thomas laughed. "I think that's why karaoke is great. No one cares if you sound terrible, it's just for fun. All that matters is if that you get up there and sing. If you sound great, people will tell you, but if you don't—no one cares."

"Prove it."

"You want me to sing? Right here? Tonight?"

"What's wrong? If you think karaoke is so great, you should have no trouble getting up there and singing."

Monica brought over their drinks and a basket of chips. Celia took one of the fries and dipped it into a small cup of ketchup. Thomas stared at her, a mischievous look on his face. He took a quick drink of his beer and sat it down.

"Remember, you wanted me to do this," he said.

He walked over to the employee playing the karaoke songs for the patrons. As *Blue Christmas* finished and the young man walked off the stage, Thomas took his place.

"This is for you," he said, winking at Celia.

Celia immediately recognized the song as the music started— Mariah Carey's *All I Want for Christmas is You*. She hastily pulled out her phone and started recording. Thomas' voice was, surprisingly good. He wasn't able to hit all of Mariah's high notes, but he fared better than the drunken patron before him. Thomas' face suddenly reddened. The song carried on without him as he coughed uncontrollably. Celia sat her phone down and went to him. He firmly grasped her arm, struggling to stand still as he coughed. By the end of the first chorus, Thomas had regained his composure;

however, his desire to sing appeared to be gone. Without a word he walked back over to their table. His expression was deflated, his eyes hollow. It made Celia's stomach churn, she hated seeing him like that—defeated. Instead of returning to the table, she grabbed the microphone and cupped it. Her eyes were locked on him as she took over. Thomas started clapping with the beat, and several of the pub's patrons joined him. The light returned to his eyes, and he was smiling. His smile was reassuring and her singing grew louder with the second chorus. She couldn't hear herself, partially due to the loud music and partially due to tuning herself out. Her focus was on Thomas and his smile. In that moment, it was all that mattered to her.

Thomas and the other patrons clapped and cheered as the song finished. The heat rushed to Celia's cheek, a wave of self-consciousness washing over her again. She took a small, mock bow, and retreated back to the table.

"You're amazing," Thomas said.

"I'm pretty sure I sounded like a dying cow," Celia joked.

Thomas shook his head. "I'm not talking about your voice. Which, quite frankly, you shouldn't be shy about. I'm talking about how you did that, took over, especially after you told me about your feelings towards karaoke and your voice."

"I had to."

"No you didn't."

"Yes, I did. Sometimes you get this look in your eyes, like you're hurting, no— like you're *drowning*. I don't know if it's because how I feel about you or something else, but whenever it happens, I want to do whatever I can to bring you out of it."

"How *do* you feel about me?"

Celia's heartrate fluttered. "What do you mean?"

Before he could elaborate, Monica returned to the table with two Scotch pies. Steam floated above the crust. The mutton's scent was as overwhelming as it was inviting.

"Do you guys need anything else right now?" she asked.

"No, thank you," they both said in unison.

Celia quickly dug her fork into the pie and took a bite. It burned all the way down her throat, but she continued to eat. She was afraid Thomas was going to ask her how she felt again. She loved him, yes, but she wasn't ready to tell him. What if he didn't feel the same way? Thomas stared at her, eyes wide.

"I didn't realize you were so hungry for Scotch pie."

"It smelled too good."

Thomas smiled. "You're a terrible liar."

# Twelve

Their hotel had a view of Edinburgh Castle, one of the reasons
Thomas had booked it. The room itself was nice and cozy. A gas
fireplace sat in the far corner opposite of the kitchenette. The king-
sized bed had a wooden headboard and footboard that was stained
a rich mahogany. A green and red patterned quilt was spread out
across the bed. Two cream armchairs were positioned beside a coffee
table near the fireplace. Celia sat on the bed, scrolling through her
phone. It was a little after nine o'clock in the morning, and she was
still in her plaid pajama pants and solid red sweatshirt. Her hair was
pulled into a messy bun and she had bags under her eyes from the
lack of sleep she had gotten the night prior.

Thomas came into the room carrying a large brown paper sack
and a cardboard drink carrier housing two coffees. He was wearing
grey sweatpants, his Los Angeles Dodgers ball cap, tennis shoes,
a cat t-shirt, and a jacket. The smell of sausage, eggs, and bacon
permeated the room.

"I got us both a 'full Scottish breakfast', and to be honest, I'm
not entirely what that entails." He sat the food and coffee on the
kitchenette's counter. "What time did you get up?"

Celia rolled out of the bed. He handed her the coffee labeled,
"Extra sugar".

"About twenty-five minutes ago. If you hadn't left a note, I would have worried that some rogue highlanders had kidnapped you."

Thomas laughed. "I would be more worried about *you* getting kidnapped by a highlander. I'm sure Sam Heughan is around here somewhere ready to render aid."

"I guess that means you saw the posts?"

Celia sat down in one of the armchairs and Thomas sat down across from her. The gas fire was warm.

"What do you mean?" he asked.

"Apparently someone at the pub last night recognized us. They recorded everything and now it's all over the internet." She opened the Styrofoam food container. "The world knows we're in Scotland."

"They would have found out eventually."

Celia twirled her fork in the fried egg. She knew he was right, but part of her had hoped their adventures in Scotland would be private—only shared between the two of them.

"Are they raving about my singing voice?" Thomas asked.

"Hardly, they're speculating about your cough."

"What's the diagnosis?"

"Tuberculosis."

Thomas laughed. "That's new."

*At least it would be curable.* Celia sighed. She hadn't told Thomas that she had been secretly researching AIDS, gathering as much information as she could, after he admitted his diagnosis. From her understanding, AIDS was something a person could go on living a healthy, practically normal life so long as they kept up with their medication. Thomas seemed to be living a normal life, as normal of a life an actor could have anyway.

"Everything okay?" he asked.

"Yeah. I'm not sure how I feel about baked beans being considered a breakfast item... and what is this type of sausage?"

"I believe it is black pudding, also referred to as blood pudding."

"Well it looks as appetizing as it sounds." She pushed the sausage to the far corner of the tray.

"This could be your only time to try fine, authentic Scottish cuisine. Don't you want to try everything?"

She laughed. "I'm open to trying almost anything once, keyword is *almost*."

"Fair enough."

The sky was cloudless, painted in soft teal hues. A cool breeze swept through the air. Despite the chill, Edinburgh Castle was packed with tourists. Celia and Thomas stood in The Great Hall. The walls were painted a vibrant red, embellished with wooden accents. Dark wood intricately adorned the high ceiling. Red rope guarded a vast variety of weapons from axes to swords, shields, and suits of armor.

"Do you think they would notice if I took one of those axes as a souvenir?" Thomas asked.

"Initially, no, but the obscure shape underneath your jacket would be a dead giveaway upon reviewing security tapes."

"I could just hold you in front of me the entire time."

"I'm not being arrested as an accessory for theft in a foreign country so you can take home a souvenir." Celia walked towards the *Battle of Waterloo* painting. "Now, if you wanted to get arrested for something scandalous like streaking through downtown in the middle of the night— I'd be more interested."

"That could be arranged."

"You're the one in charge of calling my agent to let her know why we were arrested, and then fired."

Celia's phone buzzed in her pocket. She had silenced her calls before they went into the castle, not wanting to be distracted, but her phone had been going off almost non-stop for the past fifteen minutes. It was probably her mother, distraught after learning Celia was in Scotland with Christmas only two days away. They hadn't spent Christmas together since Celia was in middle school, but Jeff's absence could have her lonely. Thomas' phone rang, piercing her thoughts. He pulled his phone out of his coat pocket and walked out of The Great Hall. Celia followed him out, but stayed by the entrance, not wanting to encroach on his call.

Thomas had a peculiar look on his face, slowly pacing as he occasionally said something to whoever was on the other side of the call. *Maybe it's Gwen.* Celia's phone started buzzing again, and she reluctantly retrieved it. Her stomach was in knots when she saw the caller ID. It wasn't her mother that had been relentlessly calling, it was Amy.

"Hello," she answered, her tone barely above a whisper.

"My God, Celia, why haven't you been answering me? I've been worried." Amy said.

"I'm at Edinburgh Castle with Thomas, I had my phone on silent... why have you been worried?"

"Have you been online today?"

"Yeah, I saw someone leaked a video of Thomas and me at a pub. I didn't see a reason to call you about it, no damage was done."

"That's not why I'm calling." Amy took an audible deep breath. "Someone posted private pictures of you on *Instagram*."

"What do you mean by private pictures?"

There was a long pause. Each second ate away at Celia. She knew what Amy meant, but part of her hoped she was wrong. Thomas was still on the phone, but his gaze was focused on Celia now. The unfamiliar peculiar look still on his face.

"Topless pictures of you."

Celia turned pale and her insides hollowed. She felt frail, as if the smallest gust of wind was going to knock her off her feet. Tears were building in her eyes.

"They were reported and taken down a few minutes after they

were posted, but some people had already taken screenshots and shared them to *Twitter*, and other media outlets. I'm working on acquiring a legal team for this so we can figure out who posted the photos."

Amy kept talking, but Celia couldn't hear her. She couldn't hear anything, the world was silent. She gripped the stone exterior of the castle as she slid to the ground. *This can't be happening* echoed over and over again in her head. Celia knew who posted the pictures, there was no doubt in her mind. She had only ever sent pictures to one person—Brandon. He probably didn't get the reaction he wanted with releasing her address, nor the break-in, so he had escalated. He hit her where he knew it would hurt.

"Celia?"

"Yes," she managed to choke out.

"It's going to be okay. I'll call you with any updates, okay?"

Celia slid her phone back into her pocket without saying another word. Small crowds of tourist walked by. Some of them broke from their groups, pausing by themselves. It was hard to tell if they were marveling at the castle or the girl who just wanted to disappear into thin air. She felt exposed. *No one is ever going to look at me the same way again.*

Thomas walked over to her and sat down. Celia didn't look at him, her gaze fixed on the passing crowd, concentrating on the strangers' interactions.

"Do you want to talk about it?" he asked gently.

She didn't say anything. She knew that even the weakest attempt to speak would result in her breaking into tears. Thomas wrapped his arm around her. His fingers gently caressed her shoulder.

"It's okay if you don't want to talk, all I ask is that you listen. I'm not going to lie and say I understand what you're feeling, or that I've had it happen to me when it hasn't. You've been thrust into the spotlight these past few months and people are paying attention. Some of these people are fans, but not everyone has your best interest at heart. People can be cruel, whether it's by nature or circumstantial. They're looking for ways to hurt you, whether it's a stab at your professional life or something personal like this. This won't be the last time someone goes after you."

Celia brushed a tear off her cheek.

"If you want to cry, go for it, hit a wall, do it. You can react in any way you want, but once you've got it out of your system— move on. Come back stronger, show them they can't break you. Be like a phoenix, rise from the ashes. I know how strong you are."

"I think you overestimate my abilities," Celia said.

"No, I don't." He stood and offered his hand to her. "You underestimate yourself."

Celia finally looked at him. His face was serious. She took a deep breath before taking his hand and allowing him to pull her to her feet. She wrapped her arms around him and his expression melted into a smile.

"What do you say we get out of here? I have an idea for a nice distraction," Thomas said.

"I'd like that, but first." She took a step back from Thomas and dried her face on her sleeves. "I need to do something."

Celia approached a woman passing by with a man, perhaps her boyfriend or husband. They were dressed warm in long coats, and both had fiery red hair.

"Would you mind taking a picture of my boyfriend and me in front of the castle?" Celia asked.

"Aye, I don't mind at all," the woman said.

Celia handed her the phone and waved Thomas over. She wrapped her arms around his shoulders as the woman counted down to three, and pulled him into a kiss. Kissing him made her feel better, it was like tiny euphoric butterflies swam in her stomach. For a brief moment, she didn't have a care in the world, the leaked pictures were the last thing on her mind. She pulled away, and a smile sat on both of their faces. Celia thanked the woman and took her phone. She looked at the picture and smiled. It was beautiful, not only because the castle towering behind them, but because it was the only picture she would let define the day.

"That might be my new favorite picture of us," Thomas said as they walked to a waiting car.

"My favorite is of our kiss at the *Academy Awards*."

The electric feeling of that first kiss spread throughout her body as the memory flashed in her mind. She remembered the pain his eyes held as they pulled away from each other. He was fighting a battle she didn't know about, trying to keep a distance from anyone that could be caught in the crossfire of his disease. He didn't want to let anyone in, he didn't want anyone to get close. The closer a person got, the more likely they were to get hurt, and it seemed like Thomas was afraid of hurting anyone else.

The driver stopped in downtown Edinburgh, only a few blocks from Highlander's. The street was more crowded than the night they arrived. Children were running and shrieking as they threw snow-balls at each other. One of the children nearly ran into Celia as she waited for Thomas on the icy sidewalk. He tipped the driver and walked over. He had a goofy smile across his face.

"Don't tell me you're forcing me to do karaoke again," Celia said.

"As much fun as that was, no, I had something different in mind," he said.

Thomas took her hand and led her down the sidewalk, past the John Wilson Memorial statue towards East Princes Street Gardens. A small ice rink was set up in the middle of the garden. Speakers were placed strategically around the rink, emitting soft Christmas carols. A large sign read, "Edinburgh's Christmas Winter Wonder-land," at the back of the rink.

"Ice skating?" Celia asked wide-eyed.

Thomas nodded. "I was reading about the pop-up skating rinks in a travel blog, and I figured we had to visit one."

Celia looked nervously to the rink. Over a dozen people were skating. A few stragglers were clinging to the wall, most likely unsure about their own balance abilities, but most skaters were gliding around with ease.

"I've never been ice skating before," Celia said as Thomas handed her a pair of skates.

"Lucky for you, you've got an experienced date to show you the ropes."

Celia smiled, but his words did little to ease her concerns. If balancing on ice skates was anything like balancing in high heels, she was in trouble. After helping her lace up her skates, Thomas led her to the ice. Her heart was practically beating out of her chest. Thomas stepped onto the ice with ease, but Celia hesitated at the edge.

"Don't worry, I promise I won't let you fall," he said.

"You better not."

She took a deep breath and stepped onto the ice. Her hands were clamped on Thomas' arms, comparable to a ship captain's hands gripping the helm on a storming sea.

"Try taking short, small steps," Thomas said.

The skates were heavy. Each step she took was small and deliberate, her thoughts solely on the ice beneath her. Her death grip on Thomas loosened as they fell into a slow pace, skating counterclockwise with everyone else in the rink.

"Clearly this isn't your first time," Celia said as a teenager whizzed past them.

"My parents were firm believers extra-curricular activities were important to a child's development. From soccer and baseball to swimming and ice skating, Gwen and I were subjected to participate. I will say, I can't do any fancy spins or maneuvers, but I can glide around here with the best of them."

"Sounds like an eventful childhood. I can't say my mother shared the same beliefs."

"Did you not participate in sports or anything?"

Celia shook her head. "Acting was the only thing my mother cared about. I'll never forget the time my dad picked me up from school early to get a horseback riding lesson. Enamored with *Black Beauty* and *The Black Stallion,* I had begged and begged for riding lessons. My mother said no, horses were too dangerous and it could jeopardize my career. At eight-years-old my mother was worried about my *career.*"

"That's rough. What happened?"

"I had an amazing time, it's actually the best memory I have with my dad, but my mother was beyond livid when she found out. It was my first and last riding lesson. I didn't even get to see another horse in person until I was cast as the rancher's daughter."

"I'm sorry Celia. I understand now your hesitancy about meeting her at the coffee shop. You seemed out of sorts after you saw her."

"It was our typical strained interaction, but there is something I've been meaning to talk to you about."

Another teenager rushed past Celia, knocking her arm as he passed and throwing her forward. Thomas tried to stop her from falling, but they both ended up on the hard ice. Celia looked at Thomas and they both started laughing. The teenager, a pimple-faced boy no older than sixteen, skated over to them.

"I am so sorry. Are you two alright?" he asked.

"Yeah, we're fine." Thomas stood up. "But please try and be more careful."

"Yes sir."

The teenager stared at Celia for a moment. His eyes traveling from her face to her chest and back. His freckled cheeks, already reddened by the cold, darkened. Celia's stomach dropped and the smile evaporated from her face. Without another word, he skated off. She knew exactly why he looked at her like that.

"Are you going to hangout on the ground?" Thomas asked.

Celia hadn't even noticed he extended his hand to her until he spoke. She took his hand and carefully stood back up. Her knees were sore from falling. The teenager was standing at the far end of the rink with two other kids. All of their eyes were locked on Celia.

Thomas gently tapped her shoulder. "Is everything okay?"

"Yeah, I'm just cold."

One of the teenagers snapped a picture. Celia's desire to disappear into thin air was back and stronger than before.

"Can we get out of here?"

"Yeah of course," Thomas said.

Celia didn't say anything on the car ride back to the hotel. If Thomas had been speaking to her and not the driver, she had no idea. She tried to recall the first time she sent nude pictures to Brandon. *Had he egged me on? Or was it all my stupid idea?* She knew Brandon was to blame for leaking the pictures, but she couldn't dismiss her own guilt. After all, she couldn't say she didn't take the photos or send them. She already knew what people would say, "If she hadn't ever sent pictures in the first place, this wouldn't have happened."

Immediately upon entering their hotel room Celia stripped out of her boots and coat. She threw her hat and scarf onto an armchair before climbing onto the bed. Thomas came over and sat down next to her.

"What were you trying to tell me before we were plowed over?" Thomas asked.

"My mother is having some relationship issues and decided to move back to California while she and her fiancé take some time to 'think about things'. She moved with the intent of moving in with me without even discussing the idea with me. Typical Beth behavior— anyway, she took over the lease to my apartment."

"Does that mean you'll be seeing more of her?"

"I hope not. It does mean I can find my own apartment and move out when we get back from filming."

"Oh."

"Brandon won't have any reason to break-in if I'm not there."

Thomas furrowed his brow. "Is that why you want to move out?"

"No, but... I do worry about what he might try next."

"Is there a different reason you want to move?"

"It's not that I *want* to move, but we both discussed this would be only temporary. If I have the ability to have my own place, I need to move out. I can't keep burdening you."

"Why on earth would you think you living with me is a burden?"

"If I hadn't moved in, Brandon would have never broken into your place. It's my fault."

Thomas scoffed. "None of this was your fault. Brandon chose to break-in, Hell, he might've done that even if you hadn't moved in. There is no way to decipher what's running through his crazy head. Him releasing your address, the break-in that was all on him. I wouldn't be surprised if he was the asshole behind the leaked photos... You do realize you're a victim in this right? No one, especially not me, is blaming you."

Celia took a deep breath. She knew he was right, the guilt she felt was misplaced. She regretted sending the pictures to Brandon, but her mistake was in trusting him. She could beat up herself about taking the pictures in the first place, but it wasn't going to make her feel better, nor erase the fact that Brandon chose to release them. He was the guilty party.

"It's ultimately your choice, but you don't have to move out. Honestly, I'd rather you didn't." Thomas took her hand in his. "It's selfish, but I love having you around. I haven't been this happy in years."

Celia smiled. "I haven't either. It has been nice staying with you, and I'm not just saying that because of Scooter. Although, Scooter is a plus."

"Does this mean you'll stay?"

"Yes, I'll stay."

# Thirteen

Christmas morning brought a thick blanket of snow with it. Edinburgh was quiet, many of its residents tucked inside their homes and celebrating the day with family. Even the hotel was quiet, absent of the usual bustle of guests and concierges roaming the long corridors. Thomas stood shirtless in the kitchenette, only in his plaid pajama pants, as he iced freshly baked cinnamon rolls. Celia, also in her pajamas, sat in an armchair in front of the fireplace with a thick afghan blanket draped over her. The wood crackled and popped inside as the fire danced around it. Cinnamon and coffee permeated the air.

Thomas brought the cinnamon rolls over and set them down on the coffee table in between the armchairs. He grabbed a solid navy-blue hooded sweatshirt and sat down opposite to Celia.

"Would you have spent Christmas with Gwen if you weren't in Scotland?" Celia asked.

Thomas shook his head. "I usually spend Christmas Eve at her house, but not Christmas day. With the tension between Brett and me, I don't want to ruin the girls' holiday. Typically, I spend Christmas at home with Scooter. What is your usual Christmas routine?"

"The few times my mother was actually in the country and not on a yacht, we would spend Christmas day together. Christmas is one of the holidays where she actually tries to be decent. She'll put on a big, fake smile, spend most of the day in the kitchen making some elaborate dinner, and finish the day by giving me some extravagant gift I don't need. Last year it was some Louis Vuitton bag that cost more than a month's rent."

"Not a fan of Louis Vuitton?" Thomas took a bite of a cinnamon roll.

"I mean it's just not *me*. I don't wear or carry expensive items unless it's required for a premiere or a part of my wardrobe on set. If my mother actually cared enough to pay attention, she'd know this." Celia sighed. "I'm sorry, I didn't mean to ruin the mood."

"Celia, you have nothing to be sorry for. You didn't ruin anything. It's assuring that you're comfortable enough with me now to open up about personal issues like this. I want to know everything there is to know about you and I know that's not always going to be positive... There's something I've been meaning to talk to you about. I just haven't figured out the best way tell you."

"Actually, there's something I've been wanting to speak with you about as well."

"Do you want to go first?"

Celia shook her head. "This isn't easy for me. In case we're about to bring up the same subject, I'd rather you go first."

"Your agent and my agent, Bridgette, are longtime friends. They went to college together, even started out working at the same talent agency. They haven't worked together in years, and from my understanding didn't keep in touch, but they were reunited during the casting process. When Bridgette learned we were cast as the leading roles she called your agent, hoping she hadn't told you yet."

Celia felt a strange feeling bubbling in her stomach. It wasn't the butterflies she felt when Thomas kissed her or the heart-stopping electricity when he looked at her and cracked one of his killer smiles. It was a hollow feeling, as if she was climbing an old wooden ladder that was about to snap beneath her weight.

Thomas took a deep breath. "When Bridgette learned that your agent hadn't told you the news, she told her she had an idea. It was stupid, I had joked with her about it before, but I never imagined she would actually try it... or even that someone would agree to it. What I am trying to say is that the contract you signed had nothing to do with you securing the role. It was a ruse my agent came up with."

His words hit her like a sucker punch. She opened her mouth to speak, but no words came out. Even if she could've spoke, she wouldn't have known what to say.

"I didn't want to tell you, at least not like this, but I was afraid it would be brought up when we start filming and I didn't want you to be blindsided. Please believe me Celia, I had no idea how this would all play out. The more time we spent together the more I got to know you, care about you, and then I started having feelings for you. I knew the deeper we went, the worse it would be when you found out, but I didn't want to ruin what we have."

Thomas took her hand in his. Her skin was ice cold. His eyes were pleading, glistened with tears. Celia had no words. She yanked her hand free and walked over to the window. The snow was falling steadily. A child was outside riding their bike, probably a gift from Santa, on the slushy sidewalk. Their parent was following close behind. Thomas came up behind her and lightly placed his hands on her shoulders. She recoiled under his touch.

"Celia please say something."

"What do you want me to say?" Tears were in her eyes as well.

"Anything, what you're thinking, feeling... how can I make this better?"

"You can't." She turned to him. "Our entire relationship was built on a lie. I felt so guilty for lying to people, pretending while we were in a PR relationship, but we were never in a PR relationship in the first place— it was one colossal lie. I knew you were an excellent actor, but this—I didn't expect this. I let myself fall in love with you. How could I have been so stupid?"

"Celia this wasn't a game for me, I wasn't acting. I tried to fight the feelings I had for you at first, but you were like a tsunami and I was but a mere island. The more time I spent with you, the stronger the feelings grew. When I'm not around you, you're all I think about. When I'm with you, there's nowhere I would rather be. I love you Celia."

"How am I supposed to believe you when all you've ever done is lie to me?"

A tear slipped down Thomas' cheek. "Yes, I've lied to you before, but I've also been more honest with you than anyone else. I swear on my life I'm being completely transparent with you right now. If my words don't convince you, tell me what will, and I'll do it. I will do anything to assure you of this."

"I need you to leave."

"What?"

"Better yet, I'll leave."

Celia was nauseous. It was like all the air had been sucked from the room. She got her coat and hat and went for her boots. Thomas grabbed her arm before she reached them. Steady tears streamed down his cheeks.

"Please stop for a second. If you really want me to go, I'll go," he said.

Celia turned and faced him. As angry and confused as she was, seeing him cry was painful. She was torn between comforting him and shoving him as hard as she could. Without a word she walked back over to the armchair and sat down. His partially eaten cinnamon roll was still lying on the plate.

"Do you want me to go?" Thomas asked quietly.

"I don't know what I want anymore. I feel like you ripped the rug out from underneath me. Now I'm left questioning everything I thought about you, wondering what was real and what was an act."

Thomas walked over and took a seat. "Nothing was an act, it was all real, the good and the bad. The night we met, I wasn't performing, I was upset. I didn't want to be in fake relationship, PR or otherwise, but it wasn't like I could've told you. You had already agreed to the phony contract."

"That's where you're wrong. You *could* have told me right then and there. I feel like a fool Thomas. You strung me along this entire time."

"I cannot express how sorry I am Celia."

"Why did your agent even come up with this cruel idea?"

"Bridgette has been my agent for over fifteen years. We've gotten close, to the point that she's like family to me. She was one of the first people to know about my diagnosis, she saw my mental and physical decline firsthand. If I wasn't on set, working an event, or with family, I was at home—alone. As I told you previously, I had no interest in dating once I found out, and I stopped going out altogether. Bridgette and I were talking one night and she asked if I was going to live out the rest of my days as a bachelor, and I told her the only way I would ever go out with someone was if it was a PR relationship. I was clearly joking, and her response was 'that can be arranged', but I didn't think she was serious. Once I knew, it was too late, the contract had been created and you had signed off on it."

Celia stared at the fireplace, watching the logs twist and buckle helplessly as the fire consumed them. In a way she saw herself in the fleeting pieces of wood. She had gone to lengths to secure a movie role, her life shaped by her relationship with Thomas' and the agents' decisions, when in reality she didn't need to do anything at all. She had earned the role of the Witch Queen, not by her willingness to lie and pretend, but by her own sheer acting ability and talent. She knew Thomas' words were true, she had underestimated herself but she wasn't going to any longer.

"I'm at a loss for words. I need some time to wrap my head around this," Celia said after a long period of silence.

"Take all the time you need. I will be right here."

"I need to take some time *alone*."

"Oh."

Celia stood up and put on her coat. "I'm going to see about checking into my own room until filming begins."

"No." Thomas rose from his chair. "This is my mess. You can stay here and I'll find a different room."

Celia didn't argue, nor try and stop him as he packed his belongings into suitcases. She felt numb. It was like she was watching it happen from outside her body. Thomas set a small box wrapped in shiny red wrapping paper on the kitchen counter before leaving the room. Celia collapsed against the door and gave in to her tears.

# Fourteen

Celia walked alone through Holyrood Park. She was bundled up in a thick wool coat, knitted hat, and fleece gloves. A thin layer of snow covered the hiking trails and sloped landscape. Edinburgh Castle loomed in the foggy foreground. It had been several days since Celia had seen Thomas and at this point she wasn't sure if he was in the same hotel, much less Edinburgh. Part of her was relieved she hadn't seen him. Her mind was still spinning and she didn't know what to do at this point. She loved Thomas, but she didn't know if she could ever trust him again. There was no way to know if he was lying about anything else.

Lost in her own thoughts, Celia took a misstep off the trail and fell into the snow. Maybe it was due to the stress, but she couldn't help but laugh aloud at herself. She didn't even hear the stranger approach behind her.

"Are you alright miss?" a man asked in a thick Scottish accent.

Celia turned to see a man in his late twenties with his hand extended to her. He was dressed in a thick coat, jeans, and hiking boots. His face was long and freckled. Pale red hair peeked out from underneath his black beanie.

"Yeah, I just wasn't paying attention." Celia took his hand and allowed him to pull her up. "Thank you."

"You should be more careful. Are you out here to see Arthur's Seat?"

"Do I give off the tourist vibes that bad?"

He laughed. "Just a little. My name is Alastair."

"Celia."

"Nice to meet you Celia. If you'd like I can help you get to Arthur's Seat? I've hiked these hills so much I think I could do it blindfolded."

"You don't have to do that, I wouldn't want to trouble you," Celia said.

"Nonsense, it would be no trouble at all."

"Alright, then let's do it."

Celia followed him up the trail, careful of her steps. They passed others on the trail, small groups of strangers, stopping every now and again to take pictures. Small flurries were falling from the sky and a cool breeze swept through the park. The higher they climbed, the colder it got. They did not stop until they reached Arthur's Seat. The view was incredulous with the snow-capped city visible from all sides of the extinct volcano. Out of breath from the hike, Celia sat down on the snow. Alastair sat down next to her.

"So, what brought you to Edinburgh?" Alastair asked.

"It was my boyfriend's idea to spend the holidays in Scotland," she said.

"It is a wonderful time of year to visit. Are you two staying through Hogmanay?"

"I don't know what that is."

"Sorry, it's the last day of the year. It's a big deal in all of Scotland, but I think Edinburgh celebrates it best. Locals and tourist alike gather for a street party, public céilidh, and concert. It's always a fun time and the night always ends with fireworks."

"That sounds lovely, but to be honest I don't imagine I'll be in a mood for celebrating. Things haven't exactly gone as planned during this trip."

Alastair frowned. "I'm sorry."

"It's fine. I just found out some things that have made me question myself and my past choices."

"Is this why you're all out here by yourself? I've hiked these trails for years, met a lot of different folks, but never have I met a tourist by themselves."

A lump grew in Celia's throat. She wanted to vent her pent up frustrations to someone without a stake in her relationship, someone completely neutral to gauge if she was overreacting; however, she didn't want to say anything that could end up blasted on social media or all over tabloids.

"I'm sorry, I didn't mean to pry," he said.

"It's okay, I don't mind, it's just—complicated."

"Love always is."

"Have you been in love before?"

Alastair held up his left hand, revealing a gold band on his ring finger. "Aye, I've been married to the love of my life for almost four years now. We were high school sweethearts, so we've known each other for fourteen years. I can assure you it wasn't always perfect or happy during the course of our relationship, but we managed and we're still going strong."

"How did you do it?"

"With a great deal of patience, understanding, and forgiveness. If I'm not overstepping, I would like to give you some advice."

Celia nodded. "Please."

"Don't have any set expectations on what a relationship is or should be. We're all human, all perfectly imperfect."

When Celia arrived back to the hotel there was a bouquet of two-dozen red roses placed outside her door. She took the flowers and went inside the room. A small note was sitting in the middle of the flowers. It read,

"Celia,

This has been the longest four days of my life. I keep thinking about everything that happened and all the mistakes I've made. I know I can't go back and change what I did, and honestly I don't know if I would. If it hadn't been for the contract I don't know if I would've gotten the chance to know and fall in love with you. You have every right to be mad, and I understand if you don't want a personal relationship with me, but I'm really hoping you'll give me a second chance. If you're willing to give this another try, meet me at Princes Street Gardens on New Year's Eve at six o'clock.

Love,

Thomas

P.s. If you haven't already, open your Christmas gift

P.P.S. I know you're not a rose girl, but I couldn't find any sun-flowers around here."

The parchment smelled like him, his typical earthy cologne. She had forgotten how much she loved the way he smelled, always warm and inviting. She slid the note into her pocket and set the roses in a drinking glass to serve as a makeshift vase. The present the note referred to sat on the kitchenette counter where he had left it, un-touched and waiting to be unwrapped. She took the gift over to the bed and sat down. It was light in her hands.

She was hesitant to open the gift. Christmas was over and with how that day played out, she wasn't in the right frame of mind in order to open a present. Still, her curiosity toyed with her. She tore the paper off, revealing a small velvet box. Inside the box was a white-gold chain with a single charm. Tears welled up in her eyes as she took the necklace into her hands. The charm, small and shiny, was a lifeboat.

Butterflies swelled in Celia's stomach as she weaved through the large crowd gathered on Princes Street. She was wearing a black sweater dress, black leggings, riding boots, and a burgundy wool coat. Her hair was gently curled and her lips painted a vibrant shade of red. The lifeboat necklace was fastened around her neck, the charm icy against her skin.

The street and sidewalks were packed to the point of claustrophobia. Loud music played in the background but it was almost inaudible over the echoes of conversations. The majority of the crowd were armed with large beers and working towards a state of intoxication. Celia felt overwhelmed, there were *so* many people. She had anticipated finding Thomas would be easy, but now she wasn't convinced. The John Wilson Memorial statue was a welcome sight. She remembered passing it on their way to the skating rink.

Princes Street Gardens was as busy as the rest of the town. Part of the garden was sectioned off with a large and colorful stage set up. A crowd danced and sang along with the artist on stage, Paolo Nutini. Celia doubted Thomas was a part of the singing crowd, as the staged area was accessible only to ticket holders.

"Excuse me, may I have this dance?" a familiar voiced asked.

Celia turned to see Thomas standing behind her. She was taken aback by his appearance, his previously bearded face was now shaved and smooth. He wore jeans, a cream cable knit sweater, boots, and a brown leather jacket. A knitted scarf with a green and red pattern similar to a kilt was draped around his neck. He extended his hand to her, but instead of taking it, she threw her arms around him and almost knocked him back. Thomas wrapped his arms around her and squeezed.

"I missed you," Thomas whispered.

"I know." She took a step back and put her hands on his face. His cheeks were warm and flushed. She had so many things she wanted to say, but she didn't know where to start.

"I was afraid you weren't going to come, or that you might not recognize my baby face."

"It's bold of you to assume I'm not just here for Hogmanay." Celia playfully pushed him. "In all seriousness though, we really need to talk about what happened on Christmas and where we go from here."

"I agree. Why don't we get away from the crowd for a bit so we can talk?"

"Sure."

Thomas held his hand out and Celia took it. Together they carefully maneuvered through the crowd. They traveled farther and farther away from Princes Street Gardens and the happy Scots, not stopping until the roar of festivities was merely a distant chatter. Thomas and Celia sat down on a park bench outside a bookstore that had closed early for the festivities.

"Where do you want me to start?" he asked.

"The beginning. I want to know if there's anything else you're not telling me. If we're going to move past this, you have to be honest with me—about *everything*."

"Everything I told you on Christmas about the contract being fictitious was true. Only Bridgette, your agent, and I knew about it."

"What happened to the contract after I signed it?"

Thomas shrugged. "I don't know. Maybe your agent tossed it, maybe she kept it. I never really asked. The only thing that concerned me was that you had signed it and were under the impression we were in a PR relationship."

"Did you ever feel guilty?"

"The night at the beach when you told me you broke up with your boyfriend, I felt terrible. I didn't even know you had a boyfriend. I thought about it all the next day, even called Bridgette. She told me not to worry, if you had been happy in the relationship you wouldn't have ever agreed to the contract. Her words were enough to pacify my thoughts of coming clean to you."

"When I showed you the messages Brandon sent threatening to expose us, you didn't act concerned... Is that because there was nothing to expose?"

"Correct. I only became concerned with his behavior after he released your address. I was afraid he might try something else."

"Is there anything else you haven't told me?"

He shook his head. "The only secrets I ever kept from you were regarding my disease initially and the phony contract. I haven't hidden anything else from you, and I'm sorry I wasn't truthful from the beginning. If you give me a second chance, I swear to you that I will always be upfront and honest with you. No more secrets, and no more lies."

"I appreciate your honesty, I really do. I don't agree with how things were handled, but we can't go back now. I've been thinking about this since the moment you left on Christmas." She scooted closer to him and took his hands into hers. "There's no other person I would rather bring in 2017 with, so yes, I would like to give us another shot."

A smile spread across Thomas' face and no sooner than it did, he pulled Celia into his arms. His heart was beating rapidly in her ear. It was the first time since Christmas that she felt at ease. The comfort of being in his arms was enough to forget about the world around her. It didn't matter that it was New Year's Eve, it could've been any day for that matter, all that she cared about was being there in his arms, listening to his heartbeat.

"Thank you... I promise, I will spend the rest of my days making this up to you," he whispered.

# Fifteen

The first couple weeks of filming were scheduled to take place at Doune Castle. Thomas and Celia had been relocated to a hotel in Stirling, only about a twenty-minute drive to the castle. The call time for the first day was at six o'clock in the morning, which forced Celia to wake up at an ungodly hour; however, it wouldn't have mattered if it had been scheduled later in the day, as she didn't sleep at all the night prior. Her nerves were comparable to a kindergartener on their first day of class. She hardly said anything on the commute to set and her fingers rarely deviated from her hair.

They were dropped off at Basecamp, a grassy area about one-hundred yards from the castle. It was set up with trailers for the cast, a catering truck, and trailers for wardrobe as well as for hair and makeup. Numerous golf carts were scattered about to take the cast and crew from this makeshift area to set. Portable light fixtures illuminated the site, as the sun had yet to rise.

"Are you okay?" Thomas asked after the car drove away.

"Yes, the first day of filming always gives me butterflies," she said.

"There are my two stars," a man said.

The man appeared to be in his late forties or early fifties. His hair and handlebar mustache were black and peppered with grey hairs.

He was short, barely above five feet tall. What he lacked in height, he made up for in muscle.

"My name is Charles Conway, I'm one of the assistant directors. I hope Scotland has treated you both well," Charles said.

"It has, thank you," Thomas said.

"Glad to hear it. As you can see we have a nice little set up here for the cast and crew. Whenever you're needed at the castle you'll be transported by golf cart and then brought back in between takes and during your breaks. Feel free to take some time to check out your trailers and the catering truck before heading on over to wardrobe. If you have any questions or concerns, you can come find me. I'll be down here for about twenty more minutes before heading up to start getting everything ready."

"Thank you," Celia said.

Charles shook both of their hands before departing towards one of the trailers. Dozens of people were passing through, some stopping at the catering truck before driving away in a golf cart. It was slightly chaotic, but in a way it was also organized.

"You want to grab some food?" Thomas asked.

Celia shook her head. "I think I would throw up. I might go ahead and go to wardrobe, but you can grab something."

"I think I will. Want me to at least bring you a coffee?"

"Yes, thank you, I could stomach a coffee."

Thomas kissed her forehead and headed towards the catering truck. Paper signs with arrows taped to plastic posts guided Celia to the wardrobe trailer. It was, arguably, the largest trailer on site. The interior smelled like new leather and lavender. At the front of the trailer were cabinets, a stacked washer and dryer, and a sink. Exquisite costumes hung from the locking clothes racks lining both sides of the trailer. The laminate wood flooring squeaked underneath Celia's sneakers.

"Hello?" Celia called out softly.

"Just a minute." Shortly after, a woman appeared from back of the trailer. She was dressed in jeans and a black polo shirt. A measuring tape was draped around her shoulders and she wore a half-apron filled with various thread, safety pins, and needles. Her round glasses were thick, giving the impression that her eyesight was poor despite not appearing to be over the age of forty. She pulled a clipboard off the cabinet and flipped through the pages, stopping in the middle.

"You can grab a laundry bag for your clothes and start undressing while I get your costume. They're in the far-right cabinet in the middle drawer," the woman said.

While Celia undressed, the woman pulled a black and grey Victorian style gown with a leather corset. She retrieved black leather gloves and dark grey lace up boots before returning to the nose of the trailer. Celia was down to only her bra and panties.

"You won't need the bra," the woman said.

Celia hesitated. She had never felt uncomfortable changing in front of crew members before, but it felt different now that Brandon had released the pictures. Her self-conscious thoughts clung to her every move like a shadow and were overwhelmingly heavy. If she continued to allow those pictures to haunt her, it meant Brandon won—something she refused to let happen. She took a deep breath before relenting and adding her bra to the clothes pile. Without a word, the woman helped Celia into the dress. It was loose and flowy until she laced the corset. The bell-shaped sleeves fell past her wrist while the hemline was just short enough to see the tops of the boots.

"You're probably going to want a blanket for in between scenes. If there's not one in your trailer, let me know and I can find one," the woman said.

"Thank you. What did you say your name was again?"

"I didn't say it, but my name is Helen."

"Nice to meet you Helen," Celia said.

Helen didn't return any pleasantries. She tied up the laundry bag and went back to the sea of costumes. Celia exited the trailer, almost running into Thomas standing on the steps. She jumped back, slightly startled and rested her hand on her chest.

"Jesus, you scared me," she said.

"Sorry." He handed her a coffee. "That could've been a disaster."

"Tell me about it. I think Helen would've murdered me had anything spilled on this dress."

"I'm sure I could give her some puppy-dogs eyes or something to change her mind about killing the lead actress."

Celia rolled her eyes. "You haven't met her yet. She barely said anything to me, I felt more like a nuisance than a cast member."

A gust of wind blew through the lot, sending a shiver up Celia's spine. The only remotely warm pieces of her costume were the leather corset and the gloves. Not even a sip of the sugar laced hot coffee could curb the chill from her bones.

"Thank you again for the coffee, I appreciate it. I think I'm going to go to hair and makeup and then see about that blanket supposedly waiting for me in the trailer. See you in a bit?"

"Of course."

The trailer designated for hair and makeup was almost as large as the wardrobe trailer. The walls were a bright white and the floor a checkered grey vinyl. One wall was composed of mirrors with wall light fixtures dividing each section. The countertops were a light grey, covered with different hair and makeup products. Straighteners, curlers, and blow dryers were plugged into the wall. Black leather styling chairs with stuffed armrests sat in front of each block of mirror. A combination of hairspray, gel, and various shampoos floated in the air.

A man was sitting in the chair farthest from the trailer's nose. He looked to be about Thomas' age, but he was thinner and shorter.

A young woman stood behind him spiking his black hair with some gel that smelled like mint.

"You can take a seat wherever you'd like, I'll be with you in a moment," a woman called out from the back of the trailer. The voice was oddly familiar, but Celia wasn't able to put a face to it. She took a seat at the chair closest to the exit, leaving two seats vacant between her and the unknown actor. She took another sip of coffee and checked her phone. It was only six-thirty in the morning, and she knew it was going to be a long day.

The woman came over to Celia and draped a large black barber cape over her shoulders. Immediately, Celia recognized her, and a smile spread across her face.

"It's nice to see you again, Ms. Stuart," Elena said.

"I thought you sounded familiar! How've you been, it's been, what, three or four months?"

"Sounds about right." Elena sat three cosmetic bags on the counter. "I've been good, just working. I see you and Thomas are still together. I'm happy for you both."

"Thank you."

The transformation took about forty minutes. Foundation and powder made her complexion appear paler. Bronzer dusted her cheeks, defining her already high cheekbones. Eyeshadow of grey and black hues dusted her eyelids, and mascara curled her eyelashes. Her hair was tucked underneath a wig cap, hidden by a long silvery wig that fell past her lower back. Elena had taken a straightener to the bangs and a twirling wand to the length.

"Are you ready for this?" Thomas wrapped a blanket around Celia's shoulders.

They were sitting in the back of a golf cart, waiting to be taken up to the castle to film their first scene. Chill bumps were prominent on both of their arms. Thomas' costume provided less warmth than Celia's. He wore a torn white collared-shirt that was unbuttoned three-fourths of the way down, and tattered black pants. Thomas' eyes had been transformed yellow with colored contacts. His hair was tousled and splattered with fake blood.

"As ready as I will be," she said.

A production assistant drove them up to the castle. Even in the darkness, it was apparent how large and magnificent the castle was. There were a few lights set up at the entrance, but it was predominantly dark. The lower floor of the castle, where the first scene was set to be filmed, was set up to look like a dungeon. Candelabras were lit and hung up from the grey stone walls. Four sets of long chains with shackles were fastened to the walls. Sickeningly realistic fake blood was splattered about the ground. The camera crew was rehearsing their moves as Vincent Monticello and Charles watched. Vincent was a tall and thin man that appeared to be in his late forties. His heavily tanned skin was covered in freckles. He wore a hooded sweatshirt, jeans, and black sneakers. His long grey hair was pulled back into a pony-tail and red-tinted glasses hid his brown eyes.

"Good morning," Vincent called over his shoulder.

Thomas and Celia walked over to him and he shook both of their hands before turning his attention back to the camera crew. Celia's heart pounded in her chest. It was so loud she was afraid that the directors, and Thomas would hear it.

"As you both know, we're going to start with scene thirty-four today. This is one of the most pivotal scenes of the film, as it is the turning point in the relationship between Eleanor and Baldric. Thomas we're going to start off having you chained against the wall before Celia frees you, but the actions can be improvised— whatever feels right. We're still in the process of setting up lights but I want to run through this at least once before we start filming."

"Sounds good to me," Thomas said.

Celia nodded in agreement. A production assistant took her

blanket and their coffees and set them on a table against the wall. The table was already home to bottled waters and packaged snacks for the crew. Thomas walked to the middle set of chains and sat down. Celia waited in a corner that would be off camera during filming.

"Ready?" Celia asked.

Thomas nodded. She took a deep breath and stepped forward. Her entire focus was on Thomas, as if the crew and directors were invisible. All that mattered was being in character, in the moment. Thomas had the shackles on with his hands in his lap. Eyes shut, his expression was defeated.

"Why didn't you tell me?" Celia walked towards Thomas.

"I didn't want to taint your image of me, I was afraid you would think I was a monster." Thomas raised his arms and the chains clanked loudly. "I wasn't wrong, was I?"

"You are wrong. It would take more than old horror stories to make me find any race monstrous, let alone you. This wasn't my idea to have you imprisoned."

"Does the King know you're down here?"

She shook her head.

"Please don't risk your safety for me, it's not worth it."

"Why do you assume your life has less value than mine?" she asked.

"Because it does to me. I knew you were special the moment I saw you. I would live a thousand lives in this dungeon if it meant keeping you safe."

Celia kneeled next to him and placed her hands on his arm. He put his hand over hers. His skin was warm, smoothing her goosebumps.

"I'm sorry I didn't tell you," Thomas said.

"It's alright, all that matters now is getting you out of here."

Celia held her hands up and whispered incoherent words, a

fictitious spell, under her breath. She knew editors were going to add effects to the scene to make it appear that the 'spell' had released his chains during post-production. Thomas slipped his hands from the cuffs and stood up, pulling Celia up with him.

"What is your plan?" Thomas asked.

"I have a horse saddled and ready for you at the stable. Ride to Aeris Forest and go to the abandoned cabin by the lake. I have some provisions waiting. I will meet you tomorrow as soon as I can."

Thomas frowned. "You're not coming with me?"

"The King is expecting me at any moment. I'm afraid if I leave tonight, he would send an army after us. He was already acting suspicious, I have to pretend everything is normal and wait until the time is right."

"If he's acting suspicious you may already be in danger, we should leave together. We wouldn't get much of a head start, but I don't feel comfortable leaving you alone with that bastard."

"I can handle myself. What do you think I was doing before I met you?"

"The scars on your body say otherwise Ellie."

Tears filled Celia's eyes. "Asa wasn't always this way. He was kind and gentle before his father died. I don't know what changed but he did love me at one point, and I loved him too."

"I know, it's okay." Thomas put his arms around her. "Please don't cry. We're going to get through this."

"I need you to make me a promise."

"Anything for you."

Celia stepped back, so she could look him in the eyes. Tears streamed down her cheeks.

"Promise me that if I am not at the cabin by nightfall tomorrow, you'll leave without me."

"No, absolutely not. There is no way I'm leaving without you."

"If something happens to me and you die, this will all be in vain! Please don't let my actions be meaningless."

Thomas sighed. "I promise, no, I swear on my life, that I will leave at nightfall if you haven't arrived."

"Good." She wiped a tear off her cheek. "You're going to need to ride to Vulcan and find my cousin Elshir. He's a popular merchant so you shouldn't have trouble finding him. I already sent him a letter and he's expecting us. Regardless of what happens to me, he will help you. Now, you must hurry. If Asa realizes I'm gone he'll come looking for me."

Thomas pulled her into a tight embrace, his chin resting on the top of her head. Celia squeezed her arms as tightly around him as she could.

"Remember, this isn't goodbye. I will see you tomorrow."

"I know," Thomas said, his words ending the scene.

Celia stepped back. Already out of character, they both had ridiculously large smiles on their faces. Her nerves had melted during the scene, leaving excitement in their place. She was excited for the scene, the movie, and most of all— for working with Thomas. It was only practice, but if filming went this smoothly, it was going to be one hell of a process.

"Do you want to run through it again?" Thomas asked.

"Absolutely."

# Sixteen

The sun was shining, but it did little to chase away the cold afternoon temperatures. Thomas and Celia sat huddled together in a large barn in Stirling, on a short break. The barn was old, its wood weathered by age, but it had enough stalls to house twelve horses along with a spacious storage room for hay and grain. Each stall had a leather halter and lead hanging outside the door. Eight of those stalls were occupied by horses: five Friesians, and three Andalusians. A solid dark bay Andalusian mare by the name of Ravenna was set to be Celia's scene partner throughout the film.

Celia was dressed in a plum colored Victorian gown with black accents. She wore black gloves, and black riding boots. A leather choker with a garnet pendent was fastened around her neck. Realistic bruises were painted on her wrists and forearms. Thomas wore a solid white billowy shirt, tan britches, and tall black riding boots. His shirt was stained with dirt.

"Are you guys ready for another round?" Evan asked.

Evan McConnell was a young actor, only a few years older than Celia, cast to play the cruel king. His golden blond hair was long and curly. He was a little shorter than Thomas, but was as lean and fit. He wore a black long sleeved shirt, charcoal vest with red accents, black pants, and black boots. A shiny black crown with garnet crystals matching Celia's choker sat upon his head. Lavish rings adorned four of his long fingers.

Celia smiled. "Let's do this."

Thomas stood outside of Ravenna's stall with a pitchfork in his hand while Celia and Evan waited at the entrance of the barn. Charles and Vincent stood behind one of the cameras, a hint of excitement sparkling in their eyes.

"Scene eight, medium, take four." A camera assistant struck the clapperboard in front of the camera. He quickly moved out of frame. It was quiet, the only noise to be heard was the horses nibbling hay in their stalls. Celia took a deep breath and exhaled slowly.

"Action," Vincent called out.

Celia and Evan walked towards Thomas.

"Baldric come here," Evan said.

Thomas leaned the pitchfork next to the stall and met them in the middle of the barn. One of the Friesian horses hung his head over the stall and nuzzled Thomas' shoulder.

"Yes, Your Majesty?"

"I would like to introduce you to the Queen, my wife, Eleanor." Evan gestured to Celia. "Eleanor this is Baldric, our new stable hand."

Thomas bowed. "It's a pleasure to meet you."

"The pleasure is mine." She curtsied.

"Recently she has been having some issues with her horse," Evan said.

He walked to Ravenna's stall with Celia and Thomas following closely behind. Celia stood behind Evan, her smile gone and replaced by an uneasy expression. The horse stood quietly in the stall, her eyes fixated on the actors.

"What are the issues she's having?" Thomas asked.

"She's been bolting. Damn near ran over a member of my infantry," Evan said.

Thomas looked to Celia. "Has she done this with you before?"

Celia shook her head. Evan stepped forward, resting his hand on the stall door. His fingers traced an indention in the wood.

"As you may be aware, the Kingdom of Marabella is preparing for war. My men are training daily, I'm working to secure allies and am busy organizing a strategy. I don't have the time to chase down a loose horse, and neither do my knights. Despite my wife's wishes, if this behavior cannot be corrected, the animal will be destroyed. This nag can be replaced anyway."

"I understand. I will work with Her Majesty and the horse," Thomas said.

"Good. I will leave you both to it."

Evan grabbed Celia's face and kissed her roughly, biting her lip as he pulled away. Celia wiped her mouth on her sleeve as soon as his back was turned. Her sleeve slipped down to her elbow, revealing the fake bruises. Thomas nervously glanced at her, not moving until Evan had exited the barn.

"She doesn't bolt," Celia said after a tense moment of silence. She took the halter off the door and entered the stall. Ravenna turned to Celia and allowed her to put the halter on. Thomas watched her closely. The horse lowered her head, relaxing as Celia stroked underneath her forelock. Despite the cold weather, the horse's coat was slick. She had been clipped and blanketed by her owners before being brought to set. Celia noticed him staring a shot him a glare.

"Are you going to fetch my saddle or just stand there gawking?" she asked.

"My apologies, Your Majesty."

Thomas quickly retreated to the storage room. Celia sighed before leading the horse out of the stall. She brushed a lone shaving off of Ravenna's back with her hand. Thomas returned with a blanket, saddle and bridle. Celia watched him silently as he saddled and bridled the horse.

"Did your hands get tangled in the reins when she bolted?" Thomas asked.

Celia raised an eyebrow. "Excuse me?"

"The bruises." He gestured to her arms. "I saw them on your arms. I wasn't sure if maybe you got your hands wrapped in the reins or perhaps when you fell off."

"I didn't fall, but *how* I got these are none of your business. You're here to take care of the horses— not worry about me."

"My apologies, Your Majesty. Would you like me to ride her first?"

"No." Celia took the reins from him. "And please stop referring to me as 'Your Majesty'. I go by Ellie."

Thomas nodded. "As you wish."

Celia climbed into the saddle and trotted the horse out of the barn. Thomas wiped the sweat from his brow and followed her. The frosted field outside was vast with no visible fences aside from a small round pen next to the barn. Paid extras, all dressed in medieval armor, were standing in the distance. They had swords and shields. Two of the extras sat on horseback as a part of the Calvary. The horses, both Friesians, were costumed in armor. An actor stood at the front, shouting directions incoherently at the extras. Evan briefly exchanged words with the actor before marching out of sight. Celia sat on Ravenna beside round pen. She was leaning over, stroking the horse's neck when Thomas walked out.

"Where's your horse?" she asked.

"I don't understand. I'm supposed to be helping with *your* horse."

"If you're insistent on watching me ride, you better saddle a horse. It would be impossible for you to keep up on foot and I'm not waiting around."

Thomas opened his mouth to say something, but Celia had already turned Ravenna around. The horse transitioned into a lope as they headed in the opposite direction of the extras.

"Shit." Thomas ran back into the barn.

"And that's a cut," Charles said.

It was almost two o'clock in the afternoon when Celia arrived at the trailer for a break after filming two scenes. The trailer was a double-banger, assigned to her and Thomas. Both spaces were fitted with a fabric couch, bathroom, television, small fridge, desk, and a chair. The fridge was stocked with various beverages from sparkling waters to bottled soft drinks. A deck of playing cards were spread out on the table, left over from a game of Go Fish Thomas and Celia had played earlier.

Celia changed out of her gown into sweatpants and a hooded sweatshirt. She retrieved a Dr. Pepper from the fridge and collapsed on the couch. She hadn't been sitting for more than a minute when someone knocked on her trailer door.

"It's open," Celia said. She wouldn't admit it to Thomas or anyone else who was a part of the cast or crew, but she was sore from riding Ravenna. It had been a few years since she last rode a horse, and her muscles were unforgiving. Evan entered the trailer, still dressed in costume, carrying a package under his arm.

"I hope I'm not bothering you," he said.

"Not at all. What brings you by? Do you have some downtime between scenes too?"

"No, I came down to grab a quick bite before heading back to set. The mail was delivered and you had a package, so I figured I'd bring it to you first."

"Thank you, I appreciate it. I wasn't expecting anything."

Evan shrugged. "Maybe it's fan mail?"

He handed the package to her and took a seat on the other end of the couch. The package was small and light with no return address listed. As soon as she pulled off the packing tape a foul smell filled the air. She opened the package and screamed. A decapitated dead bird, covered in dry blood and small insects, was inside. She threw the package onto the laminate floor and covered her face with her hands.

Evan rushed to his feet. "What the fuck?"

"Please get that out of here!"

"Of course." He picked up the package.

Celia pushed by him and ran to the bathroom. She vomited into the toilet until there was nothing left inside her stomach, and then she dry-heaved. Her body was trembling as her stomach churned. She splashed water onto her color-drained face before rinsing her mouth out with Listerine. Evan was gone when she came out of the bathroom. She sat back down on the couch and grabbed the blanket from behind her. The trailer was warm with the heater running, but she couldn't stop shivering. She jumped as someone knocked on the door.

"Hey, it's me again," Evan said.

"Come in."

Evan came in and sat back down on the couch. Celia was re-lieved that he was empty handed this time. He had a sympathetic expression on his face.

"I told one of the production assistants and gave them the box. They're getting in contact with security and are going to try to find out if that was brought in with the outside mail or a stupid prank by someone on set. I'm sorry I brought it over," he said.

Celia shook her head. "It wasn't your fault, please don't blame yourself. I don't know if they'll be able to find any information on where it came from, but I know it wasn't anyone on set."

"I mean I'd hope not, but how can you be sure?"

"I have been harassed by my ex-boyfriend since last year. He leaked my address, broke in and trashed Thomas' house among other things I'm trying to forget myself. Every time I think he's done, he does something else. It's been a rough couple of months."

"I can imagine. Sounds like he needs to get over himself and move on. Is this why everyone was so secretive about the location prior to filming?"

"Yeah. It's more than a little troubling that he knows I'm here."

Evan put his hand on her shoulder. "Don't stress too much. Between the security guys, not to mention Thomas and me, you have nothing to worry about. A package may have gotten through, but there's no way he could get anywhere near Basecamp or the set for that matter."

"You're probably right."

"I'm always right." He stood up. "I have to get back to set, but if you need anything let me know."

"I will, thank you."

Evan paused in the doorway. "Listen, a few cast members are going to a pub tonight. You should come, it might help take your mind off things. I'm going to mention it to Thomas too when I get back to set."

"I'll think about it."

"Alright."

The door clicked as it shut. Celia took her Dr. Pepper to the sink and poured it down the drain. The color had returned to her cheeks, but she was still trembling. She sat back down on the couch and cocooned herself in the blanket. She tried closing her eyes to rest, but the headless bird invaded her thoughts. Part of her hoped that Brandon had just stumbled upon the creature and decapitated it postmortem, but given everything he had done thus far, there was no way to know. It was like with every attempt he made, she began learning who he really was. The kindness and sensibility he had shown previously were a charade. *Way to be a great judge of character.*

She was ready for the day to be over already. She wanted to be back in her hotel room, cozy under the plush comforter and inaccessible to Brandon. More than anything, she wanted Thomas. Only twenty minutes had passed, so Thomas would still be on set for at least another hour. Part of her hoped Evan would tell him what happened, so she wouldn't have to. She knew it was only going to be a matter of time before everyone else on set knew too. With security and crew members involved, the news would spread faster than dandelion seeds on a windy day. Maybe it would be a good idea to go to the pub. She could tell the story of what happened before it was twisted and worsened from being retold by second-hand sources.

Although Celia refused to admit it, she wasn't feeling better by the time they got to the pub. The pub had a 'hole in the wall' atmosphere. There were only a handful of tables besides the bar seating with the majority of the floor space occupied by pool tables. Despite the late hour, it was packed. Evan had managed to push three small tables together in the back corner by the dart boards. There were two pitchers of beer, multiple glasses, and a basket of chips with a variety of sauces. Four actors sat at the tables: Evan, Jillian, Leslie, and Matt. All were practically unrecognizable, their casual appearances a stark contrast from their costumes on set.

"Look who decided to make it," Evan said.

Celia forced a smile, and Thomas gave him a side hug before taking their seats. Jillian, who was the same age as Celia, passed her a glass of beer. She had dirty-blonde hair that was fashioned into a pixie cut. Out of the group, she was the quietest, seemingly shy until she was in character. Celia thanked her for the beer but didn't take a drink. Her stomach was still in knots.

"Evan was just telling us about the *eventful* day you both had," Matt said. Matt was the actor Celia had first seen in the hair and makeup trailer. He was a jokester, and if anyone would have been suspected of playing a prank—it would be him.

Leslie roughly elbowed Matt in the ribs, making him wince. Leslie was in her early thirties. She had brown skin and dark curly hair. She was a petite woman, but her personality was larger than life.

"Please excuse his rudeness." She shot him a glare. "How are you? Are you doing okay?"

Celia nodded. "I'm okay. I'm glad Evan was there when it happened, I don't know what I would've done had I opened it on my own."

"Please refrain from opening any future random packages without some muscle there," Evan said.

"It would have been nice if there had been some muscle there the first time," Leslie said.

They all laughed, and Evan's face reddened.

Evan rolled his eyes. "Very funny."

"I once had a fan stalk me. I first saw her at a comic con, she was a VIP ticket holder. She wore some costume and had a crazy pink wig." Matt picked up a fry. "It was cool at first, seeing her at all these events and being able to recognize her, but then she started showing up at the airport, outside hotel rooms, pretty much anywhere I was. She'd always come up and try to hug me or engage in conversation and then get upset when I told her I was busy. After months of this crazy dance, I finally had to file a restraining order. The last time I ever saw her was in a courtroom."

"Yikes," Leslie said.

Thomas and Celia exchanged a quick glance. She didn't have to say anything, his expression reflected he probably knew what she was thinking. *So much for a night out to get my mind off things.*

"It's too bad they don't have karaoke here," Thomas said.

"I had a crazy ex-girlfriend, but she never stalked me," Evan said, apparently oblivious to Thomas' attempt to change the subject.

"How crazy was she?" Matt asked.

"Showed up at a casting call unbeknownst to me. Came out on

a high after killing my audition to find my car keyed and mirrors smashed."

"Oh you think that's bad? My ex—" before Leslie could finish, Celia stood up.

All eyes were on her as she retreated to the bathroom. It was small only with only two stalls and one sink. Two women stood in front of the sink, sharing the mirror as they touched up their makeup. Celia moved behind them, tears streaming down her cheeks as she locked herself in a stall. What was supposed to be a night of fun had turned out to be nothing more than another stressor for her already frayed nerves. If her costars thought that she would find relief in their personal hellish experiences, they were wrong. All it did was bring up the question she tried her hardest to repress, *what will he do next?*

There was a knock on the stall door. "Celia?"

She wiped the smudged mascara and black tears from her face and exited the stall. Jillian was standing with her lips pursed. Leslie stood a few feet behind her, an equally concerned expression on her face. Jillian put her arms around Celia and pulled her into a hug.

"I'm so sorry, sweetie," Jillian said.

"We're all sorry." Leslie looked down at the ground. "We weren't trying to make light of what happened. I think the reason Matt started the conversation was to show that he can relate to what you're going through. I think we all can to a certain extent."

Jillian nodded. "I know it's only been a few weeks of filming, but I think I can speak for everyone when I say that we care about your well-being. If you ever need someone to talk to, we're all available."

"I appreciate you both saying that." Celia stepped back. "I know you guys didn't mean anything by what was said. Saying I'm stressed is an understatement, but I think I probably shouldn't have come out tonight. I think I'm going to go ahead and go back to the hotel."

"Please don't go. I promise there will be no more talk of crazy people or exes," Jillian said.

"I second that. If anyone even tries, they'll get a sucker punch to the gut."

"Okay, fine, I'll stay for a *little* bit longer."

Jillian and Leslie both locked arms with Celia, Jillian on the left and Leslie on the right, and escorted her back to the table. Nervous expressions were on all of the guys' faces. They were silent as she took her seat.

"Are we all good?" Evan asked.

Celia nodded.

"Good," he said.

Despite her unsettled stomach, she took a sip of beer. It was stale and unpleasant, but she thought all beer tasted the same. Thomas watched her closely, as if he suspected she was just putting up a front—which was partially true. Her smile was slightly forced.

"In case you guys didn't witness the historic event, Leslie actually rode her horse today. Vincent and Charles nearly fainted when they saw her instead of her stunt double," Evan said.

"Not everyone grew up rich in a prissy neighborhood with horses in their backyard," Leslie said.

"Hey! It was in my neighbor's backyard, not mine."

She softly punched Evan in the arm. He dramatically rubbed his arm, as if it hurt. Matt shook his head, seemingly amused.

"Are you sure you're okay?" Thomas asked softly.

"Yes, I promise."

She put her hand over Thomas' and squeezed it. He smiled, but didn't appear convinced. He was probably thinking about how terrible of a liar she was.

# Seventeen

"Why did you bring her here?" Evan asked in a raised tone.

Evan and Celia stood facing each other. She was again dressed in the black and grey Victorian style gown with a leather corset. Evan wore a heavily embroidered grey frilled shirt tucked into black pants. His crown, a staple of the king's outfit, was absent. The room was set up with multiple small beds. One of those beds was occupied by a realistic prop body with a resemblance to Leslie. A pale white sheet covered it up to the chest. The skin was painted with black designs that resembled tree roots. The eyes were painted grey, giving a glassy look. Lit candelabras illuminated the castle walls and floors. A large fireplace warmed the room.

"I had no choice, she would have died if I hadn't," Celia said.

"You may have just killed our entire coven!"

"At least then you'll be dead."

Evan pretended to slap her and Celia fell to her knees. She brought her hand to her cheek and glared at him.

"Don't you *ever* speak to me that way again, or it will be the last time you do."

Evan walked over to the fireplace as Celia stood up. She rested her hands on the side of the bed.

"Why are you being such a coward? When has a foreign ailment ever done us any harm?" she asked.

"This is not a simple ailment Eleanor, look closely at her skin." Evan walked over to her. "Those markings are of The Creature."

"The Creature? What are you even talking about?"

"There is something far worse than the war at hand. I've been sending out scouts for months, and only a few have actually returned. Of the outliers who have returned, they're lucky if they're uninfected."

An extra costumed as a knight walked onto set with a sword. Evan grabbed Celia, restraining her by her arms, and pulled her away from the bed. The extra lifted the sword in the air, leveling it with the neck of the prop.

"No, what are you doing." She fought in vain to break from his grip. "Get away from her!"

He brought down the sword, slicing through the neck as if it were butter. The faux head rolled off the bed and hit the floor with a soft thud. Evan flipped her around so they were facing each other. There was a look of madness in his eyes. His fingers dug into her upper arms.

"You bastard," Celia whispered. Tears rolled down her cheeks.

"All infected are destroyed before they have a chance to make it past the castle wall. If you spent less time at the damn stable you would know what was happening around here." He released her grip and pushed her away from him.

Another extra, dressed in dirty tattered clothes walked over to the bed. He stripped the bed of its sheets and drug the decapitated body across the floor and out of frame. The head was left untouched.

"How foolish do you think I am?" he asked.

She didn't say anything. Her hands were behind her back with her fingers moving in an ebbing motion. Special effects were going to be added later to make it appear that she was calling flames from the fire.

"I have eyes and ears all over this castle. Nothing, and I mean *nothing*, goes on that I don't know about. Which, brings me to my next question— how long have you been keeping this secret from me?"

Celia's hands fell limply to her sides. "What are you talking about?"

"Do not play dumb with me."

"I'm not, I have no idea what you're insinuating."

"For crying out loud! You can't tell me that with all the time you spent with Baldric you didn't know he was a werewolf."

"A werewolf?" Her eyes widened.

"I guess you didn't know." He shook his head. "You're more of a fool than I originally thought."

Celia was speechless. She walked over to the fireplace and sat down. The fire crackled as the flames illuminated her face. Evan walked up behind her, appearing to study her surprised expression.

"I've had him followed for a few weeks now, as I thought something might've been going on between the two of you. Saying I was surprised to hear he was transforming would be an understatement. A werewolf in Marabella? No, no, impossible I told myself. My grandfather had banned the wretched race from our kingdom more than eighty years ago. Only tales of war and horror stories kept the species from being forgotten; however, I couldn't contain my curiosity, I had to go and personally see the supposed phenomenon for myself. As I was told he would, Baldric shifted into a mangy mutt before my very eyes. I let him go, but once he returned to himself, he was apprehended."

"What did you do to him?"

Evan kneeled next to her. "Nothing yet, but you know the law. With everything going on it's not an ideal time for a public execution, *but* it offers a temporary distraction which could help boost morale."

"Where is he now?" she asked.

"He's currently getting accommodated to his new living arrangements. Hopefully, he doesn't get too comfortable, seeing how he won't be staying with us for much longer."

Celia looked like she was going to throw up, unlike Evan who wore a smug expression. He stood up and dusted off his pants. Celia didn't move, her eyes still focused on the dancing flames.

"I'm going to retire early tonight and I expect you to join me." He put his hands on her shoulders and leaned down. His breath tickled her ear. "You know how torture excites me."

He kissed the top of her head before releasing his grip on her shoulders. The smug look still on his face as he walked off set.

"And that's a cut," Charles said.

Evan ran over to Celia with wide grin on his face and extended his hand. She took it and he gently pulled her to her feet. Perspiration sat on her brow.

"Damn, I love playing an asshole," he said.

"You're a little too convincing. Should I be concerned?"

Evan shrugged his shoulders. "Can't say, I don't want to show my hand yet."

Charles approached them with a clipboard in his hand. He was dressed casually in jeans and a solid red polo shirt.

"Vincent said he wants to run through the scene one more time, but we have to get the prop fixed up first. If you two want to take a break on set or head back to Basecamp that's fine, just make sure you're back in, I'd say, no more than forty-five minutes," Charles said.

"Okay sure thanks," Evan said.

He followed Celia over to the table set up with snacks and bottled waters. She took a sip of her watered-down iced coffee. It did little to alleviate the grumbling in her stomach. They had been filming for almost two hours now, and the granola bar she ate before coming to set was all but gone.

Evan grabbed his phone off the table. "Jillian ordered a couple of pizzas from Pizza Hut and said there was plenty left. I'm going to go grab a slice, you want to come?"

"Sure."

They maneuvered through the castle, careful to avoid any props or electrical cords. Celia had already nearly tripped and fell onto the stone floor a few days prior, so she was extra cautious. Crew members were scattered around, some prepping for the scene they were going to run through again, others already focused on the next scene to be filmed. It was cloudy outside and the high breeze made it feel even cooler. The ground was dusted in a thin layer of snow. Three golf carts sat unattended with no crew members nearby. Evan walked up to the closest one and climbed into the driver's seat. The keys were waiting in the ignition.

"Come on let's go," he said.

"What are you doing? I don't think we're supposed to drive those."

Evan shrugged his shoulders before twisting the keys and bringing the engine to life. "Are you coming or what?"

Celia took a quick look around, but there was no one else nearby. Everyone was inside the castle. They were probably so busy that they wouldn't even notice one cart missing. Besides it's not like they were going to be gone for an hour or longer, it was just going to be forty minutes, if that. She scooted into the passenger seat and Evan pressed his foot to the pedal. Celia wrapped one hand around the bar on the side of her seat and held her skirt from flying up with the other as they sped down the makeshift path.

"I'm a little surprised to see you breaking the rules," he said.

"What do you mean?"

"Well, we aren't *technically* supposed to be driving these. Only possible injuring-inducing activity were allotted is riding the horses," he said.

*Great, of course.* "I meant why are you surprised?"

Evan quickly glanced at her and returned his focus back to the path. "You're noticeably quiet when you're not on set. I noticed it from the beginning, but it seems like you've gotten more reserved since the whole bird incident. Even at the bar, you didn't say much."

She looked at Evan, unsure of how to respond. *Have I really been quiet?* In all her years of acting she was never labeled the crazy outgoing cast member on set, but she was far from the quiet one. They ran over a rock and the golf cart bounced, making Celia's grip tighten on the bar.

"Sorry, I shouldn't have said anything," he said.

"No, it's fine. I had no idea I came off as quiet."

Evan stopped the golf cart. Basecamp was only about a hundred feet away, visible at the bottom of the tree line. He strummed his fingers on the steering wheel, his eyes locked forward.

"What's wrong?" she asked.

"Are you quiet because of Thomas?"

She raised an eyebrow. "No. Why would I be quiet because of Thomas?"

"I don't know if I should be saying anything, but I think Thomas might be on drugs or something."

Celia opened her mouth to argue but Evan raised his hand up. "Hear me out before you say anything. I forgot my gauntlets in his trailer yesterday. I was already running late by the time I realized so I ran over to his trailer and walked in. They were on the table where I left them, but as I was leaving, he came out of the bathroom with a needle. I didn't say anything, I pretended like I didn't even notice and left as quickly as I could. I swear, I didn't know he was even in there, I thought he was already on set."

Celia took a deep breath, hoping to mask the panic in her tone.

She knew she had to come up with something quickly—something believable. She could attempt to make him second-guess himself, creating doubt that he saw a needle by saying something like, "Are you sure he wasn't carrying a prop of some sort?", but that could go south too easily. Evan knew what he saw, and she didn't know if she could convince him otherwise. There was only one way to get out this.

"Evan, listen." Celia forced herself to laugh, "Thomas is a type one diabetic. You must've walked in on him after he gave himself an insulin shot."

"Are you serious?"

She nodded. "It's not something he likes to talk about, he's... shy. So, if you could keep this just between us, it would be best."

"Of course, yeah. I'm sorry, I shouldn't have jumped to conclusions."

Celia sighed as Evan resumed driving to Basecamp. Hopefully, he wouldn't bring it up to anyone else. Covering up a lie was one thing, but convincing people of a lie was a completely different can of worms. If the media got wind of Thomas having diabetes it could lead to the discovery of the truth. HIPAA laws or not, it wouldn't be too difficult for someone along the way to slip up and say something they shouldn't have.

There was a small foldable table outside of Jillian's trailer with three pizza boxes on top of it. The trailer door itself was ajar. Thomas was standing outside with Jillian, both still in costume. Celia followed Evan to the trailer, walking as slowly as she could so she didn't appear too eager to speak with Thomas alone. The overwhelming hunger that plagued her stomach had dwindled down, thanks to her nerves.

"How's it going?" Evan asked.

"Good," Jillian said. "I was worried you guys weren't going to show up and I would be left with all this pizza."

"What about Leslie and Matt?" Evan asked, grabbing a slice of supreme pizza from the top box.

Jillian shook her head. "Leslie isn't feeling well, and Matt was more interested in whatever fish platter the truck is serving."

Celia walked up to Thomas and he placed his arm around her. Her heart was beating rapidly.

"How was your scene?" he asked.

"Good." She glanced nervously at Evan. "Can I talk to you for a minute... in private?"

"Of course."

Thomas followed her around to the back of the trailer. She twirled her finger in her wig.

"Evan saw you in your trailer last night with your Fuzeon injection," she said.

Thomas nodded. "I know, he came in to grab some costume piece he forgot. What's the problem?"

"He didn't just see you in the trailer, I mean he saw the needle. He asked me if you were a drug addict on the drive from the castle."

"Why is it so easy to jump to that conclusion?" Thomas shook his head. "What did you tell him?"

"I... told him you were a type one diabetic."

"Jesus."

Celia shrugged her shoulders. "I didn't know what to say, I'm sorry."

"It's not your fault." He wrapped his arms around her. "I should've locked my trailer. I've been bringing all the used needles back to the hotel to throw away, so they wouldn't be found in the trash here by one of the custodians or accidentally discovered by a crew member. I thought it would be more discreet with less risk. Clearly, I was wrong."

"No, I think your only mistake was not locking the door, but even with that— Evan should have knocked first before barging in. What are you going to do?"

"I don't know. Only a handful of people know about my disease and I'm not ready to share that with anyone else."

"I told him you were shy about it and not to mention it to anyone, but I don't know what he'll do. I'm afraid if he says something people may look into it and find out what's really going on."

"I guess time will tell. There's not anything we can do about it now, and there's no point in worrying about what may or may not happen. I appreciate you being honest with me about all this and for burdening this secret with me—I know it's not always easy."

Celia kissed him softly. "I don't mind, please know I would do anything for you. I love you."

"I love you too." He tightened his grip around her. "We should probably head back over there. I know you don't have much time before you have to head back to set."

He took her hand and led her back to the front of the trailer, where Evan was already on his third slice of pizza. Jillian was inside the trailer, talking to someone on the phone. Celia's stomach audibly growled as she retrieved a slice of pepperoni. Neither Evan nor Thomas said anything. It wasn't tense, but Celia felt the weight of the words left unsaid. If Evan truly believed her lie there was a chance he felt guilty for bringing it up in the first place. Perhaps he felt as guilty as her for lying. She looked at Thomas, quietly scrolling through his phone. She couldn't help but wonder if he felt guilty too. Maybe he was so used to doing whatever it took to keep his secret hidden that lying wasn't a question of morals, only a method of self-perseverance.

# Eighteen

Celia sat on the bed in her hotel room. It was almost ten o'clock at night and her eyes were heavy with sleep. The hotel room was considerably smaller than the one they booked in Edinburgh, probably due to the fact it was meant for one person, but it was still nice. There was queen-sized bed with two nightstands on either side of it. Both nightstands had a small lamp, alarm clock, and a coaster. A small bathroom sat in the corner near the door, and a kitchenette on the opposite side. The tan walls were scarcely decorated with a hanging television and two floral paintings. Celia was partially under the thick orange comforter with her back propped up against two pillows. Her laptop was resting on her knees. Music rang out as she received a *Zoom* call from Amy. With California eight hours behind Scotland, it was only the early afternoon for Amy. She was in her ridiculously pink office, wearing a pale grey pantsuit.

"Hey, how are you? It's so good to see you," Amy said.

"I'm good." Celia smiled weakly. She still hadn't discussed the whole you-lied-to-me situation with Amy and felt slightly awkward.

"Glad to hear it. I know it's late over there, so I won't take up too much of your time. It's been a quiet few weeks since the whole leaked photo incident, but we finally have a solid lead."

Thomas walked out of the bathroom. Fresh out of the shower,

he was attired only in clover-print boxer shorts. He quietly climbed into the bed next to Celia. Amy appeared slightly surprised to see him for a moment before returning to her serious expression.

"Law enforcement was able to track the IP address and found the location of the computer that was used. It was at the Los Angeles Public Library."

"You have to have a library card to even use one of their computers—right?" Celia asked.

"Yes and no. You have to have a library card if you wish to use a one-hour internet station, but they have fifteen-minute internet stations that can be used without a card. It appears, that the person responsible, accessed a station that didn't require a card."

*Person responsible? It was Brandon.*

"What about security cameras? Surely they have those?" Thomas asked.

Amy sighed. "Yes, but the person wore a hat and sunglasses the entire time they were at the library—even when they were on the exterior. It appears that they traveled on foot, so law enforcement is going to see if any of the nearby businesses have security cameras and review their footage if they do."

"What are the *odds* of catching him and actually charging him with the crime?" Celia asked.

"I don't want to speculate—"

"Tell me," Celia's voice cracked slightly. She was on the verge of tears.

"Right now, it's not looking promising. Without a confession or any evidence that could identify the person at the library, there's nothing that can be done. It's a waiting game for now."

"Great," Celia said.

Amy apologized and attempted some motivational quote, but Celia had already tuned her out. She didn't care to hear anything else Amy had to say. Brandon was smarter than Celia gave him credit for. If he knew to wear a disguise he probably had planned the entire ordeal from start to finish—including avoiding being spotted out of disguise by any nearby security cameras. It's not like the authorities were going to spend their days watching surveillance videos from every camera down a block radius, they had bigger fish to fry.

"You okay?" Thomas asked.

"What?" Celia hadn't realized the call had ended nor that she had been sitting there staring at the greyed screen.

"Are you okay?"

She shook her head. "This isn't fair. He's just going to get away with it. Hell he's already gotten away with everything else."

"Not everything."

"What do you mean?"

"The break-in is still an open investigation, remember? They're being tight-lipped about the entire process, but I was able to get one of the guys to tell me they did find a discarded baseball bat nearby. They're dusting it for fingerprints, but that's all he would say. I don't know if they found anything when they were investigating the interior, but who knows—maybe he left some kind of evidence?"

"I don't know. He's lazy, but he seems too calculated to leave anything behind. For all we know, that bat could belong to one of the neighborhood kids."

Thomas shrugged. "I'm trying to be optimistic."

"I know, and I appreciate that," she moved the laptop over to the nightstand. "I thought when we came to Scotland he would stop. I would be out of his reach and he would be forced to move on with his life. Clearly, he didn't share the same sentiment. Filming is going to wrap up in a few weeks and we'll be right back into his territory... I'm a little scared of what's next. I know it's not a matter of *if* he does something, it's a matter of *when*."

"If you're worried because he knows where you live, we could always move."

"Move? Are you crazy? I'm not asking you to leave your home."

"It's not a big deal, really. We could find somewhere nice, maybe something close to the beach?"

"You keep saying *we*, but Thomas you know I can't afford to put any money into a home. Besides, moving would only be a temporary fix. He's resourceful, if he was able to find our filming location, it wouldn't take him long to find a new address."

"I guess you have a point... We could get married instead."

Celia's mouth fell open. "What?"

"He thinks we're in a fake relationship and he's pulling all these stunts to try and prove it. The more he escalates, the more he probably thinks he has a chance at you 'confessing'. Maybe if he sees how serious things are, he'll back off?"

"Wow," Celia scoffed. "Let's get married so my ex-boyfriend will stop harassing me—what a *terrific* idea. You don't just marry someone because you want to prove a point."

"Do you really think that's the only reason I would marry you?"

"You said it yourself."

Thomas shook his head and laughed. "God, you can be so frustrating sometimes. I would marry you because I love you and I want to. Have you been ignoring everything I've said these past months? You make my life better. It's like there's a fire in my soul, a desire to keep going—something I never thought I'd have again."

"I love you, but I don't want to have this conversation right now. It's late and we're both sleep deprived. The six AM call time is going to be here before we know it." She tossed the extra pillow onto the carpet before turning off the lamp next to her and scooting down in the bed.

Thomas sighed, but didn't say anything. After a few minutes of sitting up he relented and turned off the lamp next to him. Both he and Celia had their eyes closed, but neither were asleep. Maybe it was due to her exhaustion, but she couldn't understand what

Thomas had said. The word marriage, yes, the reasons—no. *If he truly feels this way, he wouldn't have brought it up on a whim.*

Celia felt awkward, but it had more to do with the scene than the conversation she and Thomas had the night prior. The set was made to look like the interior of an old cabin with rotting walls and uneven flooring. There was a bed resting on a wooden frame and covered in dusty sheets. A small pillow, the only item that appeared to be clean, sat at the foot of the bed. Celia was dressed in another dark Victorian gown and Thomas wore a plain shirt and pants. Vincent and Charles were at one of the cameras, reviewing film from a previous scene. The crew was still adjusting the lights.

"Have you ever filmed anything like this before?" Thomas asked.

Celia shook her head. Her nerves were apparent by the expression on her face and the slight tremble in her hands.

"It's going to be alright, I promise." Thomas took her hands into his and lightly squeezed them. "Regardless of what it may appear like on screen, there's nothing sexy about filming a sex-scene. For some of the shots they're going to be uncomfortably close. Eyes and lights are going to be on us and it's going to be hot—temperature wise, anyway. All you need to do is focus on me, ignore the crew around us."

Vincent walked up to them. "You guys ready?"

They both nodded.

"Good. I know it's a tad chilly in here, but we're going to have two cameras rolling so we can try and get this in as few takes as possible. Celia, keep in mind that this is Eleanor's first sexual experience with anyone other than Asa." He looked to Thomas, "I want to see some initial hesitation from Baldric. The attraction is there, and he feels it, but he wants to fight it. This is not just a married woman, this is the King's wife. A king he knows it vengeful and cruel."

"Understood," Thomas said.

"Perfect, let's do this." He walked back over to the camera.

"It will be okay, I promise." Thomas lightly kissed her forehead.

He took a few steps away from her and she turned her back to him. Celia took a deep breath, trying to reign in her nerves. She was terrified, but she knew he was right. This was a scene, and while it was her first sex-scene, it wasn't the first for majority of the crew. They were professionals and were going to be concerned about the scene itself, not the fact that she was nude. Not to mention that despite the fact she was filming the scene nude, the directors had assured her they weren't going to show more than she was comfortable with to audiences.

"Scene twenty-six, long, take one," a camera assistant said as he struck the clapperboard in front of the first camera. He repeated the words and action for the second camera.

"Action," Vincent yelled.

"This is what you wanted to show me? An old, rundown cabin?" Thomas asked.

"Come on, you can't seriously think that's why I brought you here." Celia spun around. A mischievous look was on her face.

He shrugged. His eyes nervously scanned the room—stopping at the musty bed. She approached him and he took a step back. He put his hands up defensively, but instead of stopping, she took his hand and held it above her chest. His face reddened.

"We shouldn't be here." He tried to pull his hand away, but she held it in place. "Ellie, have you gone mad? Do you know what the King would do to me if he even knew I was somewhere like this alone with you?"

"He doesn't know, and he's certainly not going to find out. I don't know why you're pretending like I'm the crazy one. I've seen the way you look at me, Baldric."

"I don't know what you're talking about," Thomas said. His face was contrary to his words, like a criminal caught in the act of stealing.

"Yes, you do."

She released her grip, but he didn't move. Nervous perspiration sat on his brow line. He took a deep breath.

"Even if what you're saying is true—none of it matters. You're a *queen*, a married queen at that. It was foolish to allow myself to develop feelings for you," he said.

"If you're foolish, so am I." Celia unlaced the front of her dress. Faux bruises were painted around her neck and collarbone. She pulled back the shoulders and the dress fell to her feet, leaving her naked. "In case you haven't realized, I've been looking at you in the same manner."

Thomas grabbed her face and kissed her. He tasted like Baileys Irish Cream. Both he and Celia had poured generous shots of liqueur in their coffees before heading to set—something to take the edge off for the scene. Thomas scooped her into his arms and carried her to the bed. It creaked as he sat her gently down on top of it. He pulled off his shirt and tossed it to the side. His tattoos were hidden by foundation and his muscles were expanded from the push-ups he had done minutes earlier. Celia ran her hands down his chest and stopped at his waistband.

"Are you sure you want to do this?" he asked.

She nodded. "I want you more than anything I've ever wanted."

His lips formed a devilishly handsome smile. He pulled off his pants and carelessly tossed them next to his shirt. Thomas started kissing her, his lips traveled down her body as Celia twisted her fingers in his hair. After a few moments, he sat up and pulled her close to him—chest to chest. A pillow was in between them as they began to rock back and forth. Celia focused on his eyes, as if there would be a test later to determine how blue they were. It was all she could do to block out the cameras and eyes around them while staying in character.

"And that's a cut," Charles said.

A woman who was part of the wardrobe crew quickly retrieved Celia's costume from the ground and brought it to her. Her face was flushed as she redressed. Thomas on the other hand didn't appear shy or embarrassed about being exposed in front of the crew members. Instead, he had a smile on his face.

"Was it as bad as you imagined it would be?" He picked up his clothes from the ground.

"No, but I can't say it's in my top five favorite scenes."

"Any scene I get to kiss you like that is *easily* in my top five."

Celia playfully thumped his shoulder and he laughed. As he was getting redressed, Elena came in with a portable makeup container that was almost large enough to fit a child inside. She smiled at Celia but was quiet as she ran a brush through her wig and touched-up her makeup. Charles walked over as Elena had finished and turned her attention to Thomas' appearance. Vincent hung back at his director's chair, chatting with the camera assistant.

"As soon as you guys are ready, we're going to run through it again. I want you both to take it slower this time, it felt a little rushed," Charles said. "I know this is a little awkward for you both but see if you can channel some of your real-life romantic chemistry into the scene."

Thomas and Celia exchanged a glance and her cheeks flushed. Their first time had been something comparable to the scene. The frustration of wanting each other, but afraid to cross boundaries. Attraction that had grown until it was undeniable and irresistible.

"Are you ready?" Thomas asked.

She smiled. "As ready as I will be."

They returned to their previous stances, waiting.

"Scene twenty-six, long, take two," a camera assistant said as he struck the clapperboard in front of the first camera. He repeated himself for the second camera.

"Action," Vincent yelled.

"This is what you wanted to show me? An old, rundown cabin?" Thomas asked.

"Come on, you can't seriously think that's why I brought you here." Celia turned around. Her arms were crossed but her expression was playful.

He shrugged his shoulders. He walked around the room stopping at the base of musty bed. She approached him and he took a step back. He put his arms up, and Celia grabbed his hands, her fingers interlacing with his.

"We shouldn't be here." He tried to pull his hands away, but it was in vain. "Ellie, have you gone mad? Do you know what the King would do to me if he even knew I was somewhere like this alone with you?"

"He doesn't know, and he's certainly not going to find out. I don't know why you're pretending like I'm the crazy one. I've seen the way you look at me, Baldric."

"I don't know what you're talking about," Thomas said. His words were contrary to the guilty expression on his face.

"Yes, you do."

Sweat ran down his face as he took a deep breath. The temperature in the room was warm and rising with each second.

"Even if what you're saying is true—none of it matters. You're a queen, a married queen at that. It was foolish to allow myself to develop feelings for you," he said.

Celia placed her hands on his face and pressed her forehead to his. "If you're foolish, so am I."

Thomas didn't say anything. His eyes were a shut as they kept their heads together. Celia took his hands again and placed them over the bodice of her dress. His fingers toyed with the thin leather string holding the top together.

Celia gently kissed his cheek before softly whispering in his ear, "In case you haven't realized, I've been looking at you in the same manner."

Thomas opened his eyes and kissed her gently on the lips. Slowly he unlaced her dress. His hand slipped under the fabric, caressing her skin. His lips brushed against the faux bruises before he kissed her neck. Celia untucked his shirt and slid her hands underneath, traveling up his spine. Thomas pulled away, his gaze intensely focused on her.

"Are you sure you want to do this?" Thomas asked.

"Yes," her voice barely above a whisper. "I want you more than anything I've ever wanted."

He smiled and pulled his shirt off over his head. Her fingers traced the outline of his muscles. She stopped at the waistband of his pants, a small hesitation, before pulling them down. He slid back the shoulders of her dress, slipping it down to her waist before letting it fall onto the ground. Celia kissed him as he picked her up. Her legs were wrapped around his waist as he pushed her up against the wall. Pressed against each other, their heat radiated off onto one another.

Thomas carried her over to the bed. Its familiar creak welcomed them. This time, she got on top of him. Thomas held one hand on the bed post and the other on her lower back. His fingers dug into her skin as they swayed. Sweat covered their skin as the temperature in the room continuously rose, chasing out the original chill. Panic flashed in Thomas' eyes as the pillow in between them slipped down. It was quick, but enough for Celia to notice. She halted her movements and began kissing him again.

"And that's a cut." Charles clapped his hands together. "Damn, that was *much* better. Well done."

Everyone on set looked pleased, aside from Thomas. The panicked expression had evolved to concern. He gently shifted Celia to the side of him and immediately went for his pants.

"Can we take a quick break before the next shot?" Celia asked.

Vincent and Charles both nodded. "We're going to set up for a different angle, so it'll be a minute anyway. Take fifteen," Vincent said.

"Thank you." Celia took her dress from the wardrobe assistant and quickly put it back on. Thomas was already dressed, standing off to the corner. Not wanting to waste any time, she didn't bother lacing it up. She held the top together as she walked over to him.

"Can we go outside for a minute?" she asked quietly.

"Yeah."

He followed her out of the makeshift cabin. The sun was shining, but the cool breeze was unforgiving to their sweaty skin. Celia stopped next to a large oak tree and started retying her dress. Thomas ran his fingers through his hair mindlessly. He stood there, but his mind appeared to be miles away.

"Are you okay?" she asked.

He adamantly shook his head. "That was too close."

"I know, but it's alright. We'll be more careful next time."

"We have to be. That cannot happen again." Tears glistened in his eyes. "I'm going to ask for a modesty pouch, and you need to see if they have some beige underwear you can wear during the remaining takes."

"Are you sure you're not overreacting? What will they think when we haven't been using those and all of the sudden ask for them?"

"I don't *care* what they think!"

"Lower your voice." Celia nervously looked at the cabin, but it appeared no one was paying attention nor heard what he had said.

Thomas collapsed to the ground with his back against the tree trunk. He was crying. Celia sat down next to him and took his hand into hers. It was painful to see him so distraught. She placed her hand on his cheek, offsetting the stream of tears.

"I would never forgive myself if you got sick because of me," he said.

"I'm not going to."

He shook his head. "You don't know that."

"Yes, I do. We're careful, even in the heat of things... Are you bringing this up because what happened or is there something else bothering you?"

"It's a combination of things..."

"You can tell me anything, you know?"

He nodded. "After our conversation last night, I couldn't sleep. I felt stupid for even suggesting marriage. It's not that I don't want to marry you, because honestly I have given it a lot of thought and I do; however, it's not fair of me to hold you back."

"What do you mean? You're not holding me back in any shape or form."

"If you were to marry me, we wouldn't be able to have children to-gether, let alone unprotected sex. You may say none of that matters to you, but you're young Celia, not even in your prime. Ten years from now or maybe even sooner you may realize that's not what you want. I don't want to be an anchor in your life, grounding you from everything out there. You deserve options I can't give you."

"I may be young, but I'm not naïve. I know what I want Thomas, and I want *you*." Heat rushed to the back of her head. "When I think about my future, I don't see myself with anyone but you. I knew what I was getting myself into when you told me about your disease. It wasn't on some whim that I decided to stay with you. I could have left then, or even after Christmas. If you think I would be better off without you, you're not as smart I thought."

"Celia..."

"No—let me finish. If you had asked me to marry you, I would've said yes. There wouldn't have been any hesitation on my end, what-so-ever. When I think about us, I don't see the things we can't do, I see the beauty of what we can do. I see all the memories waiting to happen, and relish in those that already have. You're not an anchor, you're my lifeboat. I didn't even know I was drowning, you see, but you made me aware of how empty I was. I thought I was happy, but I was only kidding myself. I will say it again so maybe it'll sink in—you're a fool if you think I would be better off without you."

Celia stood up and turned towards the cabin.

"Where are you going?" Thomas asked.

"To get ready for the scene. I don't have anything else to say to you about this."

He opened his mouth as if he was going to say something, but Celia had already started walking away. She didn't want him to see the tears in her eyes.

# Nineteen

Celia was sitting in her hotel room reading *Outlander* when someone knocked on her door. It was a little after ten o'clock in the morning. She was dressed casually in jeans and a t-shirt. Her hair was pulled into a messy braid. She set her book down and went to the door. It was Leslie. She was dressed in a cable knit sweater, faux leather jacket, skinny jeans, and suede booties. Her curly hair was masked by a knitted cap.

"Good morning," Celia said. She forced a smile but was unable to hide the disappointment that it wasn't Thomas.

"Hey." Leslie paused. "Were you expecting someone else?"

She shook her head. "Wasn't expecting anyone actually. What's going on?"

"I'm going into town today and was wondering if you'd like to come with me? We haven't both had the same day off yet and I feel like it's been ages since we've hung out offset."

"Yeah, I'd love to. Let me grab my coat and we can go," Celia said.

Leslie smiled. "Perfect."

The morning air was chilly. Streets and sidewalks were busy, but were nothing in comparison to the hustle and bustle of the holidays in Edinburgh. Celia and Leslie walked to a coffee shop a block away from their hotel. It was a mom-and-pop kind of shop, with a small, but cozy interior. They served a variety of coffees, lattes, and teas, along with pastries. Large windows covered three of the shop's four walls, giving view to the day-to-day life outside. Celia and Leslie sat at a small table by the entrance. Celia had her usual coffee and a cinnamon roll, while Leslie had ordered a breakfast tea and a muffin.

"I can't believe we're almost done filming." Leslie took a bite of her muffin. "It feels like yesterday I was on my way to the airport."

"I know what you mean. I'm not going to miss these cool temperatures, but I'm definitely going to miss Scotland. Thomas and I flew down two weeks early and spent the holidays here— it was amazing. If Santa was real, he would definitely have modeled the North Pole like downtown Edinburgh."

"I forgot you both came early... Listen, I don't mean to pry, but is everything okay between you two?"

"Yeah, why do you ask?"

Leslie shrugged. "I saw him coming out of his hotel room this morning. You've been sharing your room with him this entire time, so I was worried something might've happened."

Celia sighed. She hadn't spoken to Thomas since their argument the day prior. After finishing the scene, she had gone back to Basecamp, but he had stayed for a different scene. When he was still on set at nine o'clock in the evening, she had chosen to hitch a ride with Jillian and Matt back to the hotel. She had expected him to come in after she was already asleep, not to stay in a different room. Waking up without him next to her was strange and she missed his presence.

"We had a small disagreement in between takes yesterday. We're both tired and little stressed, so when I got some bad news about my ex, it made things worse," Celia said.

"Bird guy?"

Celia nodded. "I didn't want to talk about this in front of

everyone, but he posted some inappropriate pictures of me without my consent. Law enforcement has been working on building a case, but it's like he's one step ahead of them. They tracked the computer to where the pictures were posted, but it was in a public library and he was disguised. You'd think someone who failed out of college would've been sloppier about it."

"What an ass."

"Tell me about it." She sighed. "It's been almost a year since we broke up. I really thought he'd have moved on with his life by now."

"Wait... so you guys broke up right before you and Thomas got together?"

"Yes, which is why he thinks Thomas and I aren't in a real relationship."

Leslie shook her head. "I will say, when I heard about the relationship and the casting I wondered if it was some kind of PR stunt; however, when I saw the two of you together it absolved all of my doubts."

"You're probably not the only one who thought that. I know there's the age difference and we're at different levels in our careers, but I don't care about any of that. I love him."

"Well it's obvious that he loves you too." Leslie stood up. "I'm going to run to the ladies' room real quick. When I get back, you want to head out? I heard there's some retro antique shop around here and I really want to check it out."

"Sure."

Celia got up to throw away her half-eaten cinnamon roll and accidentally bumped into a man behind her.

"I'm so sorry," she said. The color drained from her as face as she looked up and saw the man's face. It was Brandon. He was wearing a black heavy coat and grey knit cap. A smug grin sat on his face.

"Hello, Celia. It's nice to see you," he said.

"You shouldn't be here," she said.

"Why not? Oh, I forgot," He thumped the palm of his hand to his forehead. "You probably assumed a piece of paper would keep me away. We're not in Los Angeles anymore."

A suffocating lump sat in her throat. She didn't know what to do or say. She looked over to the bathroom, hoping to see Leslie come out, but the door was still shut. *Leslie please hurry up.* Brandon leaned in close to her, his hot breath pressed against her ear.

"Did you like my little *gift*?" he asked.

Celia shoved him back as hard as she could. He fell back against a table, knocking a random patron's coffee off onto the floor. His face was red like a tomato as he lunged towards her, wrapping his hands around her throat. She struggled to breathe as his grip tightened. People were shouting at him, and two men struggled to pry him away from her. Her vision was blurred by the time a husky customer managed to pull Brandon back. His fingers had been entwined in her necklace and the chain snapped, sending the lifeboat charm crashing to the ground. Celia fell to her knees coughing. A young man rushed to her side and grabbed her arm. A woman grabbed her other arm and together the strangers helped her into a seat.

"You'll be sorry you did this! I swear, you just wait and see," Brandon yelled.

Leslie came out of the bathroom as Brandon was bring drug outside. Two of the men kept him restrained while the larger man appeared to be lecturing him. He waved his hands in the air as he spoke.

"What the hell happened?" Leslie asked. Her eyes wildly looking from the men restraining Brandon back to Celia.

"The lad out there attacked her," the woman said.

"Oh my God," Leslie whispered.

"Stay with her, I'm going to call the bobbies while he's restrained." The woman pulled a phone out of her pocket and walked towards the front of the coffee shop.

Celia's eyes were watery and red. She managed to stop coughing but her throat was painfully dry. She took a sip of her coffee and it burned.

"Can I have some water?" her voice was hoarse.

The young man nodded and went to the counter. Leslie picked up the necklace off the ground and slid into her pocket. Celia's neck was indented where his fingers had been.

"Are you okay?" Leslie asked.

"No." She started crying.

Leslie pulled her into an embrace and Celia pressed her face against Leslie's shoulder. Her tears stained Leslie's jacket. It hurt to cry, it hurt to breathe, but she was inconsolable. All she wanted was Thomas, but he was on set and still upset with her for all she knew.

Celia sat in the small claw foot bathtub. The bubbles were practically overflowing. It had been a couple of hours since the incident with Brandon, but her throat was still scratchy and her neck had begun to bruise. The bathroom door was cracked open and Leslie was sitting on a chair by the kitchenette. She had been hesitant to leave Celia alone by herself. There was a knock on the door. Cautiously, Leslie went to see who it was.

"Oh thank God it's you," she said.

Thomas raised an eyebrow. "What's going on? Where's Celia?"

"She's in the bath... there was an incident today."

"What do you mean? Is she alright?"

"She's a little shaken up, but she's alright, come sit down, I'll tell you what happened."

They walked by the bathroom door, but Celia didn't look. She kept her eyes, bloodshot and dry from crying, shut. Leslie reclaimed her chair and Thomas sat down across from her.

"We went to a coffee shop this morning, the one that's at the end of the block. While I was in the bathroom, she was attacked by bird guy, I mean Brandon. He was choking her... some other customers stepped in and were able to pull him off, but she had nearly blacked out by then," she rubbed her temples and sighed. "Scotland Yard came and interviewed everyone there—Celia, Brandon, and the witnesses. They took him into custody, but I don't know if they're even going to hold him. They acted like it was Celia's fault for pushing him. According to them, she 'escalated the situation'."

Thomas appeared speechless, as if he was in shock. Leslie pulled her phone out of her pocket and unlocked it before handing it to Thomas.

"To top things off, somehow *TMZ* acquired a cellphone recording of the whole thing. It's grainy, but you can clearly see Celia as well as Brandon. I don't know if we can get them to take it down, but even if they agreed, the damage has been done."

Thomas covered his mouth in disgust as he watched the video. His eyes were filled with tears as he handed Leslie back her phone.

"Why didn't anyone tell me? I had my phone with me on set the entire time. I could've done something," he said.

"Celia didn't want to distract you. Besides things were hectic. We've only been here for maybe two hours. I didn't want to leave until you got here."

"Thank you, I appreciate you taking care of her."

Leslie shook her head. "I didn't. If I hadn't gone into the bathroom, none of this would've happened."

"You don't know that. Please don't blame yourself." He stood up. "If you don't mind I'd like to spend some time with her."

"Of course. Please reach out if you need anything, I'm just a few rooms away. Oh—I almost forgot." She pulled the necklace out of her pocket and handed it to him. "This broke sometime during the struggle. Please make sure she gets it."

"Thank you, I will."

The room was quiet after Leslie left, minus the rattling of the heater. Thomas rolled the charm in his hands before setting it on the nightstand. He walked over to the bathroom door and knocked softly. A minute passed, but Celia didn't say anything. She had heard him knocking, but she was staying silent— trying her best not to fall apart. Leslie probably wasn't aware that Celia could hear her talking, or else she wouldn't have mentioned the *TMZ* video. Celia hadn't been on her phone all day and had no idea a video of the ordeal even existed.

The door creaked as it opened. As soon as Celia's eyes locked with Thomas' she started crying. Still in his jeans and button-up shirt, Thomas stepped into the bath. Water spilled onto the tile floor as he sat down and threw his arms around her. Her sobbing intensified as his hands caressed her back.

"It's okay," he whispered.

After a few minutes, she stopped crying. The bathwater was cold and most of the bubbles had dissipated. Thomas wiped a clump of mascara off her cheek. His eyes were sorrowful as he tried to resist looking at her neck.

"I'm so sorry about what I said yesterday, what happened to you today, and everything in between," his words broke the silence. "I should've never gone to sleep without talking to you first. What if something worse had happened to you today? I don't want to walk away from you when we're in an argument ever again."

Celia put her arms around his neck and held him as tight as she could. She wanted to say something but was afraid it would hurt too much to speak.

He kissed the top of her head. "We're going to get through this, I promise."

# Twenty

The cameras were rolling as Celia sat with her back propped against the stone wall. Her arms and legs were bound with thick rope. Faux bruises were painted on her cheek, and her lips were stained a pale grey. Her gown was torn and stained with fake blood. Synthetic skin partially covered her neck and shoulder. Evan stood in front of her. His costume was unblemished, but his hands were stained red. A cot-shaped green mat was on the ground a few feet behind him. An extra costumed as a knight stood statuesque next to a wooden table. The table was covered in various weapons, ranging from a double-bladed sword to a mace-and-chain. Thomas stood outside of the camera range. He wore a VFX motion-capture body-suit. Both directors were intently watching the scene unfold from their chairs.

"I can't say that I'm pleased you freed the mutt." Evan leaned down, his face a mere inch from hers. "But at least I'll get the chance to hunt him down and slaughter him however I see fit."

He kissed her roughly, biting her lip as he pulled away. Celia spat in his face. Fake blood and spit covered his nose as he smiled deviously. There was a look of insanity in his eyes, but his face was absent of anger of any sort.

"Keep it up, love. Hate me while you can, it'll make this all the more enjoyable." He held his hand out towards the extra and snapped his fingers. "Bring me something sharp."

The extra grabbed the jagged-edge dagger from the table and walked over to Evan, his armor clanking with each step he took. Evan greedily wrapped his fingers around the prop's handle. The extra returned to his previous spot at the table without a word.

"Don't worry—this'll hurt, but it won't kill you."

Evan grabbed her by the back of her wig. She winced as he pressed the blade into the synthetic skin, drawing out faux blood. He withdrew the dagger and plunged it again into the skin. Tears ran down her cheeks and her breaths were labored.

"I want to hear you scream my name," he whispered.

The extra grabbed a sword from the table as Thomas rushed at him. He clumsily waved it in the air towards Thomas' chest and shoulders. Thomas carefully dodged each blow.

"Kill him you fool," Evan yelled.

The extra lifted the table and thrusted it towards Thomas, scattering the weapons across the ground. A small blade landed within reach of Celia. She grabbed it and cut through the bindings around her wrists and ankles. Evan was preoccupied with the fight between Thomas and the extra, he didn't appear to realize she had freed herself. Celia stuck the blade into his left calf and he fell to one knee. He dropped the dagger and used both hands to remove the small blade. Fake blood oozed from the puncture.

"Stupid whore." He threw his hands out in front of him and her back stiffened as if she was being held against the wall. "Did you forget who you're dealing with?"

Thomas caught the sword with his hands and pushed the extra into the corner. He groaned as he pressed the sword's edge into the extra's neck. The extra's hands fell limp before he crashed to his knees. The armor and sword clanked against the stone floor. Thomas looked at his hands, where the blood would be added during post-production, before turning towards Evan. He gritted his teeth as he ran towards him. Evan cast his left hand towards Thomas and he stopped in his place as if he were frozen.

"So lovely of you to join us Baldric," Evan sneered. "I think, given the circumstances, we don't have time for a public execution. I'm going to kill you right now for my beloved Queen to see. And then, I'm going to finish her off."

He squeezed his hand into a fist and Thomas writhed in pain. Celia yelled for him to stop, but Evan didn't budge. He laughed as Thomas appeared to be in more pain with each passing second. Celia screamed. She slowly rose to her feet and moved her arms forward, as if the ties that had her to the wall were weakening. She snapped her hands forward and Evan fell backwards onto the mat, while Thomas collapsed onto the ground.

"I believe you're the one who forgot who *you* were dealing with," Celia said.

She walked towards Evan, whispering a fictitious spell. Evan clawed at his neck, gasping for air as if he was choking. The closer she got, the more he struggled. She pulled her arms in together and Evan's arms went limp against his chest. His labored breaths ceased and his eyes held an empty stare.

"You're not half the man your father was, he was a great king," she whispered.

Thomas rose to his feet and walked over to Celia. She jumped as he lightly put his hand on her shoulder. She circled him, her eyes studying his appearance. Cautiously, she touched the side of his face.

"Is that really you Baldric?"

Thomas stepped back and dropped his arms to his side. Editors were going to make him appear as if he had transformed back to his human form. Celia threw her arms around him and pulled him into a tight embrace. Tears streamed down her cheeks.

"You were supposed to go to Vulcan." She shook her head. "You promised me you would go. What are you doing here?"

Thomas stepped back and placed his hands on her shoulders. "I know, I'm sorry. I got to the edge of the forest, but I couldn't go any further. I had this feeling in the pit of my stomach—I knew something was wrong."

"That was reckless, but I appreciate you coming to my aide. How were you able to get past the guards?"

"There were no guards... I actually didn't see anyone until I got inside the castle."

Celia's eyes widened. "What are you talking about? The men aren't heading out until tomorrow. They should be here."

She walked over to the wall and stood on her toes in an effort to see out of the window. She walked over to the extra and carefully removed his helmet. His face was painted with the black root designs, just like the prop. Celia dropped the helmet, its crash echoed throughout the room.

"Ellie?"

Celia walked back over to Evan and kneeled next to him. She grabbed the top of his shirt and tore it open. His chest was painted with the markings, only they were smaller and less noticeable—as if the transformation was just beginning.

"What are those markings?" Thomas extended his hand to her and helped her stand.

"I don't know. I found a woman marked like this, but she was alive. Her skin was ice cold and her eyes were glasslike, but she was breathing. It was as if she were imprisoned in her own body. Asa had her beheaded before I could attempt to make any diagnosis. He didn't admit it, but I could tell he was frightened. I don't know if he was overreacting, but I think it's best we leave before we find out."

"I agree. I left my horse at the stable and saddled yours, just in case."

"Thank you. I need to grab some items from my chambers before we go. Can you meet me at the stable in ten minutes?"

"I would rather we stay together," Thomas said.

"Yes, but I can't let someone in the castle see me with you." She placed her hand on his cheek. "I will be fine, I promise."

Thomas sighed. "If you're not there in ten minutes, I'm coming back."

"I'll hold you to that."

Thomas and Celia rushed out of frame as Evan's hands began twitching. After a few moments, his eyes shot open.

"And that's a cut." Charles exchanged a quick glance with Vincent. "Actually, no, that's a wrap. We're done here folks."

The camera and production crew clapped and cheered. Wide smiles were plastered on their tired faces. Thomas picked Celia up and spun her around, their smiles were arguably the biggest. He kissed her before setting her back on the ground. Evan ran over and threw his arms around the both of them.

"Guys, you know what this means right?" Evan asked.

Celia shrugged her shoulders.

"It's time to celebrate! And by celebrate, I mean get shit-faced one last time in Scotland. I know of the perfect place."

"I think, I'll pass," Celia said. She hadn't seen Brandon since he attacked her three weeks ago, but it didn't mean he had left the country. Scotland Yard hadn't appeared concerned with the matter, as if he was justified in his actions—an eye for an eye. She had pushed him first, but her actions paled in comparison to his response. The bruises on her neck were gone, but the incident still haunted her dreams.

"I'm with Celia. It's probably best not to go out given the circumstances," Thomas said.

Evan frowned. "Come on, guys. We'll be heading back to the states soon, this will be the last chance we have to hang out with everyone until the press tour. It'll be a huge group of us, and we can make sure you're not left alone under any circumstances."

Celia looked at Thomas, hoping he would know what to say, but he simply shrugged his shoulders.

"It's your call," he said.

"Please?" Evan asked.

"One drink." She held up her hand. "But, if at any moment I feel uncomfortable, I'm leaving. No ifs ands or buts. Deal?"

Evan smiled. "Deal."

Celia and Thomas stood waiting outside of an old pub. Celia was dressed in a black dress and a denim jacket. Her lips were painted red, and her hair was pulled into a tight ponytail. Thomas was wearing jeans, a plaid long-sleeved shirt, and his favorite Los Angeles Dodgers hat. The night sky was cloudless and glittered with stars. A gentle breeze swept through town.

"I have something for you. Close your eyes," Thomas said.

Celia flashed him a suspicious smile before closing her eyes. Thomas pulled the lifeboat necklace out of his pocket and carefully clasped it around her neck. The white gold gave a familiar chill to her bare skin.

"Okay, you can open your eyes now."

She looked down at the necklace and her face lit up. "I don't know if you realize how much this means to me. Thank you for getting it fixed."

"All it needed was a new chain. Lucky for me, there's a jeweler a few streets over and he had an almost identical replacement."

He kissed her before pulling her into a tight embrace. Evan and Matt walked up to them with Leslie and Jillian following close behind. The women were dressed for a night on the town while the guys appeared more casual. Jillian wore a sequin-adorned gold dress and heels. Her lace jacket was more for a statement than warmth.

Leslie was attired in a black bodysuit with pleather pants over it. Both Matt and Evan wore t-shirts and jeans.

"Did you guys already start celebrating without us?" Matt asked.

Celia rolled her eyes.

"You're late," Thomas said.

"Actually." Evan pulled out his phone. "We're right on time. You kids must've been eager to get started."

"You told us earlier—actually, never mind." Thomas laughed. "Come on."

They joined the small line of people waiting to get inside. A bouncer was at the door, checking ID's. The street was quiet for a Friday night, but it was only a little after nine, and perhaps too early for the drinking crowd.

Thomas fished through his shirt and jean pockets. "Shit."

"What's wrong?" Celia asked.

"I think I left my wallet back at the hotel."

Jillian and Leslie had already entered the pub, and Matt was in the middle of having his driver's license checked by the bouncer. The bouncer was a large man, over six-feet tall. He was almost as muscular as he was tall. His long red beard was scraggly.

"I don't think you can get in without it," Evan said.

"You can't enter without a proper form of identification," the bouncer said, apparently in tune to their conversation.

"It's not a big deal, I'll walk back with you to go get it," Celia said.

Thomas shook his head. "I don't want you to have to walk all that way, just to come back. You're not dressed for that."

He wasn't wrong. She had already admitted how uncomfortable her shoes were from not being worn often; however, she didn't want him to go alone.

"Do you want me to come with you?" Evan asked.

"Honestly, I'd rather you stay with Celia. It's only a few blocks, I'll be back in no time," Thomas said.

"You sure?" Celia asked.

He kissed her on her forehead. "Positive."

"Okay, see you soon."

She watched him merge in with the passing strangers on the sidewalk, before turning back to the pub's entrance. The bouncer checked her ID and let her pass. Contrary to the small crowd outside, the interior of the pub was packed. The bar had patrons lined all around it with all the counter seats taken. All of the pool tables were occupied, and only a few small tables were open. Rock music blared from the speakers, forcing conversations into yelling matches. Leslie and Jillian had secured a table near the bar, while Matt was in charge of ordering drinks. Evan locked his arm with Celia's and helped her navigate to the table through the crowd.

"Where's Thomas?" Leslie asked.

"What?" Celia asked.

"I asked, where's Thomas?" she repeated.

"Oh. He forgot his wallet and had to go back to the hotel for it." Before she could say anything else, Matt came to the table with a pitcher and glasses. A barmaid followed him and placed a tray of shots on the table.

"What's this?" Jillian asked, inspecting the shot glass.

Matt shrugged. "I asked for their best beer and a few of their best shots."

Everyone grabbed a shot glass, but Celia hesitated. She had agreed to *one* drink, not one drink and a shot.

"Come on Celia don't be a Debbie downer. Have some fun with us tonight," Evan offered her a shot.

"Okay, fine." She took the glass.

"What should we toast to?" Jillian asked.

"Wrapping up?" Matt offered.

Leslie shook her head.

"How about we toast to witches, werewolves, and a damn good film?" Evan suggested.

"I'd toast to that," Celia said.

"Same," Jillian said.

"Alright, to witches, werewolves and a damn good film it is!"

They clanked their glasses with one another before slamming them onto the table. In unison they drank the shot. It was bitter, burning all the way down Celia's throat. She coughed and quickly poured herself a glass of beer. It wasn't her ideal choice of a chaser, but she needed something to alleviate the burning.

"You're not much of a shot taker, are you?" Leslie asked.

Celia shook her head. "I'm not much of a *whiskey* drinker. On the occasions that I do take a shot, I make sure it's something fruity. I'm not a fan of beer either."

"You want to get something else then?"

"No, I think I'll wait for Thomas. Hopefully the crowd around the bar will die down some by then."

"Is anyone else going to miss Scotland?" Jillian asked.

Leslie and Celia both nodded.

"I wish we had started filming in May. The weather is so beautiful right now," Jillian said.

"I agree," Celia said.

"I'm definitely not going to miss the food." Evan took a sip of beer. "I would give anything for a good ole fashioned American cheeseburger right now."

"I know. Last week I was so desperate I went to McDonald's," Matt said.

Celia laughed. "That does sound pretty desperate."

"Come on guys, McDonald's isn't *that* bad," Leslie said.

"It depends on what you're comparing it too—like haggis for example," Matt said.

They all laughed. Celia's phone buzzed inside her jacket pocket.

It was so loud inside the pub, if she hadn't had her phone in her pocket, she wouldn't have realized.

Thomas had texted her, "On my way back."

"Better hurry ♥," she replied.

"Fancy a game of pool?" Evan asked.

She slid her phone back in her pocket. One of the pool tables had opened up and, like vultures, Matt and Leslie had swooped in. Leslie was placing the balls in the rack while Matt secured two cue sticks.

"I can play, but I'm not very good," Celia said.

"That's alright, your teammate is." Evan winked at her. "Jill you going to be alright by yourself?"

Jillian nodded, but didn't appear to be paying attention. Her gaze was focused on a young Scottish woman sitting a few tables down. Eyes locked with Jillian, she appeared to be ignoring her friends as well.

"Alright who wants to break?" Matt asked as he handed a cue stick to Evan.

"I think it should be one of the ladies," Evan said.

Leslie and Celia looked at each other.

"You can go for it," Celia said.

"Watch and learn boys." Leslie took the cue stick from Matt. She quickly rubbed chalk on the tip before taking a stance at the end of the table. She leaned over, careful not to hit anyone standing too close behind her and hit the cue ball. The balls popped as the cue ball smacked into them, scattering them in different directions. The three-ball teetered on the edge of the corner pocket before falling in.

"Solids." She walked around the edge and took aim at the seven ball. The cue ball hit it, but it ricocheted off the wall of the table and knocked in the nine-ball.

"Thank you," Evan teased. He turned to Celia. "Would you like to do the honors?"

"Sure." She took the cue stick and walked over by Leslie. There was no easy shot to make. She could take a chance and aim for the two striped balls by the corner pocket, but the eight-ball was dangerously close. Her other option was to aim for the thirteen-ball to break up the cluster and set up for the next shot. Evan walked up beside her.

"Want a suggestion?" he asked.

She nodded.

"Don't worry about the eight-ball. You have a greater chance of getting the thirteen or ten in the pocket and sending the eight-ball back towards the middle."

"Alright, I'll give a try." She gently tapped the cue ball and it glided across the table. It knocked the thirteen-ball into the pocket and pushed the eight-ball towards the cluster.

Evan gave her a high-five. "Nice one."

"All about the teamwork," she said. She aimed her next shot for the ten-ball, but hit too hard, and the ball rebounded off the end pocket.

"That one was all you, not the team," Evan joked.

She playfully rolled her eyes as she handed him the cue stick. Matt took a swig of his beer before taking his turn. Leslie cheered as he knocked in two solid balls in one shot. His second shot wasn't as lucky. He narrowly missed the pocket and set Evan up for an easy score. One-by-one he sent the remaining striped balls into pockets, leaving only the solids and the eight-ball.

"Far right pocket," he called out before taking his shot.

For a brief moment, Celia was so focused on the game it was like the noise around her had become no more than a quiet whisper. It all returned as the eight-ball fell into its designated pocket and she and Evan cheered. Matt shook his head, muttering something about luck, while Leslie laughed cheered with them.

"You want to play another round?" Evan asked.

Celia shook her head. "I'm good."

She walked back over to the table where Jillian was in deep conversation with the beautiful stranger.

"I don't mean to interrupt, but have you seen Thomas?" she asked.

Both women shook their heads. Celia checked her phone, but there were no new notifications. More than twenty-minutes had passed since her last text message and he should've been there by now. She walked around the bar, but he was nowhere to be seen. Evan came up behind her as she was heading towards the door.

"Where are you going?" he asked.

"To see if Thomas is outside."

"I'll come with you."

An uneasy feeling was brewing in the pit of her stomach. *He probably met some fans as he was walking back and took some pictures or something. Perhaps he's just outside, waiting in line. He's going to tease me for worrying.* A long line stretched around the outside of the pub, but Thomas wasn't in it. Nor was he on sidewalk or across the street. Celia's hands were shaky as she dialed his number. Each ring felt like an eternity, but she knew at any second he was going to answer. She was going to hear his voice and her worries would be absolved. He didn't answer. Instead, the robotic-sounding recording told her to leave a message. She tried to say, "Thomas, please call me back," but her words were cut short by the Scottish ambulance's sirens as it whizzed by.

# Twenty-One

Celia and Evan sat in the emergency room's waiting area. A paramedic had answered her fourth distressed phone call to Thomas' phone and told her he was being taken to a nearby hospital. The paramedic hadn't given any inclination to what was wrong, only that Thomas needed medical treatment. Her vague response and hurry to end the call, only fueled Celia's concerns.

The hospital was large, but the waiting room was small and suffocating. Its walls were painted an eggshell white, and the tile floors were white with colored specks. The majority of the blue fabric clad chairs were empty, save for a small family nestled in the corner. A young girl who appeared to have a broken or fractured arm sat with her eyes glued to the cartoon playing on the television.

An older gentleman came out of the swinging doors carrying a clipboard. He wore a white medical coat and a gold stethoscope rested around his neck. His blue eyes were plagued with dark circles. He spoke softly to the woman at the receptionist area, who pointed towards Celia and Evan, before approaching them.

"Hello, are you here for Mr. Richardson?" he asked.

"Yes," Celia said. She and Evan both stood up.

"My name is Dr. McTavish." He shook both of their hands. "I'm overseeing Mr. Richardson's care. What is your relationship to the patient?"

"I'm Celia Stuart... his fiancé, and this is our friend Evan."

She was afraid if she hadn't lied, the doctor wouldn't have disclosed Thomas' condition. She was the closest person to Thomas in the country, but she wasn't family.

"It's nice to meet you both."

"How's Thomas?" Celia wasn't in the mood for pleasantries.

"He lost a lot of blood, but he's stable."

"What happened?" Evan asked.

"Mr. Richardson suffered three gunshot wounds: one to the stomach, and two to the leg."

Celia's skin paled and she nearly fell, but Evan grabbed her arms. Her entire body was numb as tears streamed down her cheeks. So many questions flooded her mind, the most prevalent was how had this even happened? All he was doing was retrieving his wallet from the hotel. She pictured him, sliding his phone back into his pocket after he texted her, only to be confronted by a man dressed in all dark clothing. The man demanded Thomas give him his wallet but ended up shooting him anyway. *But he was shot three times. Why would a robber shoot him that many times? Unless it wasn't a robbery at all, no, perhaps he had been targeted for a different reason.* Suddenly the image of Brandon flashed in her mind, yelling as he was pulled from the coffee shop yelling, "You'll be sorry you did this! I swear, you wait and see!"

The doctor flipped through the pages on the clipboard. "We were able to stop the bleeding, and it appears no major organs were damaged, but we still need to run some tests. He's been unconscious since the ambulance picked him up. Would you mind answering a few questions?"

Celia nodded feebly. Her stomach ached with nausea and the whiskey was at risk of crawling back up her throat.

"Is Mr. Richardson allergic to anything?"

"Not that I'm aware of."

"Does he have any medical conditions?"

His words sucked the oxygen right out of her body. She couldn't lie to him, he was a doctor, and it could put Thomas' health at risk if he didn't know the truth; however, Evan would become another keeper of this secret. The more people who knew, the higher the risk was for his condition to come to light.

"Ma'am? Are you alright?"

"Yes, sorry." She took a deep breath. "He has Acquired Immune Deficiency Syndrome."

Dr. McTavish wrote an illegible note on Thomas' chart, but his face was unreadable. Celia was afraid to look at Evan. She didn't want to know what he was thinking and was afraid there would be unfair judgement in his eyes.

"Is he on any medications?"

She nodded. "He gets an injection of Fuzeon twice daily, but I don't know the dosage."

Celia kept her eyes focused on the ground as Dr. McTavish made more notes. Evan was quiet. His arms were still holding Celia steady.

"Thank you for all the information, you've been helpful." Dr. McTavish slid the pen underneath his clipboard. "As I mentioned previously, we still have some tests to do, so it'll be at least a couple of hours before you can see him. I suggest you go home and rest. You can leave your information with Ms. Clark at the receptionist desk, and I will call as soon as I have an update on his condition."

He shook both their hands before he went back through the doors by the receptionist desk. Evan and Celia were both quiet. The cartoon and the child's soft laughter were the only audible noise in the waiting room.

"What do you want to do?" Evan asked.

Celia shrugged. "I don't want to leave, but I know I'm not doing him any service just sitting here. Might as well go back to the hotel and get some of his things."

"Alright. Why don't you go leave your information like the doc said, and I'll get us a ride to the hotel."

The cab dropped Celia and Evan off a block away from the hotel. Scotland Yard had barricaded the street and part of the sidewalk in front of the hotel where Thomas had been shot. News crews, policeman, a handful of witnesses, and curious spectators were everywhere. Innovative evidence identification markers were placed around the blood-stained sidewalk and by bullet casings. Celia could see the commotion from her hotel room window. Everything felt surreal, like it was part of a movie set, but there were no cameras and Thomas wasn't waiting nearby for his next scene. It was all real.

Evan sat in one of the kitchenette's chair with an untouched cup of coffee in his hands. His expression was peculiar, but unreadable. It was like he was trying to figure out what to say, if there was anything that should be said. Celia sat down next to him. Her eyes were red, and tears stained her cheeks.

"I'm sorry I lied to you about Thomas having diabetes. I didn't know what to say that day, but I knew it wasn't my secret to share."

"You don't have to apologize, I understand." He shook his head. "I'm trying to process everything, but it's overwhelming. Thomas having AIDS pales in comparison to what transpired. He was *shot*."

"It doesn't feel real. I knew better than to let him go by himself, but not even in my darkest nightmares did I imagine something would happen to him. It was supposed to be me."

"What do you mean it was supposed to be you?"

Celia took a deep breath. "Do you remember the day I was attacked by my ex in the coffee shop?"

He nodded.

"When he was being restrained by the group of strangers he yelled, 'you'll be sorry you did this, I swear, you wait and see'. He had this crazed look in his eyes, and the way he said it, I was terrified. I knew he was planning to finish what he started one way or another."

"This is why you've been a bit of a recluse these past few weeks?"

"Yeah." She choked back tears. "I wasn't sure if he was still in Scotland or if he'd gone back to Los Angeles. Scotland Yard wouldn't tell me anything, so I was afraid to venture out. I only ever left the hotel to go to set, and I always returned without stopping anywhere in between. Thomas went out a few times though. He'd go get us something to eat and once he even brought me flowers, but nothing ever happened to him. I never imagined he would be a target."

"You don't know if your crazy ex was the one that shot Thomas, but even if he did— it's not your fault. You can't blame yourself."

Celia nodded. "You're right."

"I know, don't act so surprised." He smiled softly. "Why don't you get some rest, we can go back to the hospital tomorrow if there hasn't been an update by then?"

"I'll try, but I don't know how much sleep I'll be getting. Thank you for all your help today."

"Anytime."

It was late when Celia finally crawled into bed, but she wasn't tired. Even if she had been, sleeping would've been difficult. Every time she closed her eyes, she pictured Thomas lying on the hard sidewalk, gasping for air as pain consumed his entire body. She thought about calling Gwen, it was still in the afternoon in Los Angeles, but she didn't want to call her prematurely. Gwen would want to know everything, and Celia didn't even have a basic outline of what happened. Besides, there was no use in getting her all worried when she was halfway across the world and nothing she could do to help her brother. *I will call her as soon as I have an update, or perhaps Thomas will be able to call her himself. It would be better coming from him than me.*

She grabbed the remote and flipped on the television. An old black-and-white sitcom was playing, something far too cheery for her mood. She surfed the channels, but nothing took her interest, until she reached the news channel. All in red and capitalized the running-headline said, "Breaking News: Suspected Gunman Caught While Attempting to Board Plane".

Celia's mouth fell open and the remote crashed onto the floor. Hastily she retrieved the remote from the floor and turned up the volume. A pretty blonde with a thick Scottish accent was sitting behind a large white desk. A grainy picture of a man taken from security video appeared next to her on screen. He was dressed in all black, wore sunglasses and a black cap. The only identifiable feature was the blond hair that peeked out from underneath the man's cap.

"Witnesses say the alleged suspect pulled out a handgun and opened fire on a man as he walked down the street. He led authorities on a wild chase that ended at the airport, where the man was attempting to board a flight to Los Angeles. The identities of the alleged suspect and victim are not being released at this time, but authorities say that the victim is currently stable and at the hospital for treatment to his injuries. If you have any information about this case, please contact Scotland Yard at the number listed below."

Celia barely made it to the toilet in time before the shot, the little beer she had drank, and her dinner were purged into the bowl. Her throat burned, almost like when Brandon had choked her. She flushed the toilet and tried to stand, but her legs were too weak. There had been little doubt in her mind that someone besides Brandon had shot Thomas, but the confirmation from the news anchor still hit her like a truck. She didn't need a better-quality photograph or even for the news to utter his name. His destination, Los Angeles, was the great reveal.

The hospital was crowded on Saturday morning. Almost all of the seats in the waiting area were occupied. The sounds of children's coughs and cries echoed off the high ceilings and overshadowed conversations between the staff and parties trying to inquire about their loved ones. Celia stood against a far wall in a vain attempt to avoid the chaos. She wore jeans and a sweatshirt. Her hair was messily pulled into a braid and her face was absent of any makeup. Circles sat underneath both her eyes, a testament of her sleepless night. Her arms were tightly wrapped around a stuffed bear she had purchased from the gift store for Thomas. Evan walked up carrying two coffees. He was also dressed casually in jeans and a t-shirt.

"I know you said you didn't want anything, but I got you a coffee anyway." He handed her one of the coffees. "The barista put an ungodly amount of sugar in it, so it should be to your liking."

"Thank you." She was still nauseous from the night prior, but she forced herself to take a sip of the coffee. Her entire body stiffened as Dr. McTavish walked through the swinging doors. He stopped by the receptionist desk before approaching Celia and Evan.

"Good morning, I was just about to call you when I was informed you were already here." Dr. McTavish smiled. "Thomas regained consciousness earlier this morning and has been doing well despite his injuries. He has been speaking coherently and was able to eat breakfast."

"Can I see him?"

The doctor nodded. "He's finishing up with an officer from Scotland Yard, but he's able to have visitors now. I ask that you limit your interactions to one person at a time, and don't say or do anything that could upset him. He doesn't need to get worked up."

"Understood." Celia looked at Evan. "Do you mind if I go?"

"Are you kidding me? Go on."

She mouthed, "Thank you," and followed Dr. McTavish back through the swinging doors and to the elevator. It slowly ascended to the third floor and it felt like an eternity before the elevator's doors opened.

"He's in room 314B," Dr. McTavish said as they entered the hallway.

It was quiet. The hushed conversations, soft footsteps, and beeping of EKG's were a welcome break from the hectic environment of the waiting room. Celia picked up her pace as she passed an officer in the hallway, but lost her nerve at the doorway to 314B. She knew Thomas was in there, but in what capacity? Dr. McTavish said he was doing *well*, but a doctor's interpretation could be different from her own.

"It's okay, you can go in," Dr. McTavish said gently.

Celia took a deep breath and opened the door. Thomas wasn't immediately visible from the entrance into the room. It was set up with a small hallway that had the bathroom to the left, and a sink with cabinets to the right. A television on the right wall was turned onto a movie, but the volume was muted. The far wall had a large window with chairs pushed under it. Thomas was lying in a bed on the left. His eyes were shut and his skin was sickeningly pale. An IV was connected to his inner right elbow and quietly dripped. There was an EKG on the left side of his bed and a small dresser on the right. A whiteboard on the wall had his vitals recorded by the night shift nurse, along with his pain level, and a list of medications. Next to the board was a computer the nurses utilized.

"Thomas?" her voice was barely above a whisper, but he immediately opened his eyes and his lips curved into a smile.

"Hey you," he said.

Tears streamed down her cheeks as she rushed to his side, nearly spilling the coffee onto the floor. She sat the coffee onto the dresser next to a water cup and pulled a chair over to his bedside. Thomas tried to sit up and winced.

"Don't move," Celia said.

"There's a control for the bed on my right side. Would you mind raising the top half so I can sit up?"

She nodded. Carefully she reached over him and pressed the button, slowly bringing the top of the bed up to where he was almost sitting up.

"Thank you." Thomas extended his free hand to her as she sat down. They interlocked their fingers. "You don't know how good it is to see you."

Dr. McTavish stepped forward. "How are you feeling?"

"Like I was shot three times."

"Well you were." He walked over to the computer and logged in. "You're a lucky man, Mr. Richardson. None of the bullets hit any major organs or arteries. Two of the bullets went straight through your leg and the third bullet is lodged in soft tissue above your small intestine. Due to its location, we are not going to attempt to remove it."

"You're just going to leave it in there?" Celia asked.

Dr. McTavish nodded. "The risk of causing further damage during surgery to remove the bullet is too high. Leaving the bullet in place should not cause any pain nor discomfort for your fiancé, and scar tissue will eventually form around it."

Thomas glanced at Celia and her cheeks flushed. Of all the information Dr. McTavish was saying, it appeared that the only concern of his was the word fiancé.

"I will be back tomorrow afternoon to check on your condition. In the meantime, a nurse will be checking in on you every few hours and providing pain medication as needed. If you need anything, you can press that red button on the end of the control and it will notify the nurses up front."

"Thank you," Thomas said.

Dr. McTavish nodded at both Thomas and Celia before leaving. The door clicked loudly behind him. Celia set the plush bear next to Thomas and kissed his forehead. He was sweating but his skin was icy cold.

"Fiancé huh?"

Celia rolled her eyes. "What else was I supposed to say? I figured he wouldn't release any information to someone who wasn't family."

"Sure." He winked at her. "Does Gwen know?"

"No, I wanted to wait until I knew more about your condition. I also figured it might be better coming from you, since it was my ex who shot you."

"Brandon was the one who shot me?"

"You don't remember?"

He shook his head. "I remember being at the bar, but I wasn't able to get in so I went back to the hotel to get something. Everything else in between leaving the hotel and waking up here is a blank. I didn't even know I was shot until a nurse told me."

"I'm so sorry, I shouldn't have let you walk back alone last night."

"I'm glad you weren't there. If he shot me, who knows what he would've done to you. Did the authorities catch him?"

"Yes. He was trying to board a flight back to Los Angeles. Neither his identity nor yours has been released to the public yet, but I'm not sure how long that will last," she took a deep breath. "There's something else I need to tell you and I don't know how to say it."

"What is it?"

"Evan knows."

He raised an eyebrow. "Knows what?"

"The truth. He knows you don't have diabetes."

"Oh."

"He was with me when Dr. McTavish was inquiring about your medical history. I didn't know what to do, you were unconscious, and I was afraid if I wasn't honest the doctor might give you something that wouldn't mix well with your medication." She started crying. "I'm not trying to make excuses, I know I broke my promise and I understand if you want me to walk out that door and never come back."

"Are you done?"

She nodded.

"Good. I'm not mad at you, you did nothing wrong. If Evan decides to tell people, so be it, it won't be your fault."

"I don't think he will."

"All the more reason not be upset then. Also, if I had wanted to get rid of you, I would've done it *before* I was shot. You're stuck with me now."

She smiled. "I'm perfectly okay with that."

"As am I."

# Twenty-Two

The crowd of paparazzi outside the Los Angeles International Airport was worse than usual. How they knew when Celia's and Thomas' flight was scheduled to arrive was unknown, but security had been amplified in preparation. It had been over a week since Thomas was shot. He was discharged and given medical clearance for the flight, but he still wasn't one-hundred percent himself. His body was bruised around the entry and exit wounds, and where the IV had been. His leg was incredibly sore and he walked with a limp whenever his pain medication wore off. The sutures were healing, but he still had another week before his stitches could be removed.

Gwen was standing alone in the airport terminal. Her foot anxiously tapped the floor. She was dressed casually, but her expression was serious. She had been standing in that exact spot for almost an hour. She scanned every crowd that dispersed through the terminal looking for Thomas. Her expression softened when she finally saw him. If it wasn't public knowledge he had been shot, he could've been easily mistaken as a man with a cold. His skin was pale. He was wearing sweatpants and a hooded sweatshirt. Celia followed close behind with their carry-on bags.

"Thomas!" Gwen threw her arms around him and he winced.

"I'm sorry." She released her grip and stepped back. "You look like Hell. Are you alright?"

"I appreciate the confidence boost, but I'm fine. How are you?"

"I've been better. It was a zoo trying to find parking this morning and I was afraid I would be late, but I ended up being early."

Celia stood silently behind him. She felt like an outsider as she watched them, like she shouldn't be there. She had come to terms that the shooting wasn't her fault, but it didn't mean other people felt the same. Celia had overheard the conversation when Thomas told Gwen what had happened, and Gwen was clearly upset at more people than just Brandon. She had scrutinized security, his co-stars, and ultimately Celia. She was likely unaware Celia had overheard the conversation, but she wasn't hiding her feelings.

"Why don't you go ahead and get your luggage? I'll bring my car around and we can get out of here."

"That's fine."

Gwen hugged him again, nodded at Celia, and walked towards the exit. Thomas waited until she was gone before he turned to Celia.

"I'm sorry. Give her some time and she'll be back to her normal self. She is quite fond of you, but she's not handling the situation very well."

Celia shrugged. "I don't think there's a textbook way to handle your brother being shot by his girlfriend's crazy ex."

"Touché."

Police officers and armed security guards were lined up outside the airport like a human barricade. Traffic was momentarily at a standstill to allow Celia and Thomas to safely leave the vicinity. Still, the idea of stepping through the airport doors into the chaos was daunting. Thomas took Celia's hand into his own and pushed through the doors. Immediately the shouting began.

"Thomas! Mr. Richardson! How are you feeling?"

"Celia do you feel guilty Thomas was shot by your ex-boyfriend?"

"Have either of you spoken to Brandon since the incident?"

"Care to tell your side of the story?"

One of the security officers loaded their luggage while Celia and Thomas climbed inside the backseat of the vehicle. Led Zeppelin was screaming on the radio, but it merely dulled their shouts. Celia couldn't even concentrate on her own thoughts, her heart felt like it was going to burst out of her chest. The officer closed the trunk and gave Gwen a thumbs up. The tires screeched as she pressed the gas pedal and the vehicle peeled away from the curb. A few determined cameramen attempted to run after them, but were stopped by the traffic. Gwen lowered the volume on the radio. The lull of the road and passing cars was a welcome change from the paparazzi.

"That was intense," Gwen said.

"Yeah, no kidding." Thomas sighed. "I hope that's the end of the media circus, but something tells me it's far from over."

"At least it's not the worst headline you've been in."

Thomas rolled his eyes. "That's debatable."

"I'm glad you're back... *both* of you." She glanced at Celia and smiled.

"Thank you, it's good to be back," Celia said.

Thomas put his arm around Celia as she rested her head on his shoulder. His heart was softly beating in her ear.

"The girls are excited as well, they wanted to come pick you up. It was a bit of a battle getting them to daycare."

"Daycare? When did the girls start going to daycare?" Thomas asked.

Gwen bit her lip and her grip tightened on the steering wheel. "They've been going to daycare since early February. I was going to wait until a few days after you got back to tell you, but a lot has changed while you were gone. I found out in early January that Brett has been having an affair on and off for years. Instead of chocolates or a dumb card, I was served divorce papers on Valentine's Day."

"What a bastard. How are Delilah and Danielle taking it?"

"That's one of the words I'd use to describe him." She sighed. "As well as to be expected for their age. They don't really understand what's going on, so I'm doing my best to try and keep it simple."

Celia was eager to get out of Gwen's car by the time they reached the house. Her words had brought back memories Celia had struggled to suppress over the years: her mother screaming at the top of her lungs, throwing whatever was in reach at her father while he sat at the kitchen table. Celia would lock herself in her room, grab her *iPod* and turn the volume up as loud as she could. When she couldn't ignore the screams, she would sneak out of her bedroom window and walk to the library. Sometimes she would read, but most of the times she would sit in a one of the stuffed armchairs and relish in the silence.

The sun was ruthless, and the California heat was a stark contrast from the cool temperatures in Scotland. Celia was sweating by the time she and Gwen had finished carrying all the luggage inside Thomas' house. All repairs and renovations had been completed and it was practically unrecognizable from the inside. The walls were painted a pale blue and multiple cat shelves were installed on the once naked living room wall space. The soiled couches and old recliner were replaced with a brown leather recliner and a matching L-shaped couch. A plush black rug sat in the middle of the living room floor. Thomas was resting on the new couch with a purring Scooter in his arms.

"I think that's everything," Celia said.

"Next time you guys should pack lighter." Gwen wiped the sweat onto her sleeve. "Or not get hurt so you can help."

Thomas laughed. "My plan all along was to get incapacitated so I wouldn't have to handle the luggage."

"It's a good thing being shot didn't damage his sense of humor," Celia said.

"I don't know if I can agree with you on that."

Celia sat down next to Thomas and Scooter crawled into her lap. His purring amplified as she scratched underneath his chin.

"I have to pick up the twins soon, but are you sure you two are okay on your own? I brought over some bottled water when I dropped Scooter off, but your fridge is empty and I'm guessing the food in the pantry isn't in date."

"I think we can manage. We'll probably order takeout for lunch and maybe swing by the grocery store later today if not tomorrow. I'm not opposed to dining on stale graham crackers," Thomas said.

Gwen rolled her eyes.

"I'll take care of him, don't worry," Celia said.

"Thank you." She got her keys from her pocket. "I'm going to bring the girls by in a few days, so you better rest up. Please don't hesitate to call me if you need anything."

"I won't." Thomas got up and hugged her. He whispered something in her ear before stepping back. She nodded, waved to Celia, and walked out the front door. Thomas followed behind her and locked it. He waited until she was in her car before joining Celia on the couch.

"What do you think?" he asked.

"I'm tired and could use a nap."

"I meant about the furniture and repairs."

"Oh." She laughed. "I like it. It feels like a new place."

He nodded. "I like it too. It's nice that we won't have to worry about anyone trying to break in and vandalize it any time soon with Brandon locked up in Scotland awaiting trial."

"Surely if he's convicted of the attempted murder charges, he won't see the outside of a cell for a long time."

"That's if there's a trial. The evidence is damning, I wouldn't be surprised if he is offered and takes a plea bargain of some sort. Honestly, I hope he does. I don't want to travel back for a lengthy trial."

"I'd rather not talk about him, nor the possibility of a trial anymore today. For the first time we're actually free. We can go out without having to worry about looking over our shoulders. I've forgotten what that feels like."

"I know." He kissed her hand. "I want to do something special to celebrate. Would you be up for grabbing dinner somewhere tonight and walking out on the beach? I know I can't actually swim yet, but I miss the smell of the ocean air."

"As long as I get a nap beforehand, I'd love to."

He smiled. "Perfect. It's a date."


The sun was close to setting, but the air was still hot and humid as Thomas and Celia walked hand in hand down the beach. Seagulls bobbled around the edge of the coastline, squabbling at the beach goers whenever they happened to get too close. Celia was wearing a long plum colored halter dress. The cotton material was thin and airy. Her hair was pulled into a ponytail. Thomas wore jeans and a short-sleeve button-up shirt.

"I can't believe you ordered a cheeseburger." Thomas laughed.

"I can't believe you let *me* drive your Mustang to the restaurant. Didn't you say Gwen hasn't even gotten to drive it?"

"Yeah— well I didn't think it would be a good idea for me to drive in my current condition. I will say though, don't get used to it," Thomas winked.

"Duly noted." Celia squeezed his hand. "Thank you for dinner, it was nice."

"Thanks for agreeing to go out, I'm sure you're still tired."

"Yeah. The nap had the opposite effect of what I was intending, so I'll definitely be sleeping in tomorrow."

"Me too."

They passed a group of teenagers hitting a volleyball over a small net. Their laughter overshadowed the crashing waves. Thomas was growing increasingly sweaty as they walked. He was looking forward, but his mind appeared to be elsewhere. Celia stopped, bringing him back into the present.

"Are you okay? I know you haven't walked this far since before you were shot. We can head back if you need to," Celia said.

Thomas shook his head. "We're almost there."

"Almost *where*?"

"You'll see, just be patient."

"I'll try, but you should know by now that patience isn't one of my strong suits."

"Trust me, I know."

As they walked closer towards the Santa Monica Pier, red flower petals were scattered and mixed in with the sand. It was strange, but with the pier close by, Celia shrugged it off. Some aspiring social media influencer or tourist probably had a photoshoot at the beach. It was fathomable. In fact, Celia was fairly certain some type of shoot had taken place when she saw four lit torches stuck in the sand. Thomas led her into the middle of the torches, where flower petals in a heart shaped formation were lying atop the sand.

"Thomas, I don't know if we should be here. It looks like someone arranged this," she said.

"I'm sure it's fine. Do you remember in Scotland when you called me a fool?"

"Yeah." Her face flushed. "Wasn't my finest moment."

He smiled. "You weren't wrong to call me one. I was so caught up in worrying about the things we can't do, I didn't take time to imagine what we could. I know I've said it before, but this is the happiest I've been in as long as I can remember—probably even before that. When I woke up in the hospital with no recollection of what brought me there, I was terrified something had happened to you. The thought of all the things we had yet to do and all the words still to be said was overwhelming. I decided I wasn't going to let myself be held back any longer by 'what ifs'."

Thomas gritted his teeth as he got down on one knee. He fished out a ring box from his pocket and took a deep breath. Celia's face reddened. Some of the other people on the beach had stopped what they were doing and were watching them.

"Celia Anne Stuart, would you do me the honor of becoming my wife?" He opened the ring box. Inside was a thin white gold band with three delicate sapphires.

Celia was sweating now too. It felt surreal, like she was dreaming, but never in her wildest dreams did she imagine *this* would happen. She would've laughed in anyone's face if they had told her last year she would be standing on a beach with Thomas Richardson down on one knee. Then again, this past year was anything but expected. Thomas' face grew concerned with each passing second without an answer.

"Are you being serious right now? You're asking *me* to marry you?"

"I wouldn't joke about something as serious as this. What do you say?"

"I think you're crazy." She smiled as tears began running down her cheeks. "Of course, I'll marry you."

Thomas slipped the ring on her finger and she helped pull him to his feet. He threw his arms around her and pulled her into a kiss. The strangers on the beach clapped and cheered, smiles beaming on their faces. A few even snapped pictures, making Celia feel self-conscious.

"Can we get out of here?" she asked.

"Yeah of course."

Thomas interlocked his fingers with hers as they started the walk back. Beachgoers were packing up to leave as the sun was almost set.

"How were you able to set that up?" Celia asked. To her

knowledge, Thomas had been home all day, albeit she was asleep for the majority of it.

"Gwen actually did the heavy lifting. I told her what I wanted to do, and she offered to help. Granted, I asked before I knew about everything going on with Brett."

"That was sweet of her."

"Yeah, I don't deserve a sister like her." He stopped. "I am a little confused about one thing though. I thought you said you wouldn't hesitate if I proposed to you."

Celia shrugged. "I just wanted to make you sweat."

"Mission accomplished."

# Twenty-Three

Celia sat at the edge of the pool with her legs hanging off into the water. She wore a straw sunhat, and a black polka dot bikini. Her pale skin was lathered in sunscreen. The hot July sun refracted light off her ring and onto the pavement. Thomas was manning the grill under the gazebo. He wore his pineapple print swim trunks. Faint scars marked his skin where the bullets had torn through. A plastic folding table with a red, white, and blue cover was next to the gazebo. A crockpot of queso, chips, potato salad, fruit pie, hamburger and hotdog buns, plastic utensils, paper plates, and cupcakes sat atop the table. Thomas and Celia had invited several people over for a small get together, including Gwen, Meghan and her husband, and Evan, to celebrate the Fourth of July.

Evan sat down next to Celia. He wore red swim trunks, and his hair was damp from being in the pool only a few moments prior. He had a beer in one hand and a half-eaten hotdog in the other.

"I can't believe you guys have lived only a few minutes away from me and we've never ran into each other before filming," Evan said.

Celia shrugged. "There's so many people around here, maybe we did and didn't realize it."

"Quite possibly, but I think I'd remember you. Especially if I heard you snort-laughing."

Celia's face flushed and she playfully pushed his shoulder.

"Easy now killer." Evan took a sip of beer. "Listen, I'm sorry I've been a little distant. I wasn't trying to ignore you nor Thomas, I just had a lot going on."

Considering everything that happened in Scotland, Celia had assumed she and Thomas' co-stars would've remained in touch after filming had finished; however, it had been over a month, and Leslie was the only one who stayed in contact and she wasn't even in the same state. The few times Celia or Thomas reached out to Evan, he never responded. It surprised them both when Evan had agreed to come over.

"My life has been pretty much a bad country song. My girlfriend broke up with me two days after I got back. Apparently starting a new relationship right before leaving for another country is not a great idea. I had to put my dog down two weeks ago. I know she was old and arthritic, but it didn't make things any easier. On top of it all, I'm still trying to wrap my head around everything that happened in Scotland."

"I'm sorry," Celia said.

He shrugged. "It's not your fault. It was just a lot to handle. I haven't said anything to anyone, if that's what you're worried about."

"What do you mean?"

"You know." He nodded towards Thomas. "I figured the main reason you guys were checking in with me was to make sure I didn't say anything."

"Are you being serious? Do you think that's why we invited you here today?"

"You tell me."

Celia shook her head. "I think of you as a friend, not a liability. You wouldn't have been invited otherwise."

"Good. I grew quite fond of you in Scotland, and I'd be disappointed if you saw me as anything less."

Danielle screamed as Delilah splashed water towards her. Both girls wore matching swimsuits and inflatable arm floaties, making it impossible to distinguish them apart. Meghan was talking with Gwen by the patio door, while her husband Eric was tossing a Frisbee around with some guys.

"Congratulations on the engagement by the way." Evan finished his beer. "Have you guys set a date?"

"Thank you. We haven't decided on a venue yet, but we're planning for Halloween night."

"Wow, that's soon."

She shrugged. "We have plenty of time to get preparations in order. Besides, if we wait, it could get delayed with the press tour and premieres."

"Your ex's pending trial date doesn't have anything to do with the date, does it?"

"Of course not, I don't know why you would even suggest that." Celia's tone came off harsher than she intended. "Listen, I don't mean to be rude, but I don't want to talk about Brandon, think about him, or anything of the sort. I've already been harassed enough by the media about it, and I'm just ready to move on."

"Sorry, I didn't mean to upset you."

"It's fine."

Thomas came over with two plates and sat down on the other side of Celia. He handed her a plate with the cheeseburger and large helping of potato salad. His own plate consisted of chips, queso, and a mustard drizzled hot dog.

"It's nice to see you again Evan," he said.

"You too. Um, do you guys have a bathroom I can use?"

"Yeah, go inside and down the hall. It'll be the first door on your left."

"Thanks." Evan quickly got up and headed towards the house. He didn't make eye-contact with the people he passed.

"Is he okay?" Thomas asked.

Celia sat her untouched plate of food down next to her. "I don't know. He's had a bad few weeks with a breakup and losing his dog, but he thought we were only reaching out to him so we could 'keep tabs on him'."

"People handle grief in different ways. I don't understand how he could jump to that conclusion though. I know I was a little out of it with all the medication, but I thought he seemed fine the last time I saw him."

"I thought he was fine too. Do you think we need to be worried about him actually saying something?"

"All you need to worry about is what dress you're going to look stunning in at our wedding." He smiled. "For the first time since we've met, there's nothing holding us back. We don't have to worry about he-who-shall-not-be-named lurking around nor anyone else for that matter. You have nothing to be concerned about."

"You're right, thank you."

"Aren't I always?"

She rolled her eyes. "You're lucky you have food right now."

"And why's that? Is it deterring you from doing something like *this*—" He pushed her with his freehand off the edge and into the water. The water was icy cold against her skin. Thomas was laughing uncontrollably when she emerged. Her hat had floated off and her hair was soaked.

"Did you really just do that?"

He shrugged. "You looked like you could use a swim."

"You know what." A devious smile crept on her face. "I change my mind."

Before he could even attempt to flee, Celia grabbed both of his arms and pulled him in the water with her. Chips went everywhere and his hot dog sunk down next to her sunglasses. Celia tried to swim away from him but wasn't quick enough. Thomas caught her and brought her back to him.

"Remember who started this," Celia said.

"I think I'm more concerned about who sent my perfectly grilled hot dog into the deep end."

His grip around her tightened and he pulled her under the water with him. She wrapped her legs around his waist as they floated to the bottom. Thomas leaned forward and kissed her. The water dulled the noise around them. It was like they were in their own little bubble with their own atmosphere. Their oxygen shared with each kiss, all they needed was each other.

Celia sat cross-legged on the carpeted floor in Thomas' bedroom with her laptop in front of her. Her hair was pulled into a messy bun, and she was casually dressed in a t-shirt and shorts. It was early in the evening and the sun had barely set. Celia was on *Pinterest*, and the screen was cluttered with different black lace wedding gowns. The television quietly hummed in the background, but she wasn't paying attention to it. Different bridal magazines were scattered around her, and Scooter was closely watching her from the bed.

Thomas walked in carrying his wallet and keys. He was wearing a t-shirt, and jeans. His tired expression shifted to concern when he saw Celia on the floor.

"Why are you in the exact same spot you were when I left two hours ago? Please tell me you've at least eaten dinner."

"I didn't eat dinner, but I did use the bathroom once."

Thomas sighed and shook his head.

"I know I'm being a tad obsessive, but Meghan said it would go smoother at stores if I actually had an idea of what I wanted my dress to look like," Celia said.

Thomas set his keys and wallet on the dresser. "A tad is an

understatement. I swear you've been looking at the same pictures for the past two days. Did you at least get somewhat of an idea?"

"I think so. You want to see?"

"Sure." He kicked over a magazine and sat down next to her.

She opened a new internet tab and pulled up her *Pinterest* Board labeled, "Wedding Ideas". There were pictures of gothic style cakes, bouquets, headpieces, and décor. At the bottom of the page was a model wearing a two-piece dress. The top half of the dress was sleeveless, all black, and composed of lace. The bottom of the dress was fashioned out of grey, white, and black tulle. Its uneven edges drug against the ground. The woman wearing the dress was standing at the edge of a forest. Her lips were painted red and she wore a headband composed of black and grey faux roses.

"I wouldn't have my makeup done as dark as hers, but this is the style I'm looking for," Celia said.

"I think that would suit you beautifully." He caressed her lower back. "I hope you know how happy you make me. I cannot wait for you to become my wife."

"I can't wait either. How were Gwen and the girls?"

"The girls were their usual happy, energetic selves. I'm still not convinced that Gwen doesn't give them a bucket of candy on the days I visit. Gwen is doing okay given the circumstances. I think things are going to be better after the divorce is finalized next month and she can move on with her life."

"You think asking her to help with wedding stuff might be a welcome distraction?"

"Definitely. I'm sure she'd love to help, but I can't say she won't try and take the reins. Gwen has always been big on planning events. Wait until it's the twins' birthday, you'll see her in all her glory. Last year was dinosaur themed, and I swear she had props from *Jurassic Park*."

"That sounds amazing. I'll give her a call sometime this week."

Celia's stomach growled. "I guess I should probably get something to eat."

"Come on, I'll fix us both something."

"You haven't eaten either?"

Thomas shook his head. "They were eating left-over lasagna, and you know how I feel about lasagna."

"That it's a sorry excuse for pasta?"

"Exactly."

Celia powered-off her laptop and gathered up all the magazines before following Thomas into the kitchen. A carton of eggs, package of blueberries, pancake mix, and bottle of maple syrup sat on the counter.

"Are you okay with breakfast for dinner?" Thomas asked as he carried an electric griddle over to the island.

Celia smiled. "Of course."

She took a seat across from him at one of the new barstools. The kitchen was one of the rooms not targeted during Brandon's break-in, so it wasn't included during the renovation process. The only change was adding three dark stained wooden barstools to one side of the island.

"Did I see *The Thing* was on when I walked in earlier?"

"Honestly, I can't tell you. I wasn't really paying attention, I just had it on for noise."

"What? Come on Celia, it's a classic. It was the film that really got me into horror movies."

"I was so focused on dresses I didn't even realized two hours had gone by let alone what was playing on TV. How about we watch it after dinner?"

"Would you be up for it? I know horror isn't your thing." Thomas cracked two eggs over the mixing bowl. The yolk slumped into the powdery batter.

"As long as you don't judge me if I have to cover my eyes every now and again, I'll be okay watching it."

Thomas laughed. "I can't make any promises, but I'll do my best. It should be in my DVD collection if you want to go ahead and set it out."

"Sure."

Celia walked into the living room. Thomas' DVD collection was on display in a wide wooden bookshelf below the television. He had around two-hundred movies. The movies were organized by genre, and alphabetized. Horror was his largest collection, with romantic-comedies being the smallest. *The Thing* was nestled in between *The Texas Chainsaw Massacre* and *Thinner*. As Celia grabbed it a crash echoed throughout the house. She ran back to the kitchen where Thomas was on the floor with his hand pressed against his side. The mixing bowl was on the ground, whisk still inside it, and pancake batter was splashed across the floor.

"Oh my God." Celia knelt next to Thomas. "Are you alright? What happened?"

"Yeah, I think so. I was just whisking everything together when I felt this sharp pain in my stomach. I don't know if it was a muscle spasm or something but I dropped the bowl and the next thing I knew, I was on the ground."

Celia pressed the back of her hand to his forehead. It was warm and damp with sweat. "You feel feverish. Have you been okay until now?"

"Besides not having much of an appetite, this has been the first time something has been off. I haven't done anything out of the ordinary, so I don't know why I would be in pain."

"Maybe you ate something weird or you're getting sick?"

"Maybe."

Celia draped his arm over her shoulder and helped him stand. They walked over to the couch and sat down.

"I'm going to go get you some Tylenol, but I think it would be best if you took it easy for the rest of the night. I can take over dinner," Celia said.

"Can I at least help clean up the mess I made?"

"No, I can handle it." She stood up. "How about instead of cooking, I order a pizza?"

"That's fine with me."

She kissed his forehead before heading to the bathroom for Tylenol. She had an uneasy feeling in the pit of her stomach. *What would make Thomas have a reaction like that?* Thomas hadn't exactly eased back into things after his recovery, it was more like he went from zero to sixty in a matter of days. His schedule was full with auditions and wedding planning, leaving little time for him to take it easy, but he seemed fine— or at least he pretended to be. Perhaps he had been so tired of being side-lined that he was pushing himself too hard.

When Celia came back into the living room, Thomas was still on the couch. Scooter was lying next to him, purring. Thomas smiled, but his face was pained.

"Thank you," he said.

"You would tell me if you weren't feeling okay—right?"

He nodded. "I know what you're probably thinking. It has been an adjustment getting back into my normal routine, but I haven't been feeling bad this entire time. A little more tired than usual, sure, but it was nothing a cup of coffee couldn't handle."

"I just wanted to make sure." She smiled. "Are you sure you're up for a movie tonight? I wouldn't blame you if you wanted to take a raincheck and go to bed early."

"Are you really trying to get out of our agreement right now?"

"What? No. I just don't want you to stay up if you're not feeling well."

"Good because you're not getting out of this. A deal is a deal.

We're watching *The Thing* tonight, and there's nothing you can do to change my mind."

Celia shook her head. "You're ridiculous."

"I know, but you love me anyway."

"Yeah, I do."

# Twenty-Four

Celia stood at the entrance of the dress shop with Gwen and Meghan on either side of her. She was dressed casually in a t-shirt and shorts. Her hair was down and slightly tousled from the wind. Gwen wore a polo shirt and jeans, and Meghan was in a summer-dress that accentuated her new baby bump. The shop was set up more like a warehouse than a boutique. The walls and concrete floors were bland, absent of any decorations other than signs towards the fitting area and check out. Large mirrors, ten feet high by five feet wide, were placed outside of the dressing rooms and beside the accessories. Spinning racks of dresses were stationed all around the floor. All of the dresses were grouped by style, not color or size, giving an impression of chaos and disorganization. Britney Spears' *Toxic* was barely audible over the air conditioner running overhead.

"Are you sure about this place? These are more like prom dresses," Gwen said.

Celia nodded. "I have to try something different if I want to find what I'm looking for."

This was third shop they had visited in the past two weeks, and none of the shops had *the* dress. Sure, she had tried on beautiful dresses, but none of them were black nor gave her the I-am-actually-getting-married feeling a bridal gown is supposed to.

"I'm with Celia on this. This wedding is anything but traditional. We're going to have to think outside of the box to find what she's looking for," Meghan said.

Gwen shrugged. "Let's start looking then."

Celia immediately headed to the back of the store towards the fitting rooms. The store was vacant save for the two employees who were more concerned with their own conversations than Celia, Gwen, or Meghan. It wasn't like at a high-end boutique where the employees were as vulturous as cars salesmen. They'd offer sparkling water or cheap champagne in hopes it would bolster their chances of a sale and a nice commission.

Celia started shuffling through the dresses on the rack. There was a black dress nestled in between a white and red one. It was different from the one she ogled at on *Pinterest*. It had a V-neck bodice composed of black and white lace and an A-line chiffon skirt that draped onto the floor. There were two slits in the skirt that revealed a second layer of chiffon that was white in color. The back of the dress was open with sheer beige lace and fastened together by a row of shiny black buttons. Celia pulled it off the rack and traced the lace with her fingers.

"I found one I want to try, but I'm going to need help with the buttons," Celia called out.

"Alright, be over in a second," Meghan said.

Celia entered the first small stall. Of the dressing rooms, it was the only one without discarded dresses lying about from customers who had changed their minds. She stripped out of her clothes and stepped into the gown. She held it up as Meghan fastened the buttons. It was a perfect fit, flattering to her shape. Meghan fluffed out the skirt and stepped back.

"You look amazing," Meghan said.

Celia smiled. "Thank you."

She walked in front of the large mirrors. Butterflies stirred in her stomach as she stared at her reflection. Goosebumps were on her skin. She twirled around, and the chiffon skirt floated with her.

Gwen walked over with several dressed slung over her arm. "Something tells me you're not going to need these. This is by far my favorite dress you've tried on so far; however, your opinion is what matters. What do you think?"

"I think it's perfect. It feels like it was made for me." She spun around again. "This is what Charlie Chaplin must've felt like when he tried on his signature hat the first time."

"So you're saying this is the one?" Meghan asked.

"One-hundred-percent! This is my wedding dress."

Meghan clapped her hands together. "Yes! I'm so happy for you!"

"What do you say we celebrate with lunch?" Gwen asked.

"I would love to," Celia said.

"I wish I could, but you guys are going to have to go without me. I have an appointment with my OBGYN in an hour."

"Next time then?" Celia asked.

Meghan smiled. "Absolutely!"


Celia and Gwen ended up at a nearby café. It was quiet, even for an early Tuesday afternoon, with not many tables occupied. They opted for a seat outside on the patio with a view of the ocean. The salted sea air engulfed them. Their waiter, a young guy who appeared to be in his late teens, brought Celia lemonade and Gwen a sweet tea while they looked over the menu.

Gwen folded her menu up and sat it on the table. "Thank you for letting me be a part of your wedding. I'm sure Thomas put you up to this, but it's been great to be able to concentrate on something besides the divorce."

"I promise he didn't put me up to anything. It was my idea, and I should be the one thanking you." Celia smiled. "You've been a God-send. I don't know how I would've been able to do this without your help. We've already got the venue squared away, my gown and the bridesmaid dresses, and we're close to finalizing with the caterer."

"I'm happy to help. I will say, I was a little surprised you would ask me and not someone like your mother."

"I'm not close with my mother. I still haven't decided if I'm even going to invite her to the wedding."

"I'm sorry."

Celia shook her head. "It's alright. I came to terms with the fact that I would never have a traditional mother-daughter relationship with her a long time ago. What about your parents? Thomas doesn't speak much about them."

"Well, our father passed a few years ago from liver cancer. He and Thomas were really close, so it is hard for him to talk about him. Our mother moved to Florida two years ago to live with our aunt. She's not a fan of flying, so I don't see her as often as I'd like to. She calls every other week though and has become tech-savvy enough to do FaceTime calls with the twins about twice a month."

"I'm sorry about your father. My dad passed away when I was young, and there will always be a void in my life from his absence." She sighed. "Do you think your mother will be able to come to the wedding?"

"Don't worry, she wouldn't miss it for the world. She's really excited to meet you. Even being on the other side of the country, she can see how happy you make Thomas— we all can. He really loves you."

"I'm happy to hear you say that. We've certainly had our ups and downs, but he's the best thing to ever happen to me. I can't imagine my life without him."

Before Gwen could respond, the waiter walked up with a small notebook. "Are you two ready to order?"

They both nodded.

"I'll have the waffle plate," Gwen said.

"I'd like the chicken sandwich with a side of fries, but I want it plain with no mayonnaise."

The waiter quickly jotted down their orders before retreating back inside the café. Celia's phone buzzed on the table. Celia raised an eyebrow as she read the text message from Thomas. It said, "I have a surprise for you. Don't make any plans for tomorrow."

"What do you think this is about?" Celia asked, briefly showing the phone to Gwen.

"Maybe he's going to take you dancing?"

"I doubt it, he has two left feet remember? I'm not sure how our first dance is going to go, but I may need to invest in steel-toed boots."

Gwen laughed. "I guess that explains the dance lessons."

"Dance lessons? What are you talking about?"

"Thomas has been taking lessons twice a week at a studio a few blocks from my house. He usually stops by afterwards for dinner... I thought you knew."

"He told me he was babysitting Delilah and Danielle while you were at the gym." Celia laughed so hard she snorted. "I can't believe he's been taking lessons. He wasn't *that* bad at Meghan and Eric's wedding."

"Oh crap, I wonder if he was planning on surprising you."

"I don't know, but I'm relieved you told me. I've been a little worried about him lately."

Gwen looked concerned. "Why do you say that?"

"He collapsed in the kitchen a few nights ago after he felt a sharp pain in his side. I didn't have anything to take his temperature, but I'm fairly certain he had a fever. I was afraid it could be due to him overexerting himself. He's been going non-stop and I'm sure worrying about the wedding hasn't helped anything either."

The waiter brought over their food and placed it on the table.

The smell of fried chicken overtook the salty air. "Everything look alright? Do you ladies need anything else?"

"No, thank you, we're good," Celia said.

The waiter nodded and walked off. Gwen was staring at Celia, the concerned expression still on her face. Celia's stomach growled, but her appetite was fading. She thought of what Thomas said after her first meeting when Gwen, "My sister likes to make a big deal out of things she shouldn't." She hadn't known about his disease then, but if she had, would his response have been different?

"Has anything else happened since then?" Gwen asked.

Celia shook her head.

"Will you please tell me if anything else happens? Thomas has always been someone who masks when something is wrong, perhaps out of ignorance or maybe because he doesn't want to burden anyone else with his problems. It's one of the reasons his HIV progressed to AIDS, and why I worry about him so much."

"Of course. He assured me he would let me know if he wasn't feeling well and I intend to hold him to it."

Gwen relaxed her posture and smiled. "Thank you."

It was a little after two o'clock in the afternoon when Celia got back home, and it was incredibly quiet, as if no one was home. The living room was empty, save for Scooter who was asleep on one of the wall shelves. She took her dress, safely tucked away in a garment bag, and hung it up in the spare bedroom closet—the room she had been sleeping in before they went to Scotland.

"Thomas?" she called out.

No answer. She peered out the window into the backyard, but he wasn't outside. She went to the kitchen, where a half-eaten sandwich was sitting on the kitchen counter, but there was no sign of Thomas. She knew he didn't have plans, or at least if he did—he didn't tell her about them. Gwen's concerned expression flashed in her mind. *Is there a reason to be concerned?* A lump grew in her throat as she walked down the empty hallway towards the master bedroom. The door was cracked open, but the room itself was dark. It creaked as she opened it, but she didn't hear it. Her heart was thudding too loudly in her chest to hear anything else. The blinds were closed and curtains drawn, but enough sunlight peeked through to provide some visibility. Thomas was lying on top of the bed.

Celia walked over to the side of the bed. He was wearing a t-shirt and athletic shorts. She gently touched his shoulder. He didn't stir. She rocked her hand, gently shaking him, but he still didn't respond. Her heart fell to her stomach, and tears filled her eyes. She put both hands on him and shook him harder. His eyes flew open and he practically fell out of the bed as he tried to sit up. Startled, Celia fell back into the wall. He saw her against the wall and slid off the bed.

"What's wrong? What happened?"

"You scared me." Celia put her hand over her chest. Her heart was racing.

"What? How? I was napping." He extended his hand to her and pulled her off the wall. "Did something happen today?"

"No... I'm sorry I woke you up."

Celia walked towards the bedroom door, but Thomas grabbed her arm and she stopped. Her skin trembled in his grip. She turned towards him but refused to look him in the eyes. She didn't want him to see that she was on the verge of tears.

"Celia, please tell me what's going on."

She bit her lip. "You're going to think I'm crazy."

"I already do, you agreed to marry me remember?" His words were met without a laugh or even a slight curling of her lips. He frowned. "I'm sorry, I was hoping to lighten the mood."

He took her hand and gently led her to the living room. She sat down on the couch while he grabbed her a glass of water from the kitchen. Her trembling was gone, but her eyes were still heavy with moisture.

"Here." He handed her the glass and sat down beside her.

"Thank you."

"Tell me what happened."

"Gwen and I were talking at lunch and I told her about what happened the other day. She mentioned that you're not always forthright when something is wrong. She had this concerned look on her face, and it made me feel a bit uneasy. It was abnormally quiet when I got back, I wasn't even sure if you were home. I tried to wake you, and you didn't move. I thought…"

"Thought what?"

She took a deep breath. "For a brief moment, I thought you were *gone*. I'm sure it sounds ridiculous, given how healthy and young you are, but it was what my mind jumped to when I couldn't get you to respond."

Thomas nodded, but didn't say anything. Celia sat the untouched glass of water on the coffee table and stood up. She walked over to the large bay window. Her gaze was towards the yard, but she wasn't paying attention to the world outside.

"My biggest fear used to be screwing up at an audition. Sometimes I still have nightmares that I'm at a big audition and as soon as I'm supposed to say my lines, I choke. Now, nothing scares me more than the idea of losing you. Just the thought of it is crippling. I know we've gotten past the physical trauma of what happened in Scotland, but it's so easy to go back and relive the night I didn't know what your condition was."

Thomas walked over and wrapped his arms around her from behind. His chin rested on the top of her head. "I'm sorry."

"Don't apologize, it wasn't your fault."

"I'm not apologizing for taking a nap, trust me, I needed it. I'm sorry because I understand what you must've felt. If the roles had been reversed, I would've reacted the same way."

Celia turned around and wrapped her arms around his waist. "If you're only saying that to make me feel better, it's working."

"I'm not, but I'm glad." He kissed her on the forehead. "Aside from this afternoon's *excitement*, how was the rest of the day? Did you find a dress?"

"It was great, and yes—I found the perfect dress."

"Can I see it?"

"No! You know that's bad luck."

Thomas rolled his eyes. "That's a superstition."

"I don't care. Besides, if you see the dress now I won't get the same reaction from you when I walk down the aisle."

"Fair enough."

"So, what's this surprise about? You're a man of many secrets lately."

"It wouldn't be a surprise if I told you about it now, would it? You're going to have to be patient."

"Can I at least have a hint?"

He shook his head. "It's like what you said about your dress. If I tell you about it now, you won't have the same reaction tomorrow. I will say, there is something I can show you right now."

"What is it?"

"Hold on." Thomas went to the bedroom and retrieved his phone. He connected it to a small Bluetooth speaker on the bookshelf in front of the DVD's. *Laughter Lines* by Bastille started playing. Thomas extended his hand to her. "May I have this dance?"

She smiled. "Of course."

Celia laced her fingers with his and he pulled her close to him. His right hand rested on the small of her back. Their bodies were pressed against each other's as they moved with the music. His grip tightened on her hand as he spun her away from him and pulled her back in. She pressed her face to his chest. His heartbeat fluttered in her ear. The song ended, but they kept dancing, their movements off beat with the subsequent songs.

# Twenty-Five

"Where are we?" Celia asked. She was sitting in the passenger seat of Thomas' Mustang. She wore jeans, a t-shirt, and boots. Her hair was pulled into a braid and a bandana was tied around her head as a makeshift blindfold. It was Thomas' idea to prevent her from seeing anything during the drive. She didn't even know how long she had been in the car.

"You know, I can't answer that, but you can go ahead and take the blindfold off now," Thomas said.

Celia carefully untied the bandana and brought it to her lap. The sun was harsh, and she squinted as her eyes adjusted. Thomas glanced over at her and grinned. He wore his Los Angeles Dodgers ball cap, a button-up shirt, jeans, and boots. They were driving down a gravel road. Pastures secured by white fences and no-climb wire were on either side of the road. Horses and cows grazed in the tall, but manicured grass. The land was plentiful with trees and lush mountains shaped the background. Thomas parked the car in between two pickup trucks by a large barn. It was constructed of stone and a covered arena was attached to it. Several people were inside the arena on horseback. A house sat off in the distance.

Celia looked over at Thomas with a raised eyebrow. "What are we doing here?"

"You'll see soon enough," he said.

Celia followed Thomas as he walked to the entrance of the barn. The interior of the barn was furnished with forty-five stalls, a tack-room, two feed rooms, and a spacious office. Large metal fans were hung from the high wooded celling. The stalls were composed of wood and maroon piping with an opening at each door for the horse to be able to look out into the hall. A Hispanic man pushed a wheelbarrow full of alfalfa by them as Thomas stopped in front of the office. The office's large glass window had its blinds cracked, inviting a glimpse inside. Sepia colored photographs of men and women competing at rodeo events were framed and hung on the wood-paneled walls. A black and white cow-hide rug sat centered on the stained concrete floor. There was a large desk in the middle of the room. An older red-headed woman sat behind a computer screen. On the opposite side of the desk were two chairs with cow-hide cushions. Thomas lightly tapped on the closed door.

"It's open," the woman called out.

Thomas opened the door and the woman stood up. She wore jeans, a long sleeve button up shirt, and boots. A large barrel racing buckle sat on her belt. Rose-colored blush was painted on her tanned face.

She extended her hand to him and shook his. "Thomas! It's so good to see you again. I'm assuming this gal is Celia?"

"Yes ma'am. Celia this is Gloria, Gloria this is Celia."

"It's nice to meet you," Celia said.

She shook Celia's hand and smiled. "Pleasure is all mine. Let me grab a halter right quick and I'll take you both to see her. My granddaughters did a nice job of getting her ready for your arrival."

"*Her?*" Celia looked at Thomas. "What is she talking about?"

He grinned. "You'll see."

Gloria led them through the barn and out of a side entrance where the pasture was fenced off into smaller sections. Each section had a water trough, lean-to shelter, and feed bucket. In the first lot stood a beautiful black mare. The horse's shiny coat was solid black, save for a short white sock on her left hind leg. Her wavy mane fell past her neck and her tail was only a few inches from the ground. The horse walked up to the fence as soon as they approached.

"Here she is," Gloria said. "If you want to ride her, Horatio can show you Ryan's saddle. We have other saddles you are welcome to use on the East wall, but the other saddles belong to other boarders. Horatio will give you the headstall and bit we use on her as well. I will leave you to get acquainted with her, but if you have any questions or concerns— I'll be in my office."

Gloria handed the rope halter to Thomas and started back towards the barn.

"What did she mean by 'other boarders'? What's going on?" Celia asked after Gloria had disappeared.

"Well considering we have a backyard that's not even an acre, she's going to have to stay here."

"Why would we keep someone's horse in our backyard? Wait..." Celia looked at the horse and back to Thomas. He had a ridiculously wide grin on his face. "Are you telling me this is your horse?"

"No, love. This is *your* horse."

Celia's mouth fell open. Partially due to disbelief, partially due to overwhelming excitement, she was speechless. *This is my horse?* If she hadn't felt the horse's whiskers tickle her skin, she would've thought she was dreaming.

"I hope you don't mind me giving you your wedding present early, but I couldn't wait two months."

"You bought me a horse," she said as if saying it out loud would make it any easier for her brain to digest.

Thomas nodded. "I've been looking ever since you agreed to marry me. You were so good with Ravenna, and given how much you love horses, I knew it was the perfect wedding gift idea; however, I never imagined I'd find one so close to home in Santa Clarita. Ryan, her previous owner, is Gloria's nephew. He is reenlisting in the army and instead of letting her sit in a pasture, he put her for sale. She's a registered American Quarter Horse and has been used on this ranch for the past several years."

"I cannot believe you bought me a horse. You're crazy, you know that—right?"

"I've been called worse." He laughed.

He handed her the halter and opened the gate to the paddock for her. Celia stepped inside. Her heartrate was fueled by excitement. She wasn't standing in front of just any horse, she was standing in front of *her* horse. Aside from when she was a child, she never dreamt she'd have the opportunity to own a horse of her own. The horse lowered her head into the halter and Celia secured it with a cowboy knot.

"What's her name?" she asked.

"I don't remember her registered name, I'd have to look at her papers again, but they've been calling her Sky. You can change her name if you'd like."

"Would you laugh if I called her Beauty?"

Thomas smiled. "Of course not. I remember you telling me about your fondness for *Black Beauty* and *The Black Stallion*. Why do you think I bought you a black horse?"

"You never cease to amaze me." She stroked the horse's neck. "Do I have time to ride her?"

"I don't know about you, but I don't have any other plans for today."

"What are we waiting for then?"

Thomas opened the gate and Celia led her out towards the barn. Her cheeks hurt from smiling, but she couldn't stop herself. This was, without a doubt, one of the best days of her life.

"Would you mind helping me saddle her? It's been a while since

I've ridden western, and you did such an amazing job on set. Although it would be more convenient for me, I promise you won't have to do it by yourself," Celia said.

Thomas didn't respond. Her words were met only with the grass softly crunching underneath the horse's hooves.

"Whoa girl." She stopped Beauty and turned around— fully expecting Thomas to be following a few feet behind her, but he wasn't. Instead, he was still at the gate. His right arm was slung over the top rail, and his left pressed against his stomach. He was leaning forward, and his complexion appeared two shades paler.

"Are you alright?"

He turned his head to her, as if he was going to say something, and collapsed onto the ground.

"Thomas!" Celia let go of the lead rope and ran to him. Beauty took off, trotting to the barn. His skin was fiery warm to the touch and he was covered in sweat. She cradled his head in her arms. His eyes were fluttering, and he didn't appear to be conscious. She reached for her phone in her pocket, only to remember it was sitting on the Mustang's console, charging the battery. A man attired in western clothing came out of the barn. His spurs jingled with each step he took. Horatio followed him out leading Beauty.

"Is everything alright ma'am?" the man asked.

"I don't know what's happening, but something's wrong." Her voice was noticeably higher, and she was on the verge of tears. "Please call for an ambulance."


Celia sat in the hospital's waiting room. She twisted her finger in a loose strand of hair and her boot nervously tapped against the blue tile flooring. It felt like déjà vu. Most of the seats were empty, and it was quiet aside from the occasional chatter between concerned family members and the nurse at the receptionist desk. The television was muted, leaving the stories to be interpreted solely by the pictures and subtitles.

"Celia!"

She turned to see an exasperated Gwen standing in front of the hospital's entrance. She was attired in her work clothes, a black dress and grey pantyhose. Her heels clacked against the floor as she rushed over to Celia. Celia had called her as soon as the ambulance had brought them to the hospital hours earlier.

"What's going on? How is he?"

Celia stood up. "I don't know. I haven't gotten any updates from the doctor yet."

"How do they not know anything by now? I'm going to go see if the nurse will tell us something."

Before Celia could protest, Gwen stomped off to the receptionist desk. Her love for her brother was fierce; however, it wouldn't do any good to berate the nurse for information she most likely didn't possess. Celia sat back down and folded her shaky hands in her lap.

"I'm his sister, I need to know what's going on," Gwen's voice overtook the nearby conversations and people were starting to stare.

"Ma'am, I need you to go take a seat. The doctor will be out as soon as he can."

"How about you call him out *now* and I'll consider take a seat?"

An older Asian man in a doctor's coat and pale blue scrubs walked out of the nursing station. His short black hair was thinning at the top and a face mask was hanging around his neck. His expression was unreadable, impossible to decipher what news he might bring.

"Is everything alright?" he asked.

"Yes, Dr. Nguyen. I was just telling this concerned family member she needed to take a seat and wait for news."

"It's alright," he turned to Gwen. "Who are you here to see?"

"Thomas Richardson, I'm his sister."

He extended his hand to her. "I'm Dr. Nguyen. I'm looking for his fiancé. I was told she came with him to the hospital."

She gestured to Celia. "She did."

The doctor looked at Celia. His gaze sent a sickening chill down her spine. Suddenly, she didn't want to know the diagnosis. She forced herself out of the chair and numbly walked over to them. Her throat was dry, and if she had attempted to speak, no sound would've been produced.

"Hello, I'm Dr. Nguyen." He shook Celia's limp hand. "Mr. Richardson is conscious, and he would like to see you."

Gwen exchanged a glance with Celia. "Can't I see him too? What's his condition?"

"I'll let Mr. Richardson know you're here, but for right now, he's limited to one visitor at a time, and he's asked for Ms. Stuart. If anything changes, I will make sure a nurse notifies you."

Her disappointment was evident, but she didn't try to argue. She gently placed her hand on Celia's shoulder before retreating to the waiting area. Celia's stomach churned as she followed Dr. Nguyen. If she didn't know any better, she would've thought they were back in Scotland. The walls weren't the same shade of paint and the nurses were different, but the sounds were eerily similar, and the familiar fear of the unknown was overwhelming. Celia almost ran into Dr. Nguyen, not realizing he had stopped walking. She didn't remember taking the elevator or walking by the nursing station, she had been so consumed by her thoughts they could've walked to a different building and she would've been none the wiser.

Dr. Nguyen went into the room first. Thomas was sitting up in the bed, speaking with a young nurse as she tapped away on a computer. His eyes lit up as soon as he saw Celia. She ran to his side and grabbed his hand, her forehead pressed against his chest. Careful to not rip out his IV, Thomas wrapped his arm around her and caressed her back.

"Nurse, would you mind giving us a minute?" Dr. Nguyen asked.

She nodded and left the room, pulling the door closed behind her. The room was quiet, save for their breathing, the dripping of the IV, and the air conditioning. Dr. Nguyen pushed a vinyl chair from the wall for Celia to sit in and wheeled a rolling chair over for himself on the other side of Thomas. Celia sat back, her grip around his hand still tight. Thomas and the doctor both looked at Celia and her heart felt like it was on the verge of imploding.

"What's wrong?" her voice was barely audible.

Thomas took a deep breath and looked back at Dr. Nguyen. "Go ahead."

"During the CT scan, we found a mass. Upon review with an abdominal subspecialty radiologist, it was determined to be a rup-tured intra-abdominal abscess."

"Which is treatable, right?" Celia looked at Thomas, but he didn't make eye-contact. His eyes no longer reflected the same light as when she walked in, and red lined his eyelids. *Had he been crying?*

"In the early stages, yes, an intra-abdominal abscess can be treated with antibiotics and surgical or percutaneous abscess drain-age; however, as we are dealing with a ruptured abscess, the concern is the bacteria. If it spreads to other organs and tissues, it can be fatal. Given Mr. Richardson's medical history and his immune system, he is a high-risk patient. We are going to do everything in our power to keep it from spreading and fight the infection, but I want to be honest with both of you, this will be an uphill battle."

His words knocked the air out of her. It was like she had fallen off a tall swing-set and onto the hard ground. Thomas said some-thing, but she didn't hear it. The only words echoing in her mind were fatal, high-risk, and uphill battle. What was supposed to be a wonderful day, spending time with Thomas and her new horse, had soured. A pleasant surprise had been followed up by a suffocating shock. How had the day turned so easily? If this was a nightmare, she was ready to wake up.

"Celia?" Thomas squeezed her hand and pulled her back into the present.

Dr. Nguyen was gone, and they were alone. She looked at Thomas, her eyes struggling to maintain contact with his. Everything about her appearance was fragile, as if one wrong word would shatter her into a million pieces.

"I'm sorry," he said.

Tears slipped down her cheeks. "Why are you sorry?"

"Maybe if I had been proactive about my symptoms, I wouldn't be at this point."

"What do you mean you were having symptoms? Why didn't you tell me?"

"I didn't realize they were symptoms. The pain has been present for a couple weeks, but it's been more of a dull ache." Thomas sighed. "I wanted our first dance to be perfect, so I've been secretly taking dance lessons. I associated the pain and being tired with the lessons. That night in the kitchen when I collapsed was a turning point, but the over-the-counter medicine helped, so I didn't think too much of it. After all, I had been busier than normal with worrying about the wedding, dance lessons, finding Beauty, and auditions."

"I don't understand... How did this even happen?"

Thomas opened his mouth, but hesitated. It was like he was carefully mulling over his thoughts. Celia felt nauseous. Each passing second chipped away at her fragile state.

"Dr. Nguyen can't be certain, but he said it was most likely a result from being shot."

Celia broke free from his grip and ran to the small bathroom on the other side of the room. She slammed the door shut behind her and fell on her knees in front of the toilet. Her hands pressed against the pink tile as she was unable to suppress her lunch from coming up. It burned her dry throat. She flushed the toilet and forced herself over to the sink. The nausea was gone, but she was left feeling weak. Her hands clung to both sides of the sink for support. There was a small tap on the door.

"Celia, are you okay?" Thomas asked.

*Are you seriously asking me if I'm okay right now? Of course I'm not okay.* She splashed cold water on her reddened face. If this were the cruel dream she wished it was, it would've been enough to wake her up. She wiped her tears on her sleeves and walked out of the bathroom. Thomas was standing on the other side of the door with his trembling hand wrapped around the IV pole. Fear was in his eyes. Possibly from the fear of death, or from the fear of leaving the love of his life. Celia wrapped her arms around him and he broke into sobs.

# Twenty-Six

Celia was lying in the hospital bed next to Thomas. She wore jean cut-off shorts and a pineapple print crop top. Thomas had traded his hospital gown for a t-shirt and athletic shorts. There were bags underneath his eyes and his skin was pale. They were watching an old black and white film on the television. Rain gently pitter-pattered against the window. It had been almost two-weeks since Thomas was admitted to the hospital, and Celia had rarely left his side. The only times she had left for more than an hour was when she needed to shower, pick things up from the house, or to give Thomas time alone with Gwen or the occasional friend who stopped by to visit.

"I want to get married," Thomas said.

"We *are* getting married."

"Let me rephrase that, I don't want to wait to get married."

Celia sat up and turned towards him. "What do you mean?"

"I want to marry you, tonight. There's a chapel in the lower level of the hospital we could use, and the medical chaplain said he would be able to officiate the ceremony. Gwen and I talked about it yesterday and she said she'd be able to help get everything set up. Since it's impromptu, I don't expect the majority of the guests we invited to be able to make it, but I don't care. All that matters to me is that you and I are there. I already asked Dr. Nguyen and he said it would be fine. We wouldn't occupy the chapel for more than an hour or two, and if my antibiotics are administered off schedule it won't be an issue."

"You've obviously given this some thought. Is there a reason you're in a rush all of the sudden?"

"No, but you know what Dr. Nguyen said. There's no guarantee the treatment is going to work, and I don't want to risk missing my chance to marry the love of my life. I know the venue is already booked, but we can have a recommitment ceremony or something on Halloween for all those who are unable to attend tonight. What do you say?"

"When were you thinking?"

A smile crept on his face. "Seven-ish?"


Celia stood outside the hospital's chapel entrance. She looked stunning in her black gown. Her hair was gently tousled with a braid pulled over top like a headband. Small black crystals were entwined in the braid and sparkled underneath the florescent lighting. Her lips were painted a rosy pink and her cheeks lightly blushed. Meghan stood beside her in a red lace gown that was barely large enough to fit over her stomach. Gwen slipped out the double doors. She was attired in a straight red dress the same shade as Meghan's.

"Are you ready?" Gwen asked.

Celia nodded.

"Alright." She grabbed the handle of one of the doors while Meghan grabbed the opposite. Without another word, they pushed the doors in and held them open. Celia took a deep breath before stepping inside the chapel. It was small with only six rows of pews on each side. Candles were lit in remembrance as well as in decoration for the wedding. The walls were marbled grey and tan, and the floor was a sandy brown. Thomas was standing at the head of the room. He wore a black suit with dark grey embroidered designs. The suit looked one-size too large on him, a testament of his health struggles. His undershirt was a dark grey and his bowtie black. Tears glittered in his eyes as he watched Celia walk towards him.

Gwen and Meghan closed the doors and waited until Celia was standing next to Thomas before walking to their seats. Delilah and Danielle, both in matching wine-colored dresses, were standing next to Eric. On the other side of Eric was Dr. Nguyen, absent of his usual white coat. A photographer Gwen had found last minute, stood at the back. The medical chaplain was behind Thomas. He was short, barely above five feet tall, and appeared to be in his early sixties. What was left of his thin grey hair was combed over the top of his head. He wore a black shirt and black slacks. Thomas took Celia's hands into his and smiled. His hands were warm and sweaty.

"I swear, whenever I think you couldn't possibly be any more beautiful, you surprise me," Thomas whispered.

"Stop it, or else you're going to make me cry," she said.

"You may all be seated." The chaplain paused as they sat down. "We are gathered here today to celebrate the union of Thomas Richardson and Celia Stuart. From my understanding, this was not the wedding they had planned, nor could everyone who wished to attend be present, but this occasion is nevertheless joyous, and your presence is appreciated. Marriage is not something to be taken lightly, nor is it for the faint of heart. There will be good days and some not-so-good days, but you must remember to love each other through it all. You will be two people bound together as one by love and this sacred vow. Thomas, do you take this woman to be your wedded wife?"

"I do," Thomas said.

"And Celia, do you take this man to be your wedded husband?"

She nodded. "I do."

"Now, I understand that you've both written your own vows. It is time to share them with each other."

"Can I go first?" Thomas asked.

"Of course," Celia said.

Thomas released Celia's hands and pulled a folded piece of notebook paper out of his back pocket. "I'll never forget when I first saw you, your nerves were as radiant as your beauty—apparent by the stumble and rip to your dress before you had even reached the table."

Celia laughed. Her face was a bright red.

"The more I got to see you, the real you, the stronger my feelings became. I never intended to fall in love with you, but I couldn't have stopped myself even if I had tried. You are the most down-to-earth, compassionate, beautiful, humorous, and impatient person I have ever met. I couldn't imagine spending the rest of my life, however long, with anyone else." A tear slipped down his cheek. "You are my lifeboat, the light on my darkness days, and the distraction I run to. If there is a greater plan, and everyone in the world has their one true-soulmate, the person they're destined to meet and fall-in-love with, I know that my person is you. I love you more than life itself."

He folded his vows back up and slid them into his pocket. He wiped a tear off his face before taking Celia's hands again. She was smiling but her eyes glistened with tears.

"I love you," she whispered.

"I love you too."

"Please bear with me, I memorized mine." She took a deep breath. "You once told me I drive you crazy, right before you told me you were falling for me. It would've been a year ago today—if our wedding had gone as planned for Halloween night. It's safe to say not much in our relationship has gone as planned, but it's been perfect, or I guess I should say *almost* perfect considering where we're at."

A twinge of sadness flashed in his eyes. There was a slight, but noticeable shift of mood in the chapel. They could pretend it was their ideal wedding, that Thomas wasn't fighting for his life, and they were about to embark on a wonderful honeymoon to another country; however, it would be just that—pretending.

"Sorry, I'm not doing well at this am I?"

"No, you're fine— keep going."

She tightened her grip around his sweaty hands. "We cannot rewrite the things that have happened to us, all we can do is start a new chapter. I promise I will never go to bed angry with you, nor will I ever intentionally hurt you. I'll always be open and honest with you, even when it's difficult. I can't promise I won't steal all the blankets in my sleep, nor can I promise I won't always cover my eyes during scary movies. I can't wait to share a lifetime of laughs, love, and adventures with you. My heart is yours today, tomorrow, and all of the days yet to come."

Thomas leaned forward and pressed his forehead against hers. One of his tears fell on her cheek.

"May I have the rings?" the chaplain asked.

"It's your turn," Gwen whispered to her daughters.

Delilah and Danielle both stood up. Each had a ring box in their hands as they walked up to the front. The chaplain held out his hand and the girls gave him the boxes before they shyly retreated back to their mother.

"Thomas, please repeat after me— I give you this ring, as a daily reminder of my love and my commitment to you."

Thomas took Celia's ring out of the box. It had a white gold band, a large garnet stone in the middle, and two smaller sapphires on both sides. The infinity symbol was engraved inside the band. He slid the ring around her finger and pushed it back against the engagement ring.

"I give you this ring, as a daily reminder of my love and my commitment to you."

"Celia, please repeat after me— I give you this ring, as a daily reminder of my love and my commitment to you."

She picked up Thomas' ring. It was a thick band composed of dark-stained wood with a thin golden line around it. The inside was a lighter shade of wood and engraved, "Forever yours". Thomas' hand was trembling as Celia slipped the ring onto his finger.

"I give you this ring, as a daily reminder of my love and my commitment to you."

"By the power vested in me by God and the state of California, I now pronounce you husband and wife! Thomas, you may kiss your bride."

Thomas placed his hands on Celia's face and pulled her in for a kiss. His palms were damp against her skin. The camera flashed as it captured the moment, and all of the attendees clapped and cheered. His lips lingered against hers, as if he didn't want to pull away. Celia didn't want him to pull away either. She wanted to relish in the moment. It wasn't the ceremony either of them had intentionally planned, but it was theirs. It didn't matter if they did a recommitment ceremony or something of that nature later, *this* was their actual wedding.

Thomas had a tight grip on her hand as he pulled her down an empty hallway. The further they snaked through the building, the quieter it grew. No longer followed by the nurses' hushed voices or the beeping of the EKG machines, only their giggles and footsteps echoed throughout the halls. Thomas pushed through a set of double doors and past sheets of hanging plastic. The only light was from the moonlight seeping in through the windows.

"Are we supposed to be back here?" Celia asked.

"Do you really want to know the answer to that?"

"Probably not."

He stopped at the end of the hallway where it branched out to a bigger room destined to be a waiting area with a nursing station post completion. There were sawhorses, tools, and loose pieces of plywood scattered about. In the middle of the room was a pile of blankets surrounded by candles. The air was perfumed with the soft scent of lavender. A bottle of pink champagne and two glasses were in a basket next to the blankets. Chocolate covered strawberries and cheese slices sat on a platter.

"What's all this?" Celia asked.

"Since we weren't going to have any of the traditional wedding activities, I wanted to do something else to celebrate the occasion. I know it's not the same, but—" Celia kissed him before he could finish his sentence.

She caressed the side of his face and smiled. "Forget traditions. This is perfect."

Celia carefully sat down on the blanket while Thomas popped open the champagne. He poured them both a generous amount and sat down next to her.

"Should we toast to us?" Celia asked.

"Sure."

She gently touched her glass to his before taking a sip. Thomas downed his drink and immediately refilled his cup. The champagne rocked in his trembling hands.

"Are you sure it's okay for you to drink with your current antibiotics?"

"Honestly, I'm not going to worry about anything tonight except spending time with you."

His fingers traced the path of the buttons on her dress. A smile was on his face, but the familiar look of sadness, something she hadn't seen in months, haunted his eyes.

Celia sat her glass down and turned to him. "Alright, that's enough. Tell me what's going on."

"I can't say for what's going on outside of this hospital or the city for that matter, but right now I'm sitting here enjoying the company of my beautiful wife, drinking this disgustingly sweet champagne."

"You know what I meant. Something is wrong, I can see it in your eyes."

"Sometimes I forget how well you know me." He looked down at the blanket. Tears were in his eyes. "I don't want to ruin the evening."

"You won't," she said despite the growing concern of what he might say.

He finished off his second drink and sat the glass off to the side. Celia took his hands into her own. Maybe it was the air in the room, but he felt cold.

"Dr. Nguyen ran some tests two days ago, and the results weren't good. My body hasn't responded to any of the antibiotics and the bacteria has aggressively spread. My treatment plan has transitioned into hospice care."

The color completely drained from her face and a wave of numbness washed over her. It felt like an out-of-body experience, as if she was watching him speak from a distance.

"I'm going to be discharged sometime this week to continue the care at home. He said there was no reason to keep me here, as it wouldn't prolong my life nor worsen my condition from being at home. I didn't want to tell you tonight, fuck—I didn't want to tell you at all." He shook his head. "I'm sorry. I know I should've told you earlier, but I was afraid you wouldn't want to marry me."

Celia didn't respond. The feeling had returned to her body, but she was at a loss for words. What could she say? He was dying and no words could change that. She had always known this was a possibility, Dr. Nguyen hadn't sugar-coated his chances, but it didn't make it any easier to stomach.

"Please say something."

"What do you want me to say?" her voice was barely audible.

"I don't know... I hate to admit it, but I'm scared."

Celia broke into tears. "I'm scared too."

Thomas pulled her into his lap and wrapped his arms around her. Head against his chest, his heart thumped slowly in her ear.

"When were you going to tell me?" she asked.

"I don't know, but I wasn't planning on tonight. I wanted one more night of normalcy, even if it was a lie. I wanted to feel like I was the luckiest man in the word, on the verge of happily-ever-after with you. When you said you couldn't wait to share a lifetime of laughs, love, and adventures with me, I couldn't help but feel guilty. I knew I needed to tell you."

She sat back and looked at him. Her eyes were red, and black tears stained her cheeks. "Can we... try?"

"What do you mean?"

"I want you to lie to me." She started unbuttoning his shirt. "I want to pretend that this is the first night of the rest of our lives, that your only concern is someone hearing us."

"Are you sure?"

"Yes. Everything else can wait until tomorrow."

Thomas wiped the smudges from her face and began kissing her like he had never kissed her before. He knocked over the glass of champagne as he climbed on top of her. Goosebumps covered their skin. Every kiss was electric, every touch chilling. His left hand fiddled with the buttons on her dress, while she unbuckled his belt and pulled his pants down. Hastily, but carefully, they stripped each other bare. Her fingers traced the scar left by the bullet wound on his stomach. It was hard to comprehend how something so small, barely noticeable, signified remarkable and irreversible damage.

# Twenty-Seven

Thomas never made it home from the hospital. He died two days after their wedding. His funeral was a week after he passed, but Celia had no recollection of it. The past two weeks had blurred together, as if it had been one long and terrible day. Every time she was offered a condolence she felt nauseous. It didn't matter how *sorry* they were, it wasn't going to bring him back. The void his absence left in her heart was overwhelming. Every second she missed him more than the last. Her only comfort came from the things that still held his scent like their bedsheets, and his clothes.

Celia stood in the closet. It was early in the afternoon, but she was still dressed in her pajamas. Her hair needed to be brushed and her eyes were bloodshot from crying. The house was quiet, the new normal, save for the occasional pitter-patter from Scooter walking around. Her hand brushed against one of Thomas' leather jackets, the one he had worn to the rehearsal dinner in Chicago. She could still picture him in it, standing in front of her right before he grabbed her by the shoulders and pulled her in for a kiss. She wiped a stray tear off her cheek, when something white caught her attention out of the corner of her eye. It was hanging out of the pocket of her wool coat.

*Is that what I think it is?* Her heart fluttered as she pulled out the piece of paper and carefully unfolded it. It was the note Thomas left her in Scotland, still perfumed by his earthy cologne. Tears filled her eyes as she reread it. Her focus was pulled to the bottom where he had signed it,

"Love,

Thomas"

His handwriting was messy, but beautiful at the same time—just like he was. Her eyes widened as an idea popped into her head. She ran out of the closet and grabbed her phone from off the nightstand. Her clumsy fingers struggled to unlock her phone, but after two attempts she was successful and able to dial Meghan's phone number. She put the phone on speaker and began changing out of her clothes.

"Are you busy right now?" Celia asked, not bothering to wait for a "Hello".

"No, why? Is everything okay?"

"Can I pick you up in twenty minutes? There's something I need to do."

"Yeah. Of course."

"See you soon," she hung-up and ran back to the closet.

Without much thought, she grabbed a t-shirt and shorts. She ran a brush through her hair and was about to head out but hesitated at the bedroom door. Thomas' Los Angeles Dodgers ball cap sat on the dresser. She picked it up and studied the stains along the bill. *He loved this stupid hat.* She sat it back down for a split-second before grabbing it again and putting it on. The closure was stiff from being worn, but she managed to tighten it.

"Perfect."

The Pins and Needles tattoo shop was alive with the sound of buzzing needles and old rock music. The floors were red tile, and the yellow walls were covered with framed tattoo designs. Black leather couches were pressed against the windows and there was a small table with foldable chairs for patrons to sit at. The door chimed as Celia and Meghan walked inside the shop. A young woman covered in piercings and various tattoos stood behind the glass counter that displayed a collection of different plugs, navel rings, and other piercing jewelry. She wore a striped bodysuit and revealing jean shorts.

"Welcome, how can I help you?" the woman asked.

"I'm looking for Mason Brown," Celia said.

"He finished his last appointment a few minutes ago, but I think he's still here. I'll go see." The woman's high heeled boots clicked against the tile as she headed towards the back of the shop.

Meghan looked at Celia with a curious expression. "What exactly are we doing at a tattoo shop?"

Before she could answer, a short man walked to the front. He was thin, appeared to be in his mid-thirties, and had black and green hair. He wore a tropical button-up shirt that featured surfing cats and palm trees. His arms were tattooed with different *Marvel* superheroes.

"Hi, I'm Mason." He pushed his thick-framed glasses to the bridge of his nose. "What can I do for you two ladies today?"

"I was hoping I could get a tattoo," Celia said.

"Well, we do take walk-ups here, but I'm actually done for the day, so I can see if someone else would be able to assist you."

She shook her head. "I need you to do it. My... late husband told me about you, he said you did all of his tattoos."

"What's his name?"

"Thomas Richardson."

"Oh... I thought you looked familiar. I was saddened to hear about his passing, he was a great guy. Always came in with cool ideas."

Celia pulled the note out of her pocket and carefully unfolded it.

She handed it to him. "I was hoping you would be able to copy his handwriting."

Mason's eyes scanned the note. His expression was unreadable, and Celia's heartbeat was deafening. She didn't know if anyone around her could hear it, but Meghan lightly placed her hand on Celia's back. It was a small comfort, but it failed to slow her heartrate.

"Do you want the entire letter?"

"No. I just want 'Love, Thomas' on my wrist." She held out her arm. "Nothing fancy, just black ink. This would be my first tattoo, and I couldn't imagine getting this done by anyone else other than you."

Mason looked at her, and back at the note as if he was carefully studying it. Slowly he nodded his head.

"Alright, I'll do it. I'll need a few minutes to get ready and set up, so you can take a seat if you'd like. I'll let you know when I'm ready for you."

Her posture relaxed. "Thank you."

She walked over to the couch nestled in the corner and sat down. Meghan sat down next to her, her hand resting on top of her baby bump. She was wearing a bright floral t-shirt dress with slip-on shoes. A perplexed expression sat on her face.

"I was starting to worry about you." Meghan furrowed her brow. "You haven't responded to any of my messages or returned my calls in a few days. I was surprised to see your name pop up on my caller ID today. Never expected we would end up at a tattoo shop."

"Nothing turns out how we expect it to, does it?" She sighed heavily. "I haven't been intentionally ignoring you, I just don't know what to say. Everyone keeps asking if I'm okay, as if my answer is going to be any different than the day before. I keep waking up with the hope that this was all one bad dream, only to be disappointed by the reality of an empty house. I find myself looking for him, as if he's simply in another room. If he's not in the kitchen, he must be in the living room. He's not in the living room, so of course he's outside. It's the same damn charade every day of me looking for him, only to be left to face the facts that I'll never be able to see him again."

"I'm so sorry. I can't imagine what you're going through... I want you to know that I'm here for you—always. Whatever you need, you can call me any time—day or night. Honestly, you are more than welcome to come stay with Eric and me for as long as you'd like. Maybe getting out of his house will do you some good."

Celia shook her head. "It was, even if only for a brief amount of time, *our* house. I appreciate the offer, but I feel closest to him when I'm there. Besides, you two need all the alone time you can get before the little one gets here."

Mason walked around to the back of the counter and motioned for Celia to come over. On top of the counter was an agreement for her to sign. He handed her back the letter.

"Can I see your license?" he asked.

"Yes." She handed it to him.

He wrote down her license number on the paper before placing it in the scanner behind him. Celia skimmed over the contract before signing her name. Why a tattoo shop needed to clarify that tattoos were permanent was beyond her.

Mason gave her license back to her. "It'll be ninety dollars even. Is that doable?"

"Yes."

"Sweet. You can follow me back."

The shop had small sections for each artist. There was a half wall in between each section, and a curtain hung from the ceiling to provide privacy for those tattoos destined for more risqué places. Mason's work area was colorful with artwork, action figures, and a battery-operated lucky cat. Transfer paper featuring his tattoo designs, including Thomas' phoenix tattoo, were pinned to the walls.

There was a rolling stool for him and a black hydraulic tattoo chair for his customers.

"Which wrist did you want it on again?" he asked.

She held out her right arm to him. "My right."

"Alright."

He gently cuffed her wrist as he cleaned it with antibacterial soap. It was cold against her skin. He shaved the area with a disposable razor, before applying the transfer paper. Carefully he peeled off the paper, leaving "Love, Thomas" imprinted on her wrist in blue ink.

"Why don't you go check it out in the mirror? Make sure it's what you want and where you want it."

Celia nodded and walked over to the tall mirror next to the bathroom. She turned her wrist from side-to-side as she watched in the mirror—studying the outline. It was strange seeing his writing on her wrist, but it looked, without a single doubt, perfect. For the first time since Thomas' death, she couldn't help but smile. Mason was putting on gloves as she walked back over.

"What do you think?" he asked.

"It looks great— it's perfect actually."

"Sweet! If you can take a seat right here, I'll get started."

She sat down on the chair. The right arm rest was slightly elevated, and a paper-towel separated her skin from the faux leather. Black ink was sitting in an ink cap on the counter, along with a cup of water, and Vaseline. Mason took a glob of Vaseline and gently rubbed it over the outline.

"Are you ready for me to start?" he asked.

Celia took a deep breath and nodded. She closed her eyes as the machine started buzzing and Mason pressed the needle against her skin. Her body was numb with grief, and the vibrations of the needle were felt without pain. She had always thought if she ever got a tattoo, Thomas would be sitting by her side. He would hold her hand and tell her funny stories to distract her from the pain. He wouldn't complain about how hard she squeezed his hand, he wouldn't even acknowledge it. A tear rolled down her cheek. She would give anything to see him again or to simply feel his skin against hers.

Celia's eyes shot open as Mason squirted cold water onto her wrist. Carefully he brushed a paper towel against her reddened skin.

"I'm finished," Mason said.

"Already?" The clock on the wall read three-fifteen. *Has it really been thirty minutes?* It felt like she had closed her eyes for only a few minutes.

"Pieces like this don't take as long. Go check it out in the mirror and let me know what you think."

Celia stood up on wobbly legs as the feeling returned to her feet. A soft burning sensation encased her wrist. Each letter of Thomas' writing was slightly elevated from swelling. She didn't have to look in the mirror to appreciate it, she could already see, even with the swelling, its brilliance. The sloppiness of the "T," how the top of the "V" connected with the "E," it was as if it had been written directly on her skin, instead of being transferred over from the note. She wondered how Thomas would've reacted to the tattoo. Would he have teased her about it? She could see him playfully nudging her shoulder as he said, "Really? That's what you wanted to get as your first tattoo?" Perhaps he would've been touched by the gesture with a smile on his face as he said, "You must really love me to do something crazy like that."

*Trust me, I do.*

Kendal is currently living in Texas. She graduated from the University of North Texas in 2017 with a BA in English - Creative Writing. Aside from writing, she enjoys spending time with her dog Bucky, and three cats, Steve Rogers, Delilah, and Khaleesi. She loves to ride her two horses, Princess and Pepper, and compete in barrel racing competitions.

www.kendalloudickson.com

# Other Books By Kendal Lou Dickson

Broken by Design: A Short Story Collection

Whispers Through the Pines

The Story of Steve Rogers

Mercy: A Short Story Collection